The end is near.

The end of Savannah's pregnancy, that is. Less than a month to go, and she'll be the mother of what will surely be the most adorable baby boy or baby girl in the world.

But before that, there's Thanksgiving with the Martins to get through. Not to mention a little spot of murder at the group home where Mrs. Jenkins, Savannah's grandmother-in-law, lives.

A spot of murder that leaves Mrs. Jenkins covered in blood, and with no memory of who else might have hurt night nurse Julia Poole.

With Savannah's friend, homicide detective Tamara Grimaldi, investigating, and Savannah's husband Rafe insisting that the detective can't find out about Mrs. Jenkins's involvement, in case she doesn't share his rock-solid belief that Mrs. Jenkins would never kill anyone, Savannah's caught between a rock and a hard place.

Can she help Mrs. Jenkins figure out the truth before Detective Grimaldi throws them both in prison... or before the real murderer comes back to finish the job?

OTHER BOOKS IN THIS SERIES

A Cutthroat Business

Hot Property

Contract Pending

Close to Home

A Done Deal

Change of Heart

Kickout Clause

Past Due

Dirty Deeds

Unfinished Business

Adverse Possession

Uncertain Terms

Scared Money

Bad Debt

HOME STRETCH

Savannah Martin Mystery #15

Jenna Bennett

HOME STRETCH

Savannah Martin Mystery #15

Interior design and formatting: B. Gallagher
Cover Design: Dar Albert, Wicked Smart Designs

Magpie Ink

ONE

By the middle of November, I was feeling like the Thanksgiving turkey. Stuffed. I was within a few weeks of giving birth. I couldn't see my toes. I couldn't see my swollen ankles, either, although that was probably a good thing. And I waddled when I walked. My back hurt. Sleeping was impossible—good training for after the baby was born, my sister told me; she's had three, so she should know.

I couldn't wait for it to be over.

Not because I wanted to finally meet the baby, this tiny, miraculous human who was supposed to be the perfect combination of me and my husband.

No, I just wanted to go back to having a waistline and ankles that didn't hurt.

And the worst thing was that when it was all over and done with, I still wouldn't fit back into my shoe wardrobe, because my arches were history and my feet looked like they belonged to Wilma Flintstone. Flat as flapjacks. I'd be lucky to fit into a pair of Birkenstocks by the time this was over.

"You're beautiful," my husband told me, not for the first time, as we cuddled together on the sofa the Saturday before Thanksgiving.

And by cuddling, I mean that I was sitting sideways on the sofa with my feet in his lap, and he was rubbing them.

"I'm fat." I scowled at him across the mound of my

stomach. From this vantage point, I could have sworn I was giving birth to twins. Or a baby elephant. It felt like I had gestated long enough to create one.

He kept rubbing. "You're not fat. You're pregnant. And beautiful."

One hand moved past my—swollen—ankle to my calf, and massaged a little there, too. I sighed. When he moved to the back of my knee, and stroked the thin skin there, I told him, "If you want sex, it's going to have to be doggie style. It's the only way that works anymore."

He grinned. "Far be it from me to turn down doggie style, darlin', but are you sure it's safe?"

"The doctor said we could carry on as usual until the last month," I reminded him.

"And we're in the last month now."

"By a day!" Or maybe two or three. Or four.

But really, who was counting?

"I love you," Rafe said, and smoothed a hand over my thigh. I moved my leg a little. "And I love that you can't get enough of me." He grinned as his hand moved north, with no complaint from me. "But are you sure this is a good idea?"

With the way he was touching me, it seemed like a very good idea. *Very* good.

And it seemed like he might be thinking so, too, because he didn't stop.

However, I did understand his concern. And loved him more—or would have loved him more if I didn't already love him so much it hurt—for it.

But on the other hand— "It's almost a month until the baby comes. Or at least three weeks. Are you going to go without for three weeks?"

He looked thoughtful at that. "I've gone without for longer than that before, you know."

"You have?"

He arched a brow. "Two years in Riverbend Penitentiary, remember?"

"Of course, but..." I flushed. "I mean, don't things happen in prison? You hear stories..."

He chuckled. "Big Ned didn't make me his bitch, if that's what you're asking."

"Big Ned? There was a Big Ned?"

He shook his head. "No, darlin'. There was nobody named Big Ned. And I didn't have sex with the other inmates. Or the female guards."

"There were female guards?" Who'd want to be a female guard in an all-male prison?

Then again, if all the inmates looked like Rafe, I could see the temptation. But they don't.

"Lots," Rafe said. "But for the most part they didn't look like anybody I'd wanna have sex with. Although there was this one woman..."

I held up a hand. "Please."

He laughed. "I'm just messing with you. I was celibate for two years, unless you consider the company of Mary Thumb and her four sisters. I think I can survive three weeks."

"It'll be more than that. Things have to come back together after the birth, too. You're probably looking at two months."

"I waited two years," Rafe said. "I can wait two months."

"But in this case you don't have to. You may have to wait after the birth. But you don't have to wait now. It's only a week or so into the last month. I'm sure it's safe."

He arched a brow. "You want me."

"Always." And I probably always would. At least I didn't see myself getting tired of him anytime soon. "And anyway, I wouldn't cry if the baby decided to come early."

We were at a point where it was safe. A little premature, but safe. I'd had a risky early pregnancy—it was my third, and the first two had ended in miscarriages; one a year ago, one a couple of years before that—and the doctor had told me that anything after week 36 was considered full term, so I just had to hold on until then. Although with my luck, now that I was past the danger point, the baby would probably dig in and refuse to come out, and I'd have the only 10-month baby ever born.

"It'll be worth it," Rafe told me as he walked his fingers lightly up my thigh.

"You don't have to convince me." I knew what he was capable of. It would be very worth it.

He grinned. "I meant the baby. Carrying the baby. It'll be worth it once it's born. You won't remember any of this."

Easy for him to say. "Let's just get this show on the road. You know I drop off to sleep at nine o'clock these days. And it's close to that now."

"I've got it." He moved out from under my feet and onto the floor. "Just relax. I'll take care of you. If you just turn around like this..." He pulled me down to the edge of the sofa. "That'll work. Just relax and enjoy."

He gave me a smile, one where his eyes were hot and liquid.

"I love you," I told him.

"You'll love me even more after this." The smile turned into a cocky grin, and then he set to work.

He waited until I was boneless and spent, sprawled across the sofa—to the degree that a nine-months-pregnant woman can sprawl—before he told me, "We have to go visit my grandma tomorrow."

I tilted my head to look at him, wedged into the sofa next to me, as naked as the day he was born. "You didn't have to soften me up for that. Don't we usually go visit your grandmother on Sundays?"

"When we're not visiting your family."

"We're going to Sweetwater for Thanksgiving," I reminded

him, "so we're here this weekend. I figured we'd go see your grandmother. We usually do."

Or at least he usually did. I often came along. Sometimes he brought his son David instead of me.

Not because I don't like Mrs. Jenkins. I do. She's a nice old lady. But I'll readily admit that going to see her can be draining. She struggles with dementia, and we can never be sure whether she'll be lucid or not when we visit. It can change from one breath to the next, too. Sometimes she knows exactly who we are. Other times, she thinks Rafe is her late son Tyrell—the father Rafe never knew, since he was killed before Rafe was born—and I'm LaDonna Collier, pregnant with Rafe.

When we introduced David—Rafe's son from a high school fling—into the mix, things got even more complicated, since she's never sure whether David is David, or whether he's Rafe or Tyrell.

At any rate, I go along and visit Mrs. J a lot of the time. David comes along sometimes, when he isn't busy doing something else, and when his adoptive parents agree to let him spend time with his biological father and great-grandmother. Rafe goes every weekend, unless we're out of town.

"I just wanted to let you know," my husband said, with a jaw-cracking yawn.

It was my turn to grin. "Did I wear you out?"

"I had to do all the work," he informed me, with an arch of an eyebrow.

He *had* done all the work. "You volunteered."

A corner of his mouth turned up. "Guess I did. You ready to head to bed?"

I nodded.

"I'll give you a hand up." He scrambled across me and onto the floor. I took the hand he extended and planted my feet. It took effort to get upright these days. I'd never been a lightweight, and with the extra thirty pounds or so of pregnancy weight I was carrying, I imagine it must have been a lot like hauling a small hippopotamus. Good thing he's strong.

"Clothes?" I suggested when I was upright and we were both standing in the middle of the parlor in our birthday suits. Everything we'd worn earlier was scattered across the sofa, table, and floor, where he'd tossed it or pushed it when he was taking it off.

"I'll get it tomorrow." He put an arm around me and nudged me toward the hallway.

"I can't walk around the house naked!"

Especially not in my condition. What if someone was outside, looking in? They'd get quite an eyeful. Rafe is gorgeous, of course—all smooth golden skin and hard muscles—but I look like a great, white whale at the moment.

"You're gorgeous." He kept nudging me along. He's stronger than me, so I kept moving. Across the floor to the doorway, into the foyer, toward the stairs. "Just a few more steps, and then you can run up the stairs."

No way was I running up the stairs in the nude, with my naked butt jiggling. His arm around my shoulders didn't provide much cover, but it was better than nothing.

"I'll walk," I said. "With what dignity I have left."

He grinned. "That's the attitude."

Easy for him to say. He could model underwear. Or model naked. Unlike me, he'd had all of the fun and his stomach was still flat and shaped like a perfect eight-pack.

But we made it up the stairs without hearing jeers from the outside. (And no, I hadn't really expected any. People tend to avoid hanging around our house. They know Rafe carries a gun and has a legal right to use it. We rarely have to worry about trespassers. At least when we're home.)

"Bathroom," I told him when we reached the second floor. He pointed me in the direction of the door and gave my derriere a swat. It probably jiggled, because he grinned appreciatively. I stuck my tongue out at him before I went inside. It feels like the baby has taken up permanent residence on my bladder, and I have to pee every hour or two. All through the night.

That was the reason why, six hours later, I happened to look out the window into the dark gloom of a November night, and saw a shadow move among the bare trees in the yard. I was on my way back to bed from another trip to the bathroom, and just happened to catch the movement out of the corner of my eye.

I stopped and squinted, peering down into the front yard.

"Something wrong?" my husband's sleepy voice asked from the bed. He's a light sleeper. Two years in prison and another decade deep undercover will do that to a guy. I wasn't the only one not getting much sleep these days.

"Thought I saw something," I told him, still peering through the gloom.

"On the street?" He already sounded more alert.

I shook my head. "In the yard."

The bedsprings squeaked as he moved. His bare feet were silent on the wood floor. I knew he was next to me because I felt the warmth of his skin, not because he made a sound.

I kept looking down. "There."

Something had moved between the trees. Something, or someone.

"Damn," Rafe said, and turned.

"Pants," I reminded him.

"There's a pair downstairs." He ducked out the door.

So there was. Somewhere on the floor in the parlor, where he'd told me to leave them last night. Convenient.

I stayed at the window. There was definitely someone outside. A shadow flitted between the trees and bushes in the yard, making its way toward the house. But it was dark—overcast with no moon, and raining buckets—and it was hard to see the details.

I heard the front door downstairs open and close. A second later, I saw my husband's silhouette come across the grass. He was dressed—if you can call a pair of jeans in November dressed—but he was barefoot and wasn't carrying his weapon.

I thought about opening the window and yelling at him. But I was naked, and it was cold outside. And I didn't want to draw attention to myself. And it helps when I trust him. His night-vision is a lot better than mine. Maybe he'd recognized the intruder and knew there was no reason for fear.

Maybe it was David. Maybe something had happened at home, and he'd wanted to see his father. His biological father. It wouldn't be the first time. David had run away from home a couple of times before, to find Rafe. So there was precedent.

Compared to Rafe, the shadow was short. So it might be David, who was just thirteen, and not fully grown yet. He'd probably end up being tall, but he had a ways to go before he caught up to Rafe's six-three.

My husband wended his way between the tree trunks and bushes. I heard him call out, but not what he said through the closed window. It wasn't a "Hey, you!" sort of demand—more an "I see you and I don't want you to worry, so I'm speaking softly so I don't scare you off," kind of call.

The shadow froze, halfway behind a tree. Rafe stopped in front of it. I assumed they talked for a moment, and then they both began to move toward the house. I left the window to find something to wear, since I'd have to go downstairs to find out what was going on, and since I wasn't about to make the trip naked so I could put on the clothes we'd discarded in the parlor last night. That was fine for Rafe, if he wanted to do it, but I wasn't about to.

Half a minute and a nightgown plus an oversized bathrobe later, I made my careful way down the stairs. I'm so front-heavy these days, I'm always afraid that if I don't hold on and lean back, I'll topple over.

By then, Rafe had guided our visitor into the parlor and deposited her on the sofa where we'd made love last night. The front door was locked and bolted. I checked the position of the lock and the chain on my way past.

And turned into the parlor. Only to stop two steps in, aghast.

"Oh, my God! What happened?"

Speak of the devil... It was just a few hours ago that we'd been sitting here talking about going to visit Mrs. Jenkins tomorrow. Or today, now.

And here she was, sitting in the parlor.

A good ten or fifteen miles away from where she should have been at this time of night, safely tucked away into her bed.

And not only that, but she looked awful. Soaked to the skin, her hair—the consistency of a gray Brillo pad—was sticking out every which way, when it's usually neatly tamed and pinned back. She had left in her house slippers, and had walked far enough—Dear God; hopefully not the full ten or fifteen miles!—to wear holes through both soles. The parts of her feet that peeked through the holes were black from the dirt outside. A blue housecoat stuck to her skin, and just the fact that she wasn't wearing anything else was bad enough, seeing as it was November.

Now, we're talking about Nashville and not North Dakota, so it could have been worse. We weren't dealing with temperatures below freezing yet. But it got chilly at night. And she shouldn't have been out without a coat and without proper shoes and without something to cover her spindly legs.

She shouldn't have been out at all. She should have been tucked up in her dry bed in the very nice facility Rafe had found on the other side of town, where they had always taken good care of her.

Until now.

But the worst of it was the blood. Some must have washed away in the rain, or so I assumed, but there was plenty left. It was streaked across the front of her housecoat and in rivulets down her legs. The fuzzy slippers were caked with it. And there was blood on her hands and under her nails, too. There was even some on her face, probably where she'd touched herself.

My stomach objected. I got over the morning sickness—and afternoon sickness and evening sickness—sometime in the fourth month. I didn't empty my stomach every morning when I tried to brush my teeth anymore. But I'll readily admit that part of me is a little more sensitive than usual these days. I'm a bit more prone to tossing my cookies when something upsetting happens.

And this was upsetting.

I swallowed hard. "Is she hurt?"

While I'd been starting at Mrs. Jenkins, Rafe had found yesterday's T-shirt and pulled it on. Now he shook his head. "She says no."

I lowered my voice. "Whose blood is it?"

Whoever it belonged to had lost quite a bit of it. More, I'd guess, than they could easily afford to lose.

Certainly a lot more than would result from a nosebleed. Or something like a skinned knee.

To lose this much blood, someone would have to have been shot. Or stabbed. Or otherwise very badly hurt.

"Don't know." And he sounded grim.

"We have to call Tamara Grimaldi," I said.

He gave me a look of active dislike. "Why?"

Wasn't it obvious? "She's a homicide detective. If someone's dead, she'd know about it." Or she would want to know about it.

"You gonna sic the police on my grandma, darlin'?"

"It's not like Mrs. Jenkins—" I began. And trailed off.

"Have you lost your mind? Your grandmother didn't kill anyone. Why would she? *How* would she? It's not like they leave scalpels sitting around the place. Or butcher knives. And anyway, she wouldn't have had the strength to stab anyone enough times to cause this."

Don't ask me how I know. Let's just say that I've seen more than my fair share of dead bodies.

"Besides," I added, "why would she want to kill anyone? Who would she want to kill?"

"Until we figure out who's dead," my husband told me grimly, "there's no way to know."

"I still say we should call Grimaldi."

He shook his head. "I'm not talking to Tammy about this. Not until I know what's going on."

I glanced at Mrs. Jenkins. She was paying no attention to us, just sat on the sofa with her hands in her lap, staring at nothing. Dripping. Her eyes were vacant and her mouth slack. Hard to say whether she was scared, or felt guilty, or really had no idea what was going on.

I turned back to Rafe and lowered my voice. Just because she didn't look like she was paying attention, didn't mean she wasn't listening. "She wouldn't arrest your grandmother. Especially not in her condition."

"She'd put her away," Rafe responded, his own voice also low. "Into some sort of facility. Where they'd lock her in."

They would. They'd have to. She had this habit of wandering off, so the doors had been locked at the facility where she'd been staying, too.

Until some point yesterday, when she'd found a way out.

Strange that they hadn't called us—or called Rafe—to notify us that she was missing.

But he had other things to worry about at the moment, so I didn't mention that particular wrinkle. There'd be time enough to deal with it tomorrow. Or later today, since we were past midnight. Instead I went back to the main point.

"We have to call some kind of authority. With this much blood, something's happened to somebody. We can't just ignore it."

"I ain't saying we ignore it. I'll figure it out."

"I don't think you have the authority to do that," I told him. "If it's a police matter, the police are supposed to be involved. They ask you for help if they need it. Not the other way around."

My husband works for the TBI, the Tennessee Bureau of Investigation. And while he'd worked with the police on many occasions before—including with our friend, homicide detective Tamara Grimaldi—the chain of events had always started with the MNPD asking the TBI for help. Not the other way around. And certainly not with the TBI refusing to call in the MNPD on what I suspected—what he had to suspect—was a murder.

"I'll take care of it." He got to his feet. "I need you to get her cleaned up and into bed. I'll mop up the floor."

I stared at him. "Wouldn't that be destroying evidence?"

"I'm not telling you to incinerate her clothes. Just give her a shower and dry her off. I'm not calling the cops tonight. And I don't want her going to sleep with blood all over her."

It sounded like destroying evidence to me. But he was a TBI agent, and I wasn't. So while I questioned his judgment, there wasn't much I could do about it. I wasn't about to go over his head—or behind his back—and call Grimaldi, no matter how much I thought we should. "OK."

He looked relieved. Apparently he didn't like arguing any better than I did. "Thanks, darlin'."

"No problem," I said, although between you and me, I wasn't so sure. I had a feeling we were in for a bumpy ride, and I was pretty sure his actions tonight wouldn't make things any easier.

TWO

I hosed Mrs. Jenkins down and got her situated in the lavender bedroom upstairs. It had been hers during the month or two she lived here with Rafe last year, although to be honest, I couldn't tell whether she recognized it or not. I wasn't sure whether she recognized me, or knew where she was. She went along with me upstairs, and did everything I told her to do. Got undressed, got into the shower, scrubbed, dried, put on one of my (short) nightgowns—she's a lot smaller than me—and got into bed.

"We're right across the hall," I told her, as I prepared to turn the light out. "If you need anything, just yell."

"Yes, baby." She gave me a toothless smile. I turned the light out and closed the door.

A moment later, I staggered back into our room—only to find the bed empty.

I stared at it for a moment, slowly processing the thoughts.

Rafe wasn't there.

I wanted to go back to sleep, but I didn't want to sleep in an empty bed.

Rafe must still be downstairs.

I made my slow way down the stairs, and found him sitting on the sofa in the parlor. The blood was gone, and the sofa was mostly dry again. "Problem?"

He arched a brow.

"Beyond the obvious. Don't you want to come back to bed? It's still early." Or late. Not time to get up.

"Not sure I could sleep," he told me.

Lucky guy. I was dead on my feet, and couldn't wait to shut my eyes again. But I did the right thing. I staggered across the floor, in mostly a straight line, and sat down across from him. "Want to talk about it?"

He looked at me for a second. "She asleep?"

"She's in bed. I'm not sure she's sleeping. But she looked pretty beat, so I don't think it'll be long."

He nodded. "Anything I need to know about?"

"I didn't see any marks on her," I said, "if that's what you mean. No scratches, no wounds. A few bruises, but that could be from anything, really. People bruise more easily when they're older."

It didn't mean that she'd been in a fight. Not at all.

"She's wearing one of my nightgowns," I added. "I left her clothes on the floor upstairs. I thought you might want them." To run DNA on the blood, or something. "They're nasty."

He still didn't say anything, and I continued. "It took a lot of blood to make them look like that, Rafe."

He nodded. "I know."

"Could somebody lose that much blood and still survive?"

He shrugged. Hard to say whether it was anger, or helplessness, or just frustration.

"What are you going to do?"

He just looked at me for a second. I got the sense that maybe he was weighing what he wanted to tell me. Or deciding what he didn't want me to know. Or maybe he was just trying to figure things out.

"Right now," he said eventually, "I'm gonna stay down here. Just in case."

"In case of what?"

"In case she wakes up and comes downstairs. Or in case

someone knocks on the door. Who knows if someone followed her here?"

He sounded angry. Not with me, I assumed, but with the situation. Or the position it had put him in.

And me pushing him wasn't likely to help. So I just nodded. "I'm going to go upstairs and try to get some more sleep, while I still can. Maybe we can talk more about it in the morning."

He nodded, and looked relieved. Maybe he didn't know exactly what he was going to do yet, and me asking him made him worry.

I got up and went over to kiss him. "I love you."

His arms held on for a second longer than necessary before he let go. "I love you, too."

"We'll figure it out."

He nodded.

"I'll see you in the morning," I said, and headed for the hallway and the stairs. He didn't say anything to call me back, and when I glanced into the parlor on my way up the stairs, he was staring straight ahead, his face grim.

We might figure it out, but even when we did, I had a feeling the outcome wasn't necessarily going to be a good one.

I slept late the next morning. I usually sleep late, and with the excitement in the middle of the night, I was extra tired. It was past nine by the time I rolled out of bed and into the shower. Mrs. Jenkins's clothes from last night were gone from the tile floor. Rafe must have picked them up. The door to the lavender bedroom was still shut, so hopefully Mrs. Jenkins was asleep. I could hear the sound of the TV from downstairs—the news—so Rafe was awake. And maybe checking to see whether there were any breaking stories about murder overnight.

I went through my morning ritual in a hurry, and made my way downstairs, with my hair still wet and my makeup undone. By now, the door to the lavender bedroom was open, and the bed empty, so Mrs. J must be downstairs. I wondered whether she'd headed down in my nightgown, or whether she'd dug up something else to wear.

My nightgown, as it turned out. They were in the kitchen: Rafe at the stove scrambling eggs, and Mrs. Jenkins at the table, wreathed in toothless smiles. "Morning, baby," she told me when I came in.

"Good morning, Mrs. J," I said politely. Her gray hair was still sticking out every which way, but at least it was clean. And the nightgown—several sizes too big, even before I got pregnant—hung off one bony shoulder all the way down to the elbow. Her feet under the table were bare.

Her avid little raisin eyes fastened on my stomach. "How's that grandbaby of mine?"

So that answered the question I hadn't asked. And couldn't ask, because to ask would be rude, and anyway, she wouldn't be able to answer. But it wasn't her grandbaby I was carrying. Rafe was her grandbaby. This was her great-grandbaby. She was back in time today, thirty-two years or so. To when LaDonna—whom Tondalia Jenkins had never actually met—had been pregnant with Rafe.

"He's fine," I told her. "Not much longer now."

She frowned. "You sure that's a boy, baby? You're carryin' kinda high for a boy."

Rafe was definitely a boy. But of course I had no idea how LaDonna had looked pregnant. I wasn't born yet. As for my own baby, during the latest ultrasound, the tech had informed me she wasn't able to observe a penis, so it might be a girl, but the baby could just be contrary. He or she hadn't been terribly cooperative with the wand that was trying to nudge him or her around. At the moment, I had to rely on wives tales to guess the gender of my baby, and even there things were mixed. You're carrying high, so you're having a girl. You crave salty things, so you're having a boy. You're more moody than usual, so you're having a girl. You were the more aggressive partner during sex when you conceived, so you're having a boy.

For the record, I don't know who was more aggressive, because I'm not entirely sure when I conceived. These things aren't accurate to the hour, and we'd had sex a lot. I had cravings for spicy food, which aren't either salty or sweet, but I wasn't turning down ice cream or pretzels either. Often together. Logically, I should be having twins. However, I knew I wasn't. If nothing else, the ultrasound had been clear on that point.

As for being moody, I figured that was unavoidable, whatever the gender of the baby. When you walk around looking and feeling like a small hippo, it's hard to feel good about yourself, no matter how miraculous you are for growing a baby inside you.

"Show me your hands," Mrs. Jenkins demanded. I figured she was going to do some sort of woo-woo palm reading, so I extended them palms up. She crowed. "Aha! I knew it! It's a girl!"

It might be a girl. But in this case I was supposed to be LaDonna, who had definitely had a boy. He was looking at me from in front of the stove, eyebrows arched.

"Don't forget to scramble," I told him, before I addressed Mrs. Jenkins. "I'm pretty sure it's a boy, ma'am."

Her sparse brows pulled together, and I hastened to add, "We'll find out in a couple of weeks. What do you think I should call him?"

"I called my boy Tyrell," Mrs. Jenkins said, with a fond gaze at Rafe, who smiled back. She beamed. "But if I'd had a girl, I'da called her Oneida."

Oneida Collier. I rolled it around in my mouth and tried to imagine my mother's reaction. It wasn't on the—short—list of names I had in mind for a potential girl, but it wasn't bad.

I wasn't calling my potential boy Tyrell, though. Rafe might like that, but you have to draw the line somewhere. Tyrell Collier did not roll off the tongue the way I'd like it to.

"How about William? We could call him Liam. Liam's a popular name these days."

Rafe rolled his eyes. We'd talked about this before. If we named our child Liam, he'd be going to school with five more Liams, since it's one of the most popular names around at the moment. That wasn't why I liked it, but I saw his point. No proud parent wants his or her child to be one of six. We all want them to be unique.

Tyrell Collier would be unique.

Mrs. Jenkins pursed her lips. "William's all right. William Jenkins. That sounds nice."

It sounded just fine, but since the baby wouldn't be a Jenkins, it didn't matter. Liam Collier sounded all right to me.

And then I wondered if Rafe had ever considered taking his father's name. Rafael Jenkins. Rafe Jenkins.

I'd be Savannah Jenkins. The baby might be William Jenkins, if he ended up being a boy.

Rafe had never mentioned it to me, if he had. Considered changing his last name, I mean. He'd grown up as Rafe Collier, son of LaDonna Collier and grandson of Old Jim. He hadn't known his father's name until after LaDonna died. It was last summer, and at that point, Rafe had been thirty. I'm not sure he'd ever considered being anyone else.

I liked being Savannah Collier. I wasn't sure I wanted it to change.

While I'd been pondering, Rafe had served Mrs. Jenkins scrambled eggs. Now he looked at me. "Breakfast?"

I was hungry, but scrambled eggs didn't sound good. "I'll make myself some oatmeal," I said.

He shrugged and began cracking eggs into the pan for his own breakfast. I headed to the pantry for a packet of instant oatmeal. Apples and cinnamon.

Maybe I really was having a girl.

We ate in mostly companionable silence. Mrs. Jenkins shoveled in eggs like she hadn't eaten for a week. I didn't think they starved her at the place she'd been living, but if they'd let her just walk away, who knew what had been going on? It had always seemed like a nice place whenever I'd been there—Rafe wouldn't have left his grandmother in the care of anyone incompetent—but given the situation, I was starting to worry what else had been wrong that we didn't know about.

Rafe waited until Mrs. Jenkins had finished eating, and then he asked, casually, "Do you remember what happened yesterday?"

Mrs. J looked confused for a second. I could tell from her expression that she was thinking hard. Eventually, she must have remembered something, because she said, triumphantly, "We had ice cream for dessert!"

That wasn't what Rafe was looking for, of course, but at least it answered the question I'd had. No, they hadn't been starving her.

"That's great," Rafe said. "Chocolate or vanilla?"

It had been both, as a matter of fact. Or maybe strawberry.

"Neapolitan?" I suggested. Neapolitan sounded good, actually. I wondered if we had any.

Mrs. Jenkins started to look confused again, so Rafe reined the conversation back in. "Was that for dinner?"

Mrs. Jenkins nodded. Her steel-gray hair bobbed. I determined to get a comb and some pins and put it together more neatly, but not until I'd heard the end of the conversation. If she remembered dinner, and didn't remember wrong, she had been at the facility at least through the evening meal last night. Her escape must have been affected later.

It was a long way from there to here. From one side of town to the other. She couldn't have walked. There wouldn't have been enough time, even if she'd left right after dinner. And she would have gotten lost, anyway. Probably not far from the facility.

It was a minor miracle that she'd even set out in the right direction. I wouldn't have been surprised if she'd ended up in Franklin instead of Nashville.

"Do you remember what happened after dinner?" Rafe asked.

She looked confused again, and we could see her mind spinning back. She stuck her bottom lip out. I wasn't surprised when she shook her head.

"Did someone get hurt?" Rafe tried.

Mrs. J blinked at him. "Miz Bristol got hurt. She fell down the stairs."

A fall down the stairs didn't seem like it could have caused all the blood we'd seen on Mrs. Jenkins's clothes.

But maybe, if the victim—Ms. or Mrs. Bristol, in this case—had broken a femur, it had broken the skin, and opened a jugular while it was at it, I guess it was possible.

"Yesterday?" Rafe tried.

Mrs. J looked confused. She probably had no idea what had happened yesterday versus last week versus twenty or thirty years ago.

"Is Ms. Bristol all right?" I tried.

Mrs. J turned to me. "No, baby. She died. Broke her neck." She shook her head sadly.

Then that didn't sound like it would have had anything to do with the blood on Mrs. Jenkins's clothes. Unless Ms. Bristol had fallen down the stairs and cut her head open. Head wounds bleed a lot.

Maybe Mrs. Jenkins had managed to walk off in the confusion. I guess that was possible. It might even explain—maybe—why no one had noticed that she was gone. Or if they had noticed, hadn't called us—called Rafe—to let us know.

"Anything on the news?" I asked my husband.

He shook his head.

"I don't suppose you've tried calling them?"

He hadn't. "Not sure I wanna do that."

"Why not?" Didn't he want to chew someone out for losing track of his grandmother? I did. Anything at all could have happened to her out there. She might have been attacked. She might have gotten lost. She might have fallen in the river or been hit by a car or frozen to death.

Someone had to answer for that. We paid good money every month for them to take care of her. She was there because we thought she'd be safer than we could manage to keep her on our own. Rafe attracts some undesirable attention from time to time, and it was much better not to have Mrs. Jenkins around on those occasions. We couldn't trust her not to open the door to someone who wanted to hurt Rafe by hurting her. And when she'd lived here, she'd had a habit of wandering off. The big estate in Brentwood had seemed like a nice compromise. Medical staff on site, other residents she could socialize with (when she remembered who they were), and lots of green space so she'd have the opportunity to get fresh air, but in a safe—walled—environment where nothing would happen to her.

And now this. Yes, I wanted someone to answer for it.

"Until I know what's going on," Rafe said, "I don't wanna let'em know she's here."

I guess he was still worried that someone would put his grandmother in prison for murder. Even though there'd been nothing on the news about anyone being dead.

He added, "I'd feel better if they'd just call and tell me they've lost her. Then I'd have an excuse to go down there and look around."

That made sense. "If they don't," I said, "I guess we can just wait until lunchtime, and head down. We usually do on Sundays, anyway, so there's nothing unusual about it. And we can just pretend we don't know that she's gone. And see what they say."

Rafe nodded. "If they don't call, that's what I'm gonna do. You're gonna have to stay here with her."

I had figured I would. I'd rather go with him to see what kind of excuse the staff came up with for why we couldn't see Mrs. Jenkins—they might not even admit she was gone!—but someone had to hold down the fort. Mrs. J would wander off otherwise. And it wasn't like we could bring her with us. That would defeat the whole purpose.

He pushed to his feet. "I'm gonna take a shower. You two OK on your own?"

"Fine," I said. "We'll just sit here and finish brunch until you're done. And then we'll figure out what else we can do."

It wasn't my first time babysitting Mrs. Jenkins. Last year, long before we were married, and before we were even involved (except emotionally), Rafe had been in Memphis, or maybe Atlanta, and Mrs. Jenkins had wandered off. The police had had to bring her back, and since the two patrol officers who had found her wandering the streets knew who she was, and since Detective Grimaldi knew that Rafe had asked me to keep an eye on his grandmother while he was gone, she called me. And I ended up spending a couple of nights with Mrs. J until Rafe came back. We'd gone to the movies and had ice cream and she had come with me to work when I'd had something I had to do that I couldn't put off. We'd be just fine on our own for a few hours.

So Rafe took the stairs two at a time, and a minute later I heard the shower kick on. I spent a few minutes cleaning up the kitchen while Mrs. Jenkins watched me from the table. I wondered whether she recognized her old kitchen. It looked very different from what it did when she'd lived here, but she'd made it to the house last night, so she must remember the place, at least to a degree.

When the kitchen was sparkling, we moved out into the parlor, where I got Mrs. J situated in front of the TV. On the Home and Garden network, Bitsy and Bob were on a lakefront bargain hunt, and Mrs. J watched as they toured three houses and settled on one. And the renovations started. When a kitchen cabinet slipped out of Bob's hands and hit Bitsy in the head, she even laughed.

I made sure she was comfortable, and that the front door was locked and bolted, and then I ran upstairs for a minute.

Or not ran so much as waddled as fast as I could, but you know what I mean.

Rafe takes quick showers, so he was already out and dry, but with a towel wrapped around his waist.

When I burst through the door into the bedroom he arched a brow at me.

"She's watching TV," I said. A little breathlessly, both from the climb and the fact that he was practically naked and there was a bed a few feet away.

Not that we could take advantage of it under the circumstances, but a girl can dream.

And in case I haven't mentioned it, Rafe is gorgeous. In clothes and out of them. Especially out of them.

But since it was ten in the morning and his grandmother was downstairs, I resisted the temptation to push him down on the bed so I could have my way with him.

"I need to get her something else to wear," I said instead. "She can't spend the day in a nightgown." Especially one so ill-fitting.

He nodded.

"You should put on some clothes, too." It would make it easier for me to tear myself away.

He grinned. "In a minute."

"You're not making this any easier, you know."

He nodded. "I know."

"I have to get back down to her. I don't want to leave her alone any longer than I have to." Just in case she made a break for it. In my nightgown and bare feet.

He nodded sympathetically. And stood there, oozing testosterone and sex-appeal. In nothing but a towel that kept sliding lower on his hips.

Unless that was just my imagination. It might have been.

I sniffed and turned away. He chuckled and did the same. I could hear the towel hit the floor, but I resisted the temptation to peek. Mostly.

Digging through the drawers, I found a pair of thick socks for Mrs. Jenkins, since her slippers were destroyed. Her feet were a lot smaller than mine, so my shoes wouldn't do her any good, but the socks would provide some warmth and a cushion against the floor. My underwear would have to do, too, since it was all I had. And then I dug up a short T-shirt dress I'd bought in a moment of insanity at some point, when I'd wanted something comfortable to wear that didn't cost a lot. After I got it home, I'd realized it was about a foot too short, so the tag was still on it, since I hadn't bothered to take it back for a refund. The few dollars it cost just hadn't seemed worth the trip.

I added a cardigan to the pile, and turned to Rafe. He'd been taking his time getting dressed—probably pulling his socks on with his teeth, to make the process last as long as possible—so he was still only half dressed. And in the process of buttoning his jeans. As slo-o-o-o-o-wly as he could.

"Knock it off," I told him crossly. "You know we can't do anything about it. Not with your grandmother downstairs. And driving me crazy so I spend the rest of the day thinking about getting you naked when I should be focusing on keeping your grandmother safe, isn't going to help."

He must have seen the sense of that, because he grabbed a long-sleeved T-shirt and yanked it over his head. It was sad to see all those lovely muscles disappear, but having him decently covered did wonders for my peace of mind.

"Thank you," I said.

"No problem."

"I'll make it up to you."

He grinned. "No doubt."

I took the stack of clothes for Mrs. Jenkins and headed for the door. "I'll see you downstairs."

"I'm coming," Rafe said, and followed me out the door. "Let me take that, so you can hold on."

He took the clothes out of my hands and nipped in front of me. He can move fast for a big man. "I'll go first. That way, if you fall, I'll be there to catch you."

"I'm not going to fall," I told him, but I let him take the clothes and go first, and I did hold onto the banister on my way down. I didn't want to fall, either.

THREE

Rafe spent an hour or so on the sofa with his grandmother, watching Bitsy and Bob muddle their way through their lake house renovation. Eventually, the house was ready, with big, gorgeous, floor-to-ceiling windows letting in the lake view, and Rafe got to his feet. "I'm gonna go."

I nodded. "Good luck."

"I'll take the Harley, in case you wanna go somewhere."

I glanced out the window. It was chilly outside, and looked like rain. Not very pleasant for a leisurely ride. Especially a leisurely fifteen-mile ride on a bike. "You can take the car. The weather looks questionable."

He shook his head. "I'll be fine on the bike. If you go into labor and you have to go to the hospital, the two of you need the car."

He had a point. I tried to imagine maneuvering the heavy bike to the hospital, with Mrs. Jenkins hanging onto the back. The mind boggled.

"I don't expect to go into labor today," I said. "Not with three weeks to go. But leave the car, by all means. Better safe than sorry."

"That's my girl." He bent his head and brushed my lips with his. "Take care of yourself. And our baby. And my grandma."

I promised him I'd take care of everyone, and watched him

shrug on his leather jacket and head out into the chilly November day. It wasn't raining, not precisely, but the air was wet, even if nothing was specifically falling from the sky.

He took off down the driveway. I watched until he was gone, and then I went inside to Mrs. Jenkins. A new show had started, and another couple had replaced Bitsy and Bob. They wanted to buy a tiny home and live in it with their three children. All under the age of five.

Mrs. J was enthralled. I went looking for my phone.

I wasn't going to give anything away to Detective Grimaldi. Rafe was worried about his grandmother, and I could understand that. I was worried, too. I didn't think she could have killed anyone—certainly not without incurring some sort of injuries to herself—but I knew what it looked like. Somebody doesn't get that much blood on them from a nosebleed.

At the same time, I needed information. About what, I wasn't sure. But if anyone was dead, Grimaldi might know. And might tell me, if I probed carefully and without giving away why I wanted to know.

For all I knew, she might be off work this weekend, and knew nothing at all about anything. And in that case, it would just be a cordial check-in with a woman I considered a friend and who considered my brother—maybe—something more.

So I dialed. And waited for Tamara Grimaldi to pick up. On the TV, Saffron and Gus and their three kids were looking at a school bus turned into living quarters and marveling at how spacious it was.

"Just wait until the kids grow past three feet each," I wanted to tell them, but of course I couldn't. And the real estate agent didn't, just watched them with a beaming smile while almost-visible dollar signs floated around her head.

I'm a real estate agent. I like dollar signs. But I wouldn't be beaming while a family of five were talking about moving into a school bus. I'd be trying to talk them out of it.

The phone was picked up on the other end. "Savannah."

Grimaldi has finally wrapped her brain around my first name, after calling me Ms. Martin for the first year we knew each other.

"Detective." On the other hand, I've never wrapped my brain around calling her Tamara. And while Rafe calls her Tammy, no one else does. Not even her own family.

I've never asked my brother Dix what he calls her. They've been very circumspect about their relationship. To such a degree that I'm not even a hundred percent sure they have one.

"What's going on?" Grimaldi wanted to know.

"Nothing," I said.

Grimaldi didn't answer. She has the interrogation technique down pat. Don't say anything, and let the suspect squirm. I squirmed, until the silence got to be too much for me. "I'm just saying hello. It's been a couple of days since we talked."

"Is someone dead?" Grimaldi wanted to know.

That's what I wanted to know. "I'm sure a lot of people are dead. But you'd know that better than I would. Are you working on anything interesting?"

"No," Grimaldi said. "And it wouldn't be any of your business if I were."

"Just making conversation," I said. Sort of airily.

"Uh-huh. Your husband around?"

I told her he wasn't. "He's on his way to Brentwood to see his grandmother."

Mrs. Jenkins gave me a startled look over the back of the sofa. I smiled apologetically and wandered toward they foyer while I lowered my voice. She was already confused enough, poor thing. Hearing me lie about things wouldn't make her any less so. "Speaking of..."

"Yes?" Grimaldi said.

"I heard that someone fell down the stairs at the nursing home and died. A Mrs. or Ms. Bristol. Can you shed any light on that?"

"None at all," Grimaldi told me. "I had nothing to do with it. I don't know that anyone else did. First of all, depending on where in Brentwood this place is, it could be Williamson County's jurisdiction, and then the sheriff there would likely be in charge, if there were suspicious circumstances. If not, the attending physician might just have signed the death certificate and sent the body to the funeral home for cremation or burial."

"Without an autopsy?"

"There's not always an autopsy," Grimaldi said. "People die in nursing homes all the time. It's expected. Most of them expire quietly. The family can ask for an autopsy if they feel they have cause for concern, but with most elderly people, it's bag and tag."

It took me a second to wrap my brain around 'bag and tag.' When I had, I said, "What about a fall down the stairs? Would someone order an autopsy for that?"

"Maybe, maybe not," Grimaldi said. "It would depend. If someone saw her, and could testify that she just lost her footing and fell, then no. If it happened while no one was looking—an unattended death—then maybe. It would depend on the doctor. How suspicious he was that it wasn't an accident. How eager he'd be to try to make something of it. And how likely it was that she didn't just fall."

So basically, there was no way to know. Not a particularly comforting thought, that someone could push you down the stairs in a nursing home, and just because you were old, nobody would bother to investigate.

"Did your grandmother-in-law say anything to make you think it was suspicious?" Grimaldi wanted to know.

She hadn't. But then again— "You know how she is."

Grimaldi agreed that she did. "I hope everything is all right?"

"As far as I know," I said. "If it isn't, I'm sure Rafe will figure it out when he gets there."

Grimaldi said she was sure he would, too.

"So are you working today?" I asked.

Grimaldi said she was off, but on call in case anything needed her attention.

"You didn't drive to Sweetwater to see Dix?"

"No," Grimaldi said.

"Is everything all right?"

"Everything's fine," Grimaldi said.

OK, then. I could tell from her tone of voice that she didn't want to talk about it, which made me want to talk about it more, but I respected her boundaries. Sort of. Instead, I came at the matter from a different angle. "Are you coming to Sweetwater for Thanksgiving?"

"No," Grimaldi said.

"Didn't Dix invite you?"

He had.

"Do you have to work?"

"It's a family occasion," Grimaldi said. "I'm not family."

She wasn't. But Bob Satterfield would be there—Mother's beau—and he was just as much family as Grimaldi was. Emotionally attached to one of the Martins.

"I'm sure you'd be welcome. Things are going to be awkward this year anyway, what with Darcy and all."

Darcy had been my brother's receptionist for the past couple of years. That was before we realized that she was also our half-sister, through a youthful fling of my father's. Before he met Mother, naturally. But even so, Mother was a little leery around Darcy, and still royally pissed off at Audrey, Darcy's biological mother, who had known for thirty-four years that she'd given birth to my father's child, and had never mentioned it to anyone.

Every Thanksgiving for thirty-three years, Audrey had been there as part of the family. She's been my mother's best friend since Mother came to Sweetwater as a young bride.

This year, she probably wasn't invited. Darcy probably was—Mother was doing her best to be polite—but it wasn't like Darcy would enjoy it when she knew her biological mother was sitting at home alone, gnawing on a turkey-leg by her lonesome. So either way you sliced it, it would be an awkward evening.

"That's all right," Grimaldi said, as if I'd offered her a wonderful opportunity. "I usually work on holidays. That way, the detectives who have families can be home with them."

That made sense. And was very nice of her. I said so. She grunted.

"Well, we should grab lunch sometime soon," I said brightly, and then wished I hadn't. She had the day off today—unless she got called in on a case—but I couldn't have lunch with her. If she suggested it, I'd have to decline. And I couldn't tell her it was because I had to babysit Mrs. Jenkins, since she wasn't supposed to know that Mrs. Jenkins was here.

Luckily, she didn't take the bait. "That sounds nice," she said instead, politely. "I'll see what I can find out about your Ms. or Mrs. Bristol, and get back to you."

Honestly, I didn't really care what had happened to Ms. or Mrs. Bristol. She was old; she'd probably just lost her balance and fallen. Of course, if someone had pushed her, I didn't want them to get away with it. But it wasn't really any of my business, either way. It wasn't likely to have had anything at all to do with why Mrs. Jenkins had shown up in our yard in the middle of the night.

But I had brought it up, and Grimaldi thought she was doing me a favor. So I said thank you, nicely, and hung up. And went back to the parlor to watch Saffron and Gus and their three kids decide between the school bus, a tiny home trailer—"We can park it anywhere!"—and a small cabin in the woods. Neither was above three hundred square feet. I shuddered thinking about it.

Saffron, Gus, and company went with the school bus. I figured they would. And I figured, in three years, that bus would be parked in the backyard of some cookie cutter subdivision home somewhere, and the kids would be using it as a doll house.

Another show started, and I went to the kitchen to make lunch. Mrs. Jenkins scarfed down tomato soup and a cheese sandwich like she hadn't seen food in days, although it was only a few hours since Rafe had fed her scrambled eggs. I have no idea where she put it all. She was as scrawny as a bird, and it wasn't like she did much. Today, all she'd done was sit in front of the TV. Although I guess she must have expended a bit of energy yesterday, getting from Brentwood to here.

I didn't think Rafe had asked, so I decided I would. "Mrs. Jenkins?"

She nodded. "Yes, baby?"

Her mouth was full of sandwich, so it came out a little garbled.

"Can you remember what happened yesterday? When you left the nursing home and came here?"

"Home," Mrs. Jenkins said. She lifted a spoonful of soup and slurped it down, loudly.

I nodded. "Right. You came home. Can you remember how you got here?"

"Walked," Mrs. Jenkins said.

"The whole way from Brentwood?"

Mrs. J looked confused, like she didn't know where Brentwood was. Or that she'd been living there for the past year.

I rephrased. "Did you walk the whole way?"

Mrs. J shook her head. "Gotta ride."

"Did you? What kind of ride? Who was driving?"

She looked confused again.

"Did you take a cab?" I asked. The trick, obviously, was making the questions simple. And sticking to one at a time. "Maybe a bus?"

Mrs. J shook her head.

"Did you hitchhike?" Would someone have picked up an old lady in a housecoat and slippers in the middle of the night, and just taken her where she wanted to go? Wouldn't they have driven her to the nearest police station, or the nearest hospital, instead?

Or maybe not. There are plenty of people out there who mind their own business. Even when maybe they shouldn't.

Mrs. J shook her head. She was slurping soup again.

"Do you know the person who gave you the ride?"

"No, baby," Mrs. Jenkins said.

No. Well, she wouldn't, if whoever it was had picked her up off the road. And she wasn't likely to be able to give a description of the person, or of the car, either. At least not a description that would help us find that person.

And what would we do if we did? He or she hadn't broken any laws. There are no laws against giving people rides. Even in the middle of the night.

I devoted myself to my own cheese sandwich, and to watching someone else squeeze their life into a couple hundred square feet.

A bit later, I heard the rumble of the Harley-Davidson's engine outside, and left Mrs. Jenkins dozing in front of the TV to greet Rafe.

The drizzle had gone from soft mist to hard, driving rain while we'd been watching TV, and he was soaked to the bone. I ordered him upstairs to take a hot shower and get into dry clothes while I whipped up another sandwich and bowl of soup. I wanted to know what, if anything, he'd discovered, but I wasn't going to make him stand in the foyer, dripping on the hardwood floors, while he told me. So I busied myself in the kitchen while I heard the shower turn on and then off again. A couple of minutes later he came down the stairs. I heard him linger in the doorway to the parlor for a few seconds, but I didn't hear his voice, so Mrs. Jenkins must still be asleep. Then he came padding down the hallway to the kitchen. And grinned at the sight of me, barefoot and pregnant, serving up soup and a sandwich at the table. "Looks good."

"I assume you're talking about the food," I said, although between us, the soup was out of a can—or at least a pouch—and the bread was store-bought.

He just winked, and took a seat at the table. I saw his nostrils flare. "Smells good, too."

"Tomato soup," I said, although that was obvious from looking at it. "Grilled cheese sandwich. Your grandmother inhaled hers, so I assume it must taste halfway decent."

Mine had, but then I'm so hungry all the time that most things taste good.

"I'm sure." He ate a couple of spoonfuls of soup and took a bite of sandwich. And made an approving noise. "M-hm."

"I'm glad," I said, and went to work loading the dishwasher with the dishes Mrs. Jenkins and I had used earlier. When I tiptoed into the parlor to fetch hers, she was snoring gently, her head tipped back and her mouth open. I tiptoed back out, making sure I didn't click the dishes together.

"She's asleep," I told Rafe when I got back into the kitchen. Mrs. Jenkins hadn't left so much as a crumb on her plate. I ran some water over it anyway, and slotted it into the dishwasher.

He nodded.

"We've just been sitting here all day. I tried to get her to tell me how she made it here last night, but I didn't get much out of her. She said someone gave her a ride, but she couldn't tell me who. I'm not sure she knew."

I pulled out the chair on the opposite side of the table—nothing more I could do until he'd finished eating, since I wasn't about to take his flatware away from him before he was finished with it—and maneuvered my bulk onto it. "You weren't gone long."

"I didn't think I would be." He popped the last crust of cheese sandwich into his mouth and chewed. After he'd swallowed, he added, "Since I couldn't spend any time with my grandma."

I put my elbows on the table and folded my arms. My mother would have frowned, but Rafe didn't seem to notice. Or care. "What did they give you as an excuse for why you couldn't see her? Or hadn't they realized she was gone?"

"They signed me right in," Rafe said. "Asked me if I knew where to go. I said yes, and headed down the hall. The room was empty, of course, so I went back to the receptionist and told her so. She didn't believe me at first. Then she called an orderly, who went back to the room with me to make sure I hadn't just overlooked something."

"But of course you hadn't."

He shook his head. "The orderly agreed that she wasn't there. He said he had no idea where she was. Maybe outside taking a walk."

I glanced at the rain-streaked window. "In this?"

Rafe lifted a shoulder. "I guess it was the best they could do. I mean, she wasn't where she was supposed to be."

No. She was on the sofa in the parlor.

"Did you get the impression they were lying?" He's good at picking up on lies.

"Those two?" He shook his head. "No."

"Someone else?"

"Someone's gotta know. Maybe one of the people I met, maybe not. But she was there for the bed check at nine last night. They mark'em all off on a chart."

"She could have been marked off without actually being there," I said.

He nodded. "Might could. I asked if he could call the night nurse and double-check, but he said he didn't wanna wake her. She'd been on till seven this morning, so she'd be asleep now."

Understandable.

"He said she's coming back in at seven tonight—she works three twelve-hour shifts every weekend—so he'd double-check then, and call me back if anything changed."

"That's helpful," I said.

Rafe grunted.

"Don't you think so?"

He shrugged. "I don't tend to trust helpful people. Specially when their own self-interest is involved."

He had a point. "I guess, if he's lost her—or rather, since he's lost her, but maybe he doesn't realize it yet—he has incentive to want to make you believe everything is copacetic."

Rafe nodded. "I asked if anybody'd checked on her this morning. If they do a bed check at night, maybe they do a check in the morning, too. You'd think they would."

You would. Since, occasionally—according to Grimaldi, anyway—some of the elderly pass on of natural causes. And since some of them probably needed help getting up and dressed. Mrs. Jenkins needed help getting dressed, as I had cause to know, having been the one dressing her both last night and this morning.

"Was she checked off on the list?"

"No," Rafe said. "The day nurse came on at seven, and spent the first hour doing bed checks and serving breakfast. By the time she got to my grandma's room, it was empty. But since she ain't confined to bed, they just assumed she was up early and was down in the dining room, eating."

It was a logical assumption, although given the facts—she'd made it out of the facility and was fifteen miles away—it seemed to me like they should have taken the disappearance a bit more seriously.

"Once they finally figured out she was gone," Rafe said, "they decided to look for her. I tried to stay, but since I ain't a medical, they can't have me walking into people's rooms and such. You and I know that she's right here, but they don't, so they're gonna look for her. From top to bottom. And all across the property. In every room. They can't explain how she coulda gotten outta the building after bed check without alerting the night nurse, so they're pretty sure she's somewhere in the building."

"Except she isn't. She's here." So she must have gotten out of the building. Without setting off the alarms.

Rafe nodded. "She wouldna remembered the codes, even if somebody'd given'em to her. And nobody would have. So somebody musta let her out."

"Who would have done such a thing? And why?"

"Not sure yet," Rafe said. "But I'm guessing it's got something to do with the blood on her clothes. She saw something. Or someone. And that someone didn't want her around to talk about it."

So that someone had made sure she couldn't.

"Any idea where the blood came from?"

"I looked," Rafe said. "I didn't see none. And there were no cops around. It didn't look like anybody came to work this morning and found a mutilated body taking up space."

That was encouraging, anyway.

"Course," Rafe added pensively, "they might not have found it yet."

"If it was outside, you mean?"

"Or if someone took it with them."

"Wouldn't there still be blood?"

"You'd think," Rafe said, and got to his feet. "I'm gonna go do like my grandma, and take a nap in front of the TV. I didn't get much sleep last night."

I nodded, and pushed myself upright, too. "You go ahead.

I'm going to finish filling the dishwasher. I'll be in later."

Rafe nodded and wandered off down the hallway. When I came into the parlor five minutes later, he was sprawled in one of the chairs with his eyes closed. I curled up in a corner of the sofa—the one Mrs. Jenkins wasn't occupying—and watched TV.

FOUR

The day passed slowly. Seven o'clock came and went without a call from the nursing home. It might have been an oversight, I guess. Maybe the staff went home, and whoever took their place didn't realize they were supposed to call Rafe. If this had been a real emergency—if Mrs. J had been missing without us knowing that she was safe—we would have been freaking out well before seven in the evening. The fact that nobody called to tell us anything was, frankly, pretty disturbing.

"I thought this was a good place," I told Rafe over dinner.

He looked grim. "Me, too. If I don't hear something tomorrow morning, I'm going down there and raising hell."

I glanced at Mrs. Jenkins, who was happily tucking into spaghetti and meatballs, and lowered my voice. I had no idea whether she knew or understood what we were talking about, but I didn't want to worry her. "Can you do that? I mean, when you know that she isn't actually missing?"

"I can raise hell about them not getting back to me. And about them letting her walk out. Which they musta done, or she wouldn't be here."

Indeed. "I don't suppose you have any idea who would have let her out? I mean, someone must have, right? She couldn't have gotten through the security on her own."

Rafe nodded. "I suppose she mighta slipped out. While somebody was busy hauling a body, say, and wasn't paying attention. If they left the door open or something."

Possible. "So it might not have been deliberate."

He shook his head. "Coulda happened either way. She saw something and snuck out while the door was open, to see what was going on. Or she saw something, and somebody figured it wasn't safe to leave her behind to talk."

"And when you say 'something,' you mean a murder."

"Most likely," Rafe said. "It was a helluva lot of blood on her dress. Not her blood. So she musta been right there when somebody was bleeding."

"Might it have been an animal? If she got out somehow, and was wandering the road, and came upon a dog or a deer someone had hit?" My stomach clenched a little at the thought. Last month, Rafe and I had rescued a dog named Pearl from a crime scene. We'd intended to bring her home with us, but instead, of all people, Pearl had bonded with my mother, and Mother with her. So Pearl had stayed behind in Sweetwater, at the Martin Mansion. Mother took good care of her, I was certain. But the idea of Pearl—or someone else's Pearl—getting out and getting hit by a car was disturbing.

Of course, if Mrs. Jenkins had been wandering along the side of the road, she might have been hit by a car, too, and that was even more disturbing. The nursing home had really dropped the ball badly on this one.

Rafe lifted a shoulder. "Mighta been, I guess. But I drove that road, and I didn't see nothing like that."

"If someone picked up the dog or the deer, and the rain washed away the blood...?"

He shook his head. "I dunno, darlin'. I suppose it's possible. I'll take the dress to the lab tomorrow and get the blood analyzed. If nothing else, it'll tell us whether it's human or animal."

That would be a step in the right direction. If nothing else, finding out that it was animal blood would allow us to stop worrying about what Mrs. Jenkins had seen—and maybe done—and whether there was a dead body somewhere that no one had discovered yet.

"If it's human," I said; Rafe's brows lowered, "it's not like anyone would consider her sane. She wouldn't end up in prison."

"She wouldn't end up in prison anyway. Because she didn't do nothing."

"Of course not. But that might be hard to prove, if she can't remember what happened."

Rafe didn't say anything to that.

"Are you sure we shouldn't contact Grimaldi? She knows Mrs. Jenkins. She'd help us figure out what's going on."

"No," Rafe said. "Bad enough that I'm gonna sneak around and lie. I ain't asking her to do the same."

He added, "And anyway, the group home's in Williamson County. If anything's going on down there, it'd be Williamson County's problem."

"All the more reason to ask Grimaldi for help. It wouldn't be a conflict of interest for her."

"I don't think it works that way," Rafe said. "Don't worry about it, darlin'. I'll take care of it. You just take care of my grandma."

Fine. "I'll take care of your grandma. But for the record, I'd like you to talk to somebody about what's going on. If you don't want to involve the police," and if it wouldn't be their case in any case, it probably didn't make much sense to do so, "at least talk to Wendell."

Wendell Craig was Rafe's handler during the years he was undercover. Now he's Rafe's boss, although they're really more like partners.

Rafe said he would. "Eat your food, darlin'. You gotta keep your strength up."

I assumed that meant we'd get busy later, after Mrs. Jenkins was asleep, and devoted myself to my spaghetti.

The next morning, he got up and out early. I was still in bed, with my eyes slitted against the sunlight pouring through the curtains, when he kissed me goodbye and grabbed the bag with Mrs. Jenkins's soiled housedress and slipped out the door and down the stairs. I heard the front door lock, and a few seconds later, the roar of the Harley-Davidson starting up outside the window.

At least the weather looked nicer today, what I could see of it. He wouldn't get wet driving to work.

I had nowhere to be today. There's a staff meeting at work every Monday morning, but it wasn't like I could bring Mrs. Jenkins with me, so I would have to skip it this week. Not like I had much to report anyway. Between you and me, I wasn't sure why I bothered pretending. I wasn't selling any real estate. I wasn't really working toward selling any real estate, either. I liked the idea of selling real estate, but when it came to the reality of it, I was doing a—pardon my French—piss-poor job of actually finding clients.

My license was up for renewal soon. Maybe I just wouldn't bother renewing it for next year. We could save the money I spent on the fees and the continuing education I had to take every year to keep the license current. Rafe didn't make a whole lot—people in law enforcement generally don't; it's a thankless job, and nobody pays you what you're worth—but we were living cheaply, and we would survive. Maybe I could find something else I'd be good at, that could bring in some money.

For the first couple of months after the baby was born, I probably wouldn't be able to work anyway.

I put my hand on my stomach, where the baby was still sleeping peacefully. And since he or she was, I went back to sleep, too.

When I woke up again, it was two hours later. After eight, sliding toward half past. And it was a case of opening my eyes, wide awake, from one second to the next. None of the leisurely stretching and waking slowly.

Usually, that happens as a result of hearing something. I focused, but didn't hear anything at all.

Which was a little suspicious in and of itself, actually. Sure, Rafe was gone. But Mrs. Jenkins was here. Or was supposed to be.

I rolled out of bed. As soon as my feet hit the floor, I figured out my balance—a little different every morning, as the baby grew bigger—and padded toward the door.

The door to the lavender bedroom stood open. I didn't even need to look inside—although I did—to know that Mrs. Jenkins wasn't there.

The bed was empty. So was the bathroom. The door was unlocked, to I was able to check.

I stuck my head into the yellow room at the end of the hall, just in case she'd decided to visit the nursery, but the room was also empty. Normally, I would have taken a second to admire the bright walls and the white crib (borrowed from my sister Catherine along with a matching dresser/changing table), and the colorful quilt hanging over the side of the crib... but today I didn't. I just turned on my bare heel and headed for the stairs to the first floor.

I guess I should have stopped to put on some clothes, or at least a dressing gown. But to be honest, I was worried. I think I mentioned that Mrs. Jenkins had a habit of wandering off. She used to do it when she'd lived here before. And I was in charge of keeping her safe. I didn't know how I'd be able to tell Rafe the news if I'd allowed his grandmother to vanish.

The hallway was empty. I stuck my head into the parlor—maybe she'd decided to come downstairs and watch some more HGTV—but the sofa was also empty. The TV screen was black.

I padded down the hallway toward the kitchen. "Mrs. Jenkins?"

On the way, I stuck my head through the door into the library. More than a year ago, when I first met Rafe again (twelve years after he left Columbia High), there'd been a dead body in this room.

Today there wasn't. Nor was there a live body anywhere.

I burst into the kitchen stomach first. When I got up to speed, my mass kept me going, and I ended up several steps into the room, looking around.

My heart sank. There was no Mrs. Jenkins here.

On the plus-side, the stove wasn't on, and we weren't in danger of burning the house down. That kind of thing can be a concern when you're dealing with people who forget what they're doing. But if she'd been in this room, she hadn't left any sign of her passing.

The basement door was locked and bolted. The back door was also locked. No one had come through here.

I headed back down the hallway to the front. "Mrs. Jenkins?"

It was stupid to think she'd answer. I'd already called for her on my way down, and she hadn't answered then. Besides, I'd checked the house, and she wasn't here. So how would she hear me?

We do have a third floor. There's one big room up there, at the top of the house. Back when the Victorian was built, in the 1880s sometime, they'd used it as a ballroom. It was possible that she'd gone up there rather than down.

I hesitated at the bottom of the stairs, debating. It was a long way up. Lots of steps. It would take a while to drag myself up there.

And then I saw that the front door was unlocked. Rafe wouldn't have left it that way. He wouldn't have been able to put on the security chain from outside, but he'd have locked the door when he left. Now it wasn't locked. Which meant that someone else had gone out.

I grabbed my coat off the hook and pulled it on over the nightgown. Then I stuck my bare feet into boots and headed out into the yard. "Mrs. Jenkins!"

She was nowhere to be seen. But if what I'd heard—the sound that woke me—had been the front door opening and closing, she had a five minute head start by now. She could be a block away.

Or she could be in the backyard, looking at her sadly decimated vegetable garden, or the overgrown gazebo.

But if she wanted to go there, surely she would have gone out the back door, wouldn't she?

I ducked back inside for long enough to grab my purse and keys. I didn't use them to lock the door, though. If Mrs. Jenkins came back before me, I wanted her to be able to get inside.

The Harley-Davidson was gone, of course, but my pale blue Volvo was parked on the gravel at the bottom of the stairs. I peered inside—maybe Mrs. Jenkins had decided to go for a ride—but the interior was empty. So I fit myself, with some difficulty, behind the wheel and turned the key in the ignition. The engine came to life, and I rolled down the circular driveway toward the street, looking left and right.

We live in East Nashville, in what my real estate colleagues would call a transitional neighborhood. It hasn't transitioned as far as some other parts of East Nashville—the areas on the other side of Ellington Parkway have become insanely expensive, especially when you cross Gallatin Road—but over here, we're still up-and-coming. There are renovations going on, and infills being built—historic-looking buildings on empty lots, that fit in with the architecture in the neighborhood—but the prices are still on the affordable side.

As a result of not being quite transitioned, we've also got

more crime and grime and general unpleasantness. There are more pitbulls chained in more yards, and more plaid couches on more porches, than across the parkway, where they take their designer dogs to doggie day care and wouldn't be caught dead sitting on plaid.

I decided to go right. It was the direction of downtown, and of the Milton House Nursing Home, down on the corner of Potsdam and Dresden, where Mrs. Jenkins had spent some weeks last fall. (Horrible place. Rafe had wasted no time getting her out of there as soon as he could prove he was her grandson.) It was also the direction of Brentwood, and where she must have come from the other night.

And anyway, one guess was as good as another. I had to pick a direction, and I chose that one.

The sunlight glinted on broken glass on the sidewalk as I made the turn. Hopefully Mrs. Jenkins had circumvented it, if she'd come this way. And hopefully she was at least wearing socks. I had no reason to think she'd put on shoes before she left—we didn't have any that would fit her; I'd have to remedy that today—but even an oversized pair of shoes would be better than none. And would slow her down some, too, which was only to the good.

I cruised slowly, looking into yards as I went.

Most of the houses around the Victorian are the cracker-boxes that were put up in the 1940s. There was less money then, and most of the houses that were built during that decade were small.

Houses had gotten progressively smaller for a while, as a matter of fact. My ancestral home, the Martin Mansion, was built around 1840, and boasts around five thousand square feet. Mrs. Jenkins's Victorian, from the 1880s, has around three thousand square feet. The 1920s and 1930s cottages and bungalows tend to be around two thousand, give or take a few hundred square feet. And by the late 1930s, the Great

Depression had made its mark, and then came World War Two, so by the mid-40s, houses were barely a thousand square feet each.

At any rate, I drove down a street lined with small houses. I'd never looked into the history of Mrs. J's house, not beyond the time when she'd bought it, but I wondered whether, if I went back far enough, I'd learn that all this land had belonged to the original owners of the house at one point, and they had sold off parcels of it in the 1940s. I wouldn't be surprised.

Mrs. Jenkins was nowhere to be seen. I passed the first cross-street and continued down toward Dresden, looking left and right.

It was still fairly early, so there was little traffic. After another block, I wound up behind a bus belching clouds of exhaust into the air.

Could Mrs. Jenkins have gotten on the bus?

She'd have had to have money for the fare, then. Or must have found a sympathetic driver who didn't care. It was possible.

I thought about following the bus into downtown.

I also thought, for a crazy second, about buzzing around it, and pulling up in front, so it would have to stop. And so that I could check and see whether Mrs. Jenkins was onboard.

Rafe would have. I could see him in my mind's eye, screeching to a halt in front of the bus and moving up the steps, flashing his badge. It was a very sexy vision that, frankly, left me a little breathless.

However, Rafe wasn't here. There was just me. And I didn't know how I'd be able to explain things to him, if I couldn't get his grandmother back.

The bus lumbered to the corner of Dresden and stopped to wait for the light to change. I idled behind it. When the bus moved forward, I did, too.

Potsdam dead-ends into Dresden, right where the Milton

House Nursing Home is located, so I had to choose to go left or right. The bus was going right, probably toward the main bus station in downtown. I did the same. And as I crept around the corner in its wake, I happened to catch a glimpse of movement out of the corner of my eye.

Something blue. Like the T-shirt dress I had lent Mrs. Jenkins yesterday.

It could have been anything, of course. The parking lot outside the Milton House was full, and I could have seen any number of people coming to visit their loved one. Or one of the nurses, beginning or ending a shift. Or a health inspector, planning to shut the place down. It needed it. I still felt horrible every time I thought about Mrs. Jenkins having been forced to live there.

At any rate, I waited until the bus moved past the entrance to the Milton House, and then I zipped across oncoming traffic and into the parking lot. And crept toward the entrance to the building while I looked around.

It was a good thing I was looking, because Mrs. Jenkins stepped out from between two parked cars with no warning. And it was a good thing the car was moving very slowly, because if I'd gone any faster, I wouldn't have had time to stop before I hit her.

My stomach met the steering wheel with an *oomph*. I ignored it and shoved the door open. And shoehorned myself out. "Mrs. Jenkins!"

She'd kept moving, and had to turn to look at me.

"It's me," I added. "Savannah."

Even when she thinks I'm LaDonna, I don't actually tell her I am. I won't argue with her, because I know I wouldn't be able to convince her otherwise anyway, but I won't tell her I'm LaDonna when I'm not.

In this case, it looked like she had no idea who I was. She blinked at me, her lower lip thrust out.

"You left without a coat," I added. "And without shoes."

The fluffy socks I'd given her yesterday were probably worn through on the bottom. She wasn't bleeding, though. Or at least I couldn't see any evidence of blood spots where she'd walked. But her skinny arms were all over goose pimples.

"We should go home, so you won't freeze."

"I live here," Mrs. J told me, with a gesture toward the Milton House.

I shook my head. "Not anymore. Rafe came, remember? Your grandson. And he brought you home. Back to the house."

No sense in confusing her with the other nursing home she'd spent the past year in. If she thought she still lived at the Milton House, she wouldn't remember the other place.

Mrs. Jenkins looked unsure.

"You remember the house, don't you? And Rafe? And me?"

I don't think she did. But I also don't think she wanted to admit it. And if nothing else, she wasn't moving away from me anymore, so maybe there was some part of her that at least subconsciously knew who I was.

"It's warm in the car," I told her. "And when we get home, I'll make you some breakfast. You must be hungry. You left before I got up."

Mrs. Jenkins hesitated, before shuffling closer. I opened the passenger side door and helped her in. Her fingers were cold enough from the walk that she needed help buckling her seat belt. Or maybe that was just because her fingers are old.

A few seconds later, we rolled out of the parking lot, through the stoplight, and back up Potsdam Street.

"What happened?" I asked Mrs. Jenkins.

She looked at me, blankly.

"Did you wake up and not recognize where you were?"

She looked faintly guilty, so maybe that was what had happened.

"Next time," I told her, as the circular tower on the corner of the Victorian came into view over the bare branches of the trees up ahead, "wake me up instead of going off. I was worried."

She didn't promise she would, and I hadn't expected she would. And then I forgot all about it, as I turned the car into the driveway and—a second too late—noticed the burgundy sedan parked in the place where the Harley usually sits, at the bottom of the stairs.

It had a couple of extra antennae, but other than that, and the government license plate, there wasn't much to distinguish it from any other car on the road.

I recognized it, though. I'd seen it before, many times. I didn't need to see the woman who opened the door and swung long legs out to know I was busted.

FIVE

Tamara Grimaldi didn't say anything. She didn't have to. She just watched while I parked the Volvo behind her unmarked police car. She didn't look surprised to see Mrs. Jenkins in the passenger seat, although her brows did arch when she saw that I was wearing my nightgown under my coat, and that Mrs. Jenkins was shoe-less and without one.

"She left while I was in bed," I explained while I helped Mrs. J out of the car. "The door opening and closing woke me up. By the time I'd checked the house and realized she wasn't there, she'd made it several blocks. I found her making a beeline for the Milton House."

"But she hasn't lived there for more than a year."

I nodded. "I know that. But she didn't remember."

We headed up the steps to the porch. "The door should be open," I told Grimaldi. "I thought that if she came back while I was out looking for her, I wanted her to be able to get in. Maybe you'd be so kind...?"

She nodded and pulled her gun out of the holster at her waist. I don't think either of us really expected anyone to have gone into the house during the few minutes I'd been out, but better safe than sorry.

While Grimaldi went through the house, I filled a basin with warm water and peeled Mrs. Jenkins's socks off.

I was right; she had worn holes right through the soles. The socks ended up in the trash can. Mrs. Jenkins's feet went into the water. I turned on HGTV to keep her occupied—hopefully between that and the basin, she'd stay in place long enough for me to run upstairs and change my own clothes.

By the time I came back down, in pregnancy leggings and an oversized sweater, with my teeth and hair brushed, Grimaldi had finished her search of the house and was sitting in the parlor with Mrs. J, her gun neatly tucked out of sight. Since there was no hogtied body lying in front of the door, I assumed the house had been empty.

"I called your husband," she told me when I came into the room. "He's on his way."

I winced. He probably wouldn't be happy. "There was no need for that. I got her back."

"That's not why I need to talk to him," Grimaldi said.

Uh-oh. "What's going on?"

"I'll tell you when he gets here. That way I won't have to say it twice."

That made sense, even if it made me nervous. "Would you like something to eat?" I asked, for something to do while we waited. "Mrs. Jenkins and I haven't had breakfast yet."

Grimaldi said she'd already eaten. She'd probably been up since the crack of dawn.

"I'm going to go fix something. I'll be right back."

She nodded. "I'll stay with her."

Mrs. Jenkins looked settled for the moment, her eyes on the screen and her feet in the water, but it was better not to take any chances. Take your attention off her for a second, and she might be gone. I nodded.

Since Rafe was coming soon, and I didn't want to miss any of the conversation, and since I was hungry and didn't feel like waiting, I made breakfast simple. Two bowls of oatmeal with cinnamon sprinkled on top and raisins folded in, and I was back in the parlor.

"I hope you like oatmeal," I told Mrs. Jenkins as I handed her one. She smiled, so she might. Or maybe she just, like most people of her generation who wasn't spoiled the way mine was, would eat pretty much anything, because food wasn't always plentiful. When you're hungry, it doesn't much matter what someone puts in front of you. As long as it's food, you don't turn it down.

I curled up in the other corner of the sofa and went to work on my own oatmeal. It's not my favorite, but I don't mind it. And I certainly don't want to come across as spoiled, although I'm sure I am. Compared to the way Rafe had grown up, in a trailer in one of the poorest parts of Sweetwater, with a single, teenage mother and a frankly pretty hateful grandfather, I'd been brought up in the lap of luxury, wanting for nothing.

So I ate my not very exciting oatmeal—it was good for the baby—and then I cleaned up the bowls and dried Mrs. Jenkins's feet. I'd found another pair of fluffy socks for her, that she could wear until we could make a trip to the store and find something better.

By the time I had finished doing that, the Harley was pulling up outside. When I heard Rafe's boots on the porch, I went to undo the security chain on the door and let him in.

I could tell he wasn't happy. He leaned down and brushed my cheek with his lips, but he didn't lean in for a lingering kiss the way he usually does, even with an audience. He did put a hand on my stomach for a second, though, warm even through the sweater. "Everything all right?"

I nodded. "Your grandmother escaped this morning, but I caught her. She was on her way to the Milton House. She thought she lived there."

His eyebrows drew down. "She all right?"

"She's fine. We just had a bowl of oatmeal each. When we're done here, I'm going to take her shopping. For a pair of shoes and some clothes that fit better than mine."

He lowered his voice. "Has she said anything?"

This wasn't about Mrs. Jenkins. We've been together long enough for me to follow the way his mind works.

I shook my head. "She said she wanted to wait until you got here. So she wouldn't have to explain twice."

"Then let's hear it."

He put a hand on my back and nudged me into the parlor ahead of him.

"So what's going on?" I asked brightly when he'd deposited me on the sofa next to Mrs. Jenkins, and was in the process of taking the chair across the table from Grimaldi.

She looked from me to Mrs. Jenkins to him. "How long has your grandmother been here?"

"Since Saturday night," Rafe said.

Grimaldi glanced at me, in time to catch my wince. "Is that true?"

I nodded. "Technically it was early Sunday, I guess. Around three in the morning. We were still asleep." Or had been, until I woke up to use the bathroom.

"How did she get here?"

"We're not sure," I said. "I know she walked part of the way, because her slippers were worn through on the bottoms. But I don't think she could have walked the whole way from Brentwood."

"Did you ask?"

I nodded. "She says she got a ride. But she can't tell me from who. Whom."

"Why?" Rafe asked.

Grimaldi looked at him. "Savannah said you went to Brentwood to see your grandmother yesterday."

I looked guilty. Rafe gave me an arched brow, but didn't say anything. Not about that. "I went to Brentwood, but not to see my grandma. Nobody called to let us know she was gone, so I wanted to see what they'd say when I showed up."

"And what did they say?"

"Nothing," Rafe said. "They acted like they didn't know she was gone. The doc in charge promised they'd do a top-to-bottom search, and let me know when they found her."

"But they haven't?"

He shook his head. "Not so far."

I glanced at the clock. It was after ten. Plenty of time for the nursing home staff to get their act together and notify next of kin that they'd misplaced a resident. The fact that they hadn't seemed significant. Of something, even if I had no idea what.

"Who told you she was here?" Rafe wanted to know, and I wondered guiltily whether I had. I hadn't admitted anything, but Grimaldi might have read between the lines.

Then again, why would she care? It wasn't a crime for Mrs. Jenkins to be here. It was her house, still in her name. Rafe had power of attorney, but Mrs. J had every right to visit. And she wasn't a prisoner at the nursing home, either. She shouldn't have been able to walk out the way she did—mostly for her own safety—but she wasn't in prison. If she'd seemed like she was unhappy, we'd have gotten her out of there long before this. She wouldn't have had to make a break for it to escape.

Grimaldi said that nobody had told her. "I didn't know she was here until I saw her. I wanted to talk to Savannah about something else."

"What's that?"

Rafe and I said it at the same time. I glanced at him, and he winked at me. At least he seemed less upset now.

"Ms. Bristol," Grimaldi said. When I didn't immediately answer, because it took me a second to remember who Ms. Bristol was, or had been, she added, "You asked me about her yesterday, remember?"

I remembered. The friend of Mrs. Jenkins who had fallen down the stairs and died. "You looked into it?"

"There wasn't anything to look into," Grimaldi said. "Her

name was Beverly Bristol. She was eighty-two. She died a week ago Saturday. The doctor in charge at the nursing home signed the death certificate. There was no autopsy, since the cause of death was obvious. She fell and broke her neck."

"Did someone see it happen?"

"I have no idea," Grimaldi said. "I pulled the death certificate—it's public property—and saw the cause of death written on it. There was no investigation, so to know more, I'd have to ask the doctor."

"Name?" Rafe asked.

She told him. "Is that the same guy you spoke to?"

Rafe nodded. "Fesmire. Doctor Alton Fesmire."

"Did you not like Alton Fesmire?" It was a logical guess, judging from his tone of voice.

"I didn't like that he didn't call me back when he said he would," Rafe said. "Any reason to think Beverly Bristol didn't die from a fall down the stairs?"

Grimaldi shook her head. "None at all. Or at least not until I investigate further. Any reason I should?"

"Not that I know of," Rafe told her. "So why are you here? We didn't know Beverly Bristol. You could have told us this over the phone. And you didn't need me."

"That's not really why I'm here," Grimaldi said, and glanced at Mrs. Jenkins.

Uh-oh, I thought.

Mrs. J was paying no attention to the conversation. There was home renovation going on on TV, and she was engrossed in watching muscular men wielding sledgehammers. Under other circumstances, I might have been engrossed myself.

I could feel Rafe tense, although nothing was visible on the outside, and his voice was just as calm as usual. "What's going on?"

"I caught a case last night," Grimaldi said. "A dead woman in a car in the Cumberland River."

"How sad." But what did it have to do with us?

"Her name was Julia Poole," Grimaldi said. "She was the night nurse at the facility where Mrs. Jenkins lives."

That explained what she had to do with us. Sort of. "What happened?"

"A boater found her," Grimaldi said, "when he was pulling his boat ashore after two days on the river. Down off one of the public boat ramps in Shelby Park."

That wasn't the info I was looking for, but it was interesting. Shelby Park is in the neighborhood. A couple of miles away, but in the same part of town that we live.

And quite a trek from Brentwood.

"Did she live around here? Julia Poole?"

Grimaldi shook her head. "Bellevue. It looks like someone drove the car to the ramp, put it in neutral, and let it roll into the river. I guess he—or she—hoped it would roll all the way in and then maybe get dragged by the current, but instead it got stuck on a rock, and didn't submerge all the way."

Lucky for Julia. Not that I figured she'd care, being dead. But it was good it had happened that way, and that she'd been found quickly instead of being lost, maybe forever.

"She'd been there approximately twenty-four hours," Grimaldi said, "according to the ME. The cold water did a good job preserving the body."

"How'd she die?"

Grimaldi turned to Rafe. "Her throat was cut."

My vision got narrow, and I closed my eyes and focused on breathing deeply.

I had, once upon a time, seen a dead body with its throat cut. In the room next to the one we were sitting in, as a matter of fact. If I'd been Catholic, I would have crossed myself, and offered up a prayer for Julia Poole's soul, as well as for Brenda Puckett's. Since I wasn't, I didn't. Instead, I just focused on not passing out. While my thoughts spun, wildly out of control, to places I didn't necessarily want them to go.

A cut throat would explain the amount of blood on Mrs. Jenkins's housecoat.

The Cumberland River would explain why she was soaked to the skin. I'd attributed it to the rain, but it hadn't been raining that hard, and the Cumberland River made for a better explanation.

It also explained how she'd made it home. Shelby Park was a lot closer to the house than Brentwood. Two miles rather than fifteen. And a more familiar area. One made up of small roads that were easier to navigate than the interstate.

The problem was going to be explaining what Mrs. J was doing in the car with Julia Poole and her throat in the first place.

For a hideous moment I wondered whether there was a correlation between Brenda Puckett having her throat cut in Mrs. Jenkins's library last year, and Julia Poole having her throat cut now.

I knew Mrs. Jenkins hadn't killed Brenda. The person responsible was in prison, and likely to stay there. He'd had nothing to do with Julia Poole's death. But was it possible, somewhere in Mrs. J's confused mind, that she'd gotten the two of them mixed up and thought she needed to kill Julia Poole because she thought Julia was Brenda Puckett?

I didn't know whether that made any sense whatsoever. A psychiatrist might be able to shed light on it. But the thought crossed my mind. And stayed there.

"Breathe," Rafe told me, his voice much closer than it ought to have been. A hand on the back of my neck pushed my head down, as close as I could get to between my knees. The stomach got in the way, but I did my best to comply with the pressure of his hand. "You all right?" he asked the back of my head.

I managed a grunt, as my stomach was squeezed into my thighs. "Careful."

The pressure let up a little. "I'll get you some water."

He was up and away before I could say anything. I heard his steps moving toward the door and down the hall. I concentrated on breathing, and by the time I heard his steps come back, I was ready to sit up. Between you and me, it's a lot harder to breathe bent over these days. It's hard to breathe, period. The baby's pushing on everything, including my lungs.

A glass of water appeared in front of me. "Sip. Careful."

I sipped. Carefully.

"OK?" Grimaldi asked. She was watching me closely.

I nodded. "Thank you. I just remembered Brenda Puckett. You know?"

"You don't see cut throats every day," Grimaldi agreed, calmly. "Most people, when they kill someone with a knife, they stab them. Or shoot them, if they have a gun. Or bash them over the head with a rock, if it's spur of the moment. Cutting someone's throat takes a little more forethought."

"Unless it happened in the kitchen," I said. "While she was cooking."

Grimaldi shook her head. "It didn't. I don't think it happened in her house at all."

I didn't say anything, just took another sip of water. Rafe arched a brow. He was perched on the arm of the sofa, next to me. Just in case I turned pale again, I guess, and looked like I would faint. "No blood?"

Grimaldi shook her head. "And if the ME's right about the time she went into the water, it would have happened when she was at work. Or was supposed to be at work."

My hand shook. The ice cubes rattled together. Rafe took the glass out of my hand and put it on the table. If he was nervous, I couldn't tell. His hand was warm and hard and perfectly steady. "I walked around yesterday. I didn't see any pools of blood or evidence that anybody'd cleaned up."

My eyes went, unwillingly, to the part of the sofa between

me and Mrs. Jenkins. She'd sat there just over twenty-four hours ago, dripping river water and blood. And Rafe had cleaned it up.

There was nothing to see now. But I still felt guilty.

"You probably didn't see everything," Grimaldi told him. "And if there was a pool of blood somewhere, they'd make sure you didn't see that."

Rafe nodded. "D'you have any evidence she was at work Saturday night?"

"I haven't been down there yet," Grimaldi said. "I wanted to talk to you first. Get your take on the place."

Rafe glanced at me. "We've always been happy with it. My grandma's seemed happy, and they seemed to take good care of her."

I nodded. That had been my impression, too. Until two nights ago. "Is it possible that someone killed Julia Poole before she went to work, so there wasn't a night nurse on duty Saturday night, and that's how Mrs. Jenkins was able to get out?"

That might be the explanation for what had happened to Beverly Bristol, too, a week ago. Maybe Julia Poole had a habit of not showing up for work. If she'd decided to stay home, and Beverly Bristol had needed help in the middle of the night, she might have left her room and fallen down the stairs to her death. And no one was around to help her.

It was Grimaldi's turn to shrug. "Who knows? I'll find out when I get there. So you haven't had any interactions with her?"

Rafe and I both shook our heads. "We're there in the afternoon," I explained, "when we go to visit. I've never been there at night. If she only worked nights, I wouldn't have seen her."

Rafe added, "If you gotta picture, I can take a look."

Grimaldi contemplated him for a second before she put her

hand in her pocket and pulled out her cell phone. She scrolled through a few photos, and handed it to him.

I craned my neck. "Gah!"

I should have expected it. It was Grimaldi's snapshot taken at the crime scene. I'm sure she'd had a professional crime scene photographer out to take all the official crime scene photos, but she must have snapped a few of her own, just to have handy.

Rafe tilted the phone out of my way, but not before I'd seen more than I wanted to. A woman's face, deathly pale—no pun intended, since she'd literally been drained of blood—and staring at nothing. Long, wet hair stuck to her head and lay in strands across her cheek. The hair was dark, but whether it was black, brown, or some shade of dark red, I couldn't tell.

She didn't look familiar.

Rafe handed the phone back. "Never seen her."

"Me, either," I said.

Grimaldi took the phone back and hesitated. She glanced at Mrs. Jenkins.

"Go ahead," Rafe said. His voice was calm, but I could hear the tension in it. "Warn her first."

Grimaldi nodded, and leaned forward to get Mrs. J's attention. "Mrs. Jenkins?"

Tondalia Jenkins looked away from the bulging muscles on the TV screen and smiled toothlessly. "Yes, baby?"

"Do you remember me?"

Mrs. J shook her head. "Sorry, baby."

She calls everybody baby. Me, Rafe, David. Detective Grimaldi.

"That's fine," Grimaldi said. "I'm Tamara Grimaldi. I work for the Nashville Police Department. We met last year."

Mrs. J nodded, but her attention was already straying back to the screen. Grimaldi hurried up.

"I'd like you to look at something. A picture. Can you tell

me if you know who this is?"

She handed the phone to Mrs. Jenkins, who looked at it for a second before a tear rolled down her wrinkled cheek.

"You recognize her?" Grimaldi took her phone back.

Mrs. Jenkins nodded.

"Can you tell me what happened to her?"

"She got hurt," Mrs. J said.

Obviously. But did she know that because she'd seen Julia Saturday night, or did she say it based on the photograph?

"Do you know who hurt her?"

"Julia's hurt," Mrs. J said. "We gotta get help for Julia."

"Did you see her Saturday night?"

Mrs. Jenkins looked blank. Grimaldi looked frustrated—and understandably so—but she reined it in. "I'm headed down to Brentwood from here. I thought you might want to come with me."

She was talking to Rafe, not me. I wanted to come along, too, but of course I couldn't. Aside from the fact that I hadn't been invited, and wasn't likely to be, I had to take Mrs. Jenkins shopping for shoes and a new housedress.

Rafe hesitated. "Yeah," he said after a second. "I still wanna know why they didn't call and tell me they'd lost my grandma."

I wanted to know that, too. And how it was, or might be, related to Julia's murder and Beverly Bristol's accident.

"I'll hold down the fort," I told them. "When the show is over," and the muscular men with the sledgehammers had finished throwing their weight around on screen, "we'll go shopping and get some lunch."

Rafe nodded. "Thanks, darlin'."

"No problem," I told him.

We both knew he'd delivered the old housedress with what was surely Julia Poole's blood all over it to the TBI lab this morning. That housedress implicated Mrs. Jenkins in the murder. Or if not quite that, it proved that Mrs. J had been in Julia's vicinity very shortly after her throat was cut. Someone with a cut throat doesn't take forever to bleed out. It's over in a very short time.

Rafe didn't want Grimaldi to put those pieces together. I didn't think he had anything to worry about—I didn't believe Mrs. Jenkins had hurt Julia Poole, and I figured Grimaldi would know that—but I understood that he had more reasons to be distrustful of the police than me, even now, when he was in law enforcement himself. He'd spent a lot of time under suspicion for this, that, or the other, just by being poor, or being black, or having a criminal record.

I wouldn't go against him on this. If Grimaldi asked me outright whether Mrs. Jenkins had had anything to do with Julia Poole's death... I'd deal with the problem of whether to lie or tell her the truth then.

SIX

The two of them took off in Grimaldi's sedan, after Rafe called Wendell to tell him what was going on. As expected, Wendell had no problem loaning Rafe to the MNPD for the duration. Under the circumstances, it wasn't surprising, although it was usually the case, no matter why the MNPD asked. The TBI is there as a resource for local law enforcement. And anyway, I wasn't sure what Wendell knew about the circumstances—or how much Rafe had told him—and with Grimaldi standing right there, it wasn't like I could ask.

Grimaldi got behind the wheel, which never makes Rafe happy. He made a face, but gave me a kiss before he fit himself into the passenger seat.

"For now," I told him before he closed the door, "maybe it's best if the two of you don't mention that we have Mrs. Jenkins here. It's not like we can send her back there, with what's going on, and when they let her walk out once already. I'd still like to know how that happened."

He nodded. "I ain't telling nobody nothing. Not until I know what's going on."

So that was that. They drove off, and I waited until the car had disappeared down Potsdam Street before I went inside and locked the door. Mrs. J was still engrossed in the TV, so I spent the time while she was otherwise occupied taming her hair and getting her ready to go. She frowned when I turned the TV off, but when I told her we were going out for ice cream, she came with me, as docile as a lamb.

She hadn't known who I was when I talked her into the Volvo in front of the Milton House this morning. I wasn't sure she knew who I was now. And yet she came along with no qualms and no protestations. Whoever had killed Julia Poole—and I refused to believe it was Mrs. J—wouldn't have had any problems getting her into the car for the ride to Shelby Park.

As Mrs. Jenkins had said, Julia had been hurt. She had to get help for Julia.

Maybe the killer had told her that. *"Help me get her in the car. We need to find help."*

I could see that happening, only too clearly. They loaded Julia in the passenger seat of the car, and Mrs. Jenkins crawled into the back. The killer—his face in shadow for the moment—got behind the wheel. And off they went.

It was a good twelve or thirteen miles from the home in Brentwood to Shelby Park. But probably a fairly quick ride in the middle of the night, with the rain and very few other people on the roads.

Mrs. Jenkins might have fallen asleep. It had been late, possibly well after midnight. The walk from Shelby Park to Potsdam Street might have taken her an hour, maybe a little more, but probably not much more than that. Call it midnight when the murder happened. A nice time for a rendezvous, midnight.

I imagined Julia sneaking out of the nursing home, into the dark and the rain, to meet someone. A boyfriend? A husband?

Or did she let him in? Maybe meet him in an empty room? Or an employee lounge or something? She must have a comfortable place to wait out the hours through the night.

Then the murder. And the discovery by Mrs. Jenkins. The explanation—"Julia got hurt. We need to get help for Julia,"—and the drive to Shelby Park. Close to thirty minutes for the drive itself, probably. That would have put them in the park around one o'clock in the morning, give or take a few minutes.

I imagined the car rolling down the ramp and into the water. The shadowy figure of the murderer watching to see it go in, but not waiting long enough to make sure it got completely submerged.

Careless of him. Or her. Julia might be gay. Or just meeting a friend at midnight for no romantic purpose.

How did the murderer get away from the park? Did he have a friend pick him up? Hail a cab? Walk?

Did he live nearby? Was that how he knew about the boat ramp?

Grimaldi would find out the answers to those questions, I imagined. Or she'd try, even though nobody was likely to have seen him. Not at that hour, in the rain.

But in the scenario I was building, the car was likely to have gone into the water at one, give or take. If Mrs. Jenkins was asleep, the cold water would have woken her up. It would have taken her a minute or two to scramble out, maybe more. The car hadn't been submerged, but she might not have been able to open the door against the force of the water. She might have had to roll down the window and shimmy out that way.

Good thing she was as small and skinny as she was. If it had been me, stuck in the back of a half-submerged car, I wouldn't have stood a chance of getting out of the window. Not the way I looked these days.

Having to wiggle through the window would explain the bruises on Mrs. J's legs, too.

And it would have given her an hour and a half, roughly to make it from the river and Shelby Park, up to 101 Potsdam Street. Which would put her in our front yard close to three o'clock.

Which was exactly when I'd come back to bed from the bathroom and had noticed her.

"Do you remember the river?" I asked, as I reached across Mrs. Jenkins's frail body to fasten the seatbelt.

She gave a shiver. "Cold."

It was, a little bit. Or maybe she was talking about the river.

"Were you asleep?" I tried.

She blinked.

"Were you in the car with Julia?"

"Julia got hurt."

I nodded. "Do you know who hurt Julia?"

Mrs. Jenkins looked frightened, and when she gets frightened, she has a tendency to shut down. So I gave up. At least for now. We had all day, and nothing to do except shop and talk. I'd get there.

Normally, when I need clothes, I go to Target, where I can find the kinds of fashions I like without breaking the bank. My days of being married to a lawyer are long gone, and so are my days of buying designer dresses. Having to dress for less in return for Rafe is a negligible price to pay, however.

I wasn't sure whether Target carried the sort of housecoats Mrs. Jenkins liked, though. They're made of thin material, often with flowers printed on them, and they have little snap buttons down the front. I'd never seen anything like that on any of the stylish racks at Target.

So we headed to the nearest Dollar Store instead. And found a rack of housecoats, as well as several pairs of fuzzy slippers for less than I would have paid for a single pair of shoes at Target. I added some socks and underwear (in Mrs. Jenkins's size, not mine), as well as a pair of knock-off Keds, since she couldn't go out to eat in the fuzzy slippers. A warm jacket completed our needs for today, and Mrs. Jenkins looked warm and happy, in clothes that fit, when we walked out.

(Yes, I made her change in the bathroom. The sooner we got her out of my ill-fitting clothes, that hung like sacks on her much-smaller frame, the better.)

"How about some lunch?" I suggested when we were back in the car. It was going on for that time, and as usual, the baby couldn't wait for sustenance.

Mrs. J was always happy to eat, as well. She nodded, grinning.

"Are you in the mood for anything in particular?"

She's not very adventurous when it comes to things like Mexican or Chinese food, so I figured we'd probably end up at a meat'n three or a diner, searching for soul food or the blue plate special.

And that was fine. When the baby got like this, I didn't care what I ate, as long as I put something in my stomach.

"Hamburger," Mrs. Jenkins said.

My eyebrows rose. Hamburger. OK, then.

Rafe has a favorite burger place, a little hole in the wall on a side street just on the edge of the gentrified part of the neighborhood. I don't feel comfortable going there without him. If Mrs. J still wanted a hamburger—another hamburger—later, he could come with us then. For now, I chose what I was comfortable with, and headed for the real estate office, at hip and happening Five Points.

There were two benefits. I'm familiar with the area. I feel safe there. I know the FinBar, just down the street from Lamont, Briggs, and Associates, has good hamburgers. And I could park for free in the LB&A lot. Parking can be hard to find in hip and happening Five Points.

It isn't a long drive. Barely more than five minutes later, we had parked outside the brick building that houses LB&A, and were on our way down the sidewalk toward the FinBar.

It's the East Nashville version of a sports bar. Lots of brass and dark wood, and big screen TVs showing soccer and golf and bass fishing competitions. And ferns. Lots of ferns.

It wasn't quite lunch hour yet, so we beat the rush. The hostess showed us directly to a table, and told us the waitress would be right with us. I shoe-horned myself into one side of the booth while Mrs. J slid into the other. She was about half my size, I noticed. My stomach butted against the edge of the table, while she had to sit on the edge of the seat to even put her elbows up. I gave the table a shove in her direction, which helped a little.

"Milkshake?" I asked her.

She nodded, beaming. She likes ice cream a lot, so it seemed a good guess that she'd enjoy a milkshake, too. And the dairy is good for the baby, or so I tell myself. When the waitress came, I ordered two. Chocolate for Mrs. Jenkins and strawberry for me. Berries are healthy. I felt virtuous, since between you and me, I really wanted chocolate, too.

Mrs. Jenkins had already let me know she wanted a burger. While we waited for the waitress to come back with the two milkshakes, I looked at the menu and tried to talk myself into a salad. It didn't work, so I ended up ordering a burger, too.

Protein. Good for the baby. Besides, there was cheese. I made sure of it. Dairy. And lettuce and tomato. Even onion. And pickles. Pickles used to be cucumbers. It was almost a salad.

With the ordering out of the way, I smiled at Mrs. Jenkins across the table. "You look nice. That's a good color for you."

It was. The housedress was sort of a muted turquoise with little yellow flowers. Her hair was neatly pinned back, and she looked rested and mostly well-fed.

She smiled at me, but didn't take the straw out of her mouth, just concentrated on slurping up the creamy goodness of the milkshake.

"They've been feeding you," I said, "where you've been living. Haven't they?"

She seemed like she couldn't get enough food. And of course she was as scrawny as a sparrow. But she always had been. She'd looked like this when I first met her more than a year ago, too.

She nodded. "Yes, baby."

OK, then. Good.

I devoted myself to my own milkshake. The creamy goodness slid down my throat in a glorious way, and I had to hold back a moan. And it was a good thing I did, because a shadow fell over the table, and a delighted voice said my name.

I swallowed. "Oh. Tim. Hi."

I fear my own voice was rather far from delighted.

It was my own fault, of course. We were just down the street from the office. I should have realized—or at least thought of the possibility—that we'd run into someone from LB&A.

And of course it had to be Tim. Timothy Briggs, who put the B in LB&A. The managing broker, now that Walker Lamont, the L, was languishing in prison for Brenda Puckett's murder. And a few other murders. Not to mention the attempted murder of Mrs. Jenkins and me.

But I digress. Tim was standing next to the table, flashing his unnaturally white, unnaturally straight teeth. "I didn't expect to see you here."

I flushed, as I'm sure he had intended. "Sorry I didn't make it to the sales meeting this morning. As you can see, I'm b... busy."

I almost said baby-sitting. That's what I felt like I was doing. But I didn't think Mrs. J would appreciate it, and anyway, she wasn't a baby. It wasn't fair to imply that she was. Even if this probably was good practice for when I had a toddler.

"This is Rafe's grandmother," I added.

Tim beamed, blue eyes twinkling. "Mrs. Jenkins! What a pleasure to meet you!" He reached for her hand.

I had to give him credit for remembering her name. It wasn't like he had any reason to, other than that he's had an unrequited crush on Rafe for the past year.

"This is Tim," I told Mrs. Jenkins. "My boss."

I'm self-employed, and licensed by the state of Tennessee, but since I have to hang my shingle somewhere, and since someone—a broker—has to be responsible for me, Tim is, for all intents and purposes, my boss. He doesn't pay me a salary, and can't tell me what to do, but if I screw something up, he's on the hook, so we have an interesting relationship, especially when you take into consideration that I've saved his life once or twice, and that he lusts after my husband. Oh, and that I kept him from being liable for a half-a-million dollar real estate mistake not too long ago.

Really, on the strength of all that, he ought to stop lusting after Rafe. But I suspect that would be impossible. I certainly can't do it, so it's hard to blame Tim.

And anyway, since Rafe doesn't seem to mind, and since Rafe married me and not Tim, and since he has never shown any indication of swinging Tim's way, I probably shouldn't give it another thought.

While I wasn't giving it another thought, Tim kissed Mrs. Jenkins's knuckles and gave her her hand back. "Delighted," he told her, while Mrs. Jenkins dropped her hand to her lap, probably so she could surreptitiously wipe it off where he couldn't see. "We love your grandson!"

There was no we, unless he was talking about him and me. Maybe he was. And the statement made Mrs. Jenkins look confused. I deduced that at the moment, she might not remember that she had a grandson.

"How was the meeting?" I asked Tim.

He gave an elegant shrug of one shoulder. "Oh, you know. Same old, same old. Listings, closings, new clients."

None of which I had. "Anything I should know about?"

Tim pinched his bottom lip between a beautifully manicured thumb and index fingers, and tugged on it. "I don't think so. Things are slow this week. Thanksgiving, you know."

I nodded. "I don't expect you'll need me to sit an open house for you this weekend, then?"

Sometimes, when I didn't have anything else to do, I'd host an open house for Tim, who had too many clients and too many listings to be able to handle them all himself. It was a way—or was supposed to be a way—to find new clients, but so far, it hadn't been too successful of an endeavor for me. And lately I'd mostly spent my weekend with Rafe, anyway. But since I hadn't been at the sales meeting, where such things were usually set up, I figured I should ask. Between you and me, though, I was hoping he'd say no.

He shook his head. Golden curls danced around his ears. "Like that? No, thank you." He directed an annoyed look at my stomach.

"It's the twenty-first century," I told him. "We don't make pregnant women hide out at home anymore."

My attempt at humor only made him scowl harder. "If I asked you to sit an open house on Sunday, you'd probably go into labor Saturday night. And then where would I be?"

Without someone to sit his open house.

I didn't say so. "I'm not going into labor on Saturday," I said instead. "I have almost three weeks to go. And first babies are usually late."

Tim shook his head. "Not a chance I want to take. Sorry."

"No problem. I didn't really want to do it anyway."

Tim wrinkled his nose. "Let me guess. You're going to Sweetwater."

I was. But I didn't expect to be there on Sunday. It was just meant to be a quick trip down on Wednesday afternoon, for Thanksgiving on Thursday, and then back up to Nashville again on Friday.

Although now, with Mrs. Jenkins staying with us and Rafe—along with Grimaldi—neck deep in a murder at the nursing home, I had no idea what would happen. I might end up having a turkey sandwich with Mrs. J at the kitchen table instead of a big party in the mansion in Sweetwater, with all my family around me.

I didn't tell Tim any of that. "I'll be back by Saturday," I said instead. "In case you change your mind."

"I won't." He glanced toward the door. "I have to go. Nice to meet you."

He gave Mrs. Jenkins another blinding smile and sashayed off, into the back part of the restaurant. I craned my neck and watched him for as long as he was in sight, but I couldn't see who he was meeting. And since it wasn't any of my business anyway, I turned around and devoted myself to my milkshake and to Mrs. Jenkins, who was looking around hungrily for her food.

The burgers arrived shortly, and we both went to work silencing the inner beast. I could almost feel the baby going, "Aaah!" when the first bite of burger went down.

It's not like I haven't been hungry before. When you're a Southern Belle, brought up by another Southern Belle, you learn early on to eat like a bird, so as not to give your companion the idea that you don't care about your figure. As my mother's said, not just once but several times, you won't catch a man that way.

So I've spent years on an empty stomach. But until I got pregnant, I never felt the kind of hunger where I got light-headed and thought I'd pass out if I didn't get something to eat soon. And that feeling had been a pretty constant companion the past couple of months. Whoever was in there, had a prodigious appetite. And had inherited Mrs. Jenkins's metabolism, it seemed.

It didn't take long to finish. Mrs. Jenkins practically inhaled her burger and fries, and I wasn't far behind.

"Dessert?" I asked brightly.

But she must have had enough with the milkshake, and burger and fries, because she shook her head. She was half my size, and had eaten as much, if not more, than I had.

"Check, please," I told the waitress, who whipped it out. I gave her my card, and she wandered off to put it through the machine. A minute later she came back, and I signed and left a suitable tip and tucked the card back into my wallet. "Ready?"

Mrs. Jenkins nodded and started to scoot out of the booth.

"Why don't we make a stop in the ladies' room before we leave?"

I tacked on a question mark, but it wasn't really a question.

I had several reasons for wanting to visit the facility. For one, I wanted to wash my hands and touch up my lipstick, and besides, the baby sat on my bladder, so I took every opportunity I could to relieve myself. If there was a bathroom in the vicinity, I used it, since I knew if I didn't, I'd only have to find another a few minutes later.

But I was also concerned that Mrs. Jenkins might not let me know if she needed to go. She wasn't talking much. About anything. And the last thing I wanted, was an accident in the Volvo. It would be embarrassing for her, and uncomfortable for me.

So I steered her toward the back of the FinBar and the restrooms. We did our business, and when we headed back out, that was when I noticed Tim.

He'd gone back in this direction after our conversation earlier, but I hadn't thought to look for him when we were going to the bathroom. Too busy herding Mrs. Jenkins in front of me, I guess. Or too focused on getting to the bathroom quickly.

But here he was, sitting at a table by the wall, surrounded by ferns, across from another man.

Lunch date? Or business appointment?

None of my business, I guess, but I tend to be curious.

About a lot of things.

The man wasn't anyone from the office. Not unless we had a new agent I didn't know about, but I didn't think so. But real estate agents often meet with all sorts of people. Clients, other agents, lenders, reps selling errors and omissions insurance—the real estate equivalent of malpractice coverage—or advertising...

This guy did look vaguely familiar, though, even from the back. I turned to look at him.

Tall, even sitting down, and dressed in a navy suit and tie. Reddish-blond hair and freckles in an angular face. A few years younger than Tim.

Kenny. The name popped into my head. His name was Kenny. Kenneth Grimes. He lived in the neighborhood. Four or five months back, his partner had been murdered. Jogging in Shelby Park, as it happened.

The victim, Virgil, had been a client of Tim's with his previous boyfriend. So in a roundabout way, this might be a business luncheon. Maybe Kenny wanted to sell his house. He'd owned it since before Virgil moved in, but maybe, now that Virgil was dead, he couldn't bear to live there anymore.

Or maybe not. They were looking at one another very intently across the table. Maybe it wasn't a business luncheon at all.

The last time I'd seen Kenny, he'd been trading punches with Virgil's ex on the floor of the funeral home, while the casket was threatening to—and eventually did—fall off its stand.

Maybe he was ready to move on.

Well, good for him, if he was. And good for Tim, too. Kenny seemed like a decent guy. He'd certainly mourned Virgil very sincerely. The brawling at the funeral notwithstanding.

I ushered Mrs. Jenkins out of the restaurant and toward the car. I'm not even sure Tim noticed us going by.

We took the long way home. By which I mean that instead of driving directly home from the FinBar to the house on Potsdam, I decided to take the scenic route. In the opposite direction. Through Shelby Park. Call it curiosity, or maybe I was hoping that it would spur some kind of memory in Mrs. Jenkins. Something to help us—or help Detective Grimaldi and Rafe—figure out who had murdered Julia Poole and tried to drown her and Mrs. J.

The road from the FinBar took us into the park on the north end, farthest from the river. We passed the golf course, and drove around Sevier Lake, where a few ducks were splashing in spite of the November temperatures. Up on the hill to our left, behind the trees, was the path where someone had lain in wait for Virgil and killed him this summer.

On the other side of the lake were the baseball diamonds, and the entrance to the Shelby Bottoms Greenway. I drove slowly past. A train rumbled by, four stories in the air on top of the railroad trestle that crosses the river and the wetlands.

There were very few people out. A jogger, as Virgil had been that evening in July. A woman with a baby stroller. In a month or two that might be me. Although, considering what I knew about Shelby Park and the bodies dumped here—Virgil's hadn't been the first, nor would Julia Poole's be the last, I was sure—I'd do my walking in daylight.

The road converged from the railroad trestle and turned west, toward downtown. Beyond the trees on the left I could see the river. The water was gray and choppy, even in the sunshine. And the river was high, maybe due to the rain we'd had over the past few days.

Just ahead of us was the boat ramp, with a small parking lot next to it. I turned off the road and into one of the spaces.

Other than us, the lot was empty. Through the trees, I could see a barge waiting on the other side of the river, laden with piles of dirt or maybe gravel. The ramp went down to the right of the car, and there was no evidence whatsoever to indicate that last night, a car with a dead body had been winched up from the river. There was no crime scene tape across the boat access, or anything like that.

I glanced at Mrs. Jenkins. "Is this where Julia's car ended up in the river?"

She looked around, blankly. It looked like she either didn't remember, or didn't recognize the place.

Unless I was wrong, and this wasn't the boat ramp. I couldn't think of another one, though. Not around here.

I reached for my door handle. "Do you want to come out, or do you want to stay in the car?"

Mrs. Jenkins wanted to stay in the car. I turned the engine off and put the key in my pocket, so she wouldn't get the bright idea to drive away without me. I wasn't sure whether she could drive—she probably didn't have a license, and she'd have to sit on a pillow to see out over the dashboard—but better safe than sorry.

And if she accidentally—or not so accidentally—locked herself in, I'd be able to unlock the doors again if I had the key.

There wasn't a whole lot to see, unfortunately. The ramp went at an angle into the water, the way boat ramps are wont to do. I stood at the top of it and imagined the darkness of one AM—there were no streetlights here, inside the park, and the lights across the river, where the barge was waiting, probably wouldn't have been on that late on a weekend. And I knew from experience that there had been no moon. That's what had made Mrs. Jenkins so hard to see in our front yard that night.

I imagined the killer getting out of the car and stepping back to watch it roll down the ramp, picking up speed as it went. Faster and faster until it hit the water. Would it splash? Or just slip in, nose first, without making much noise?

Had he had to give it a push, or had it rolled on its own?

And then what had he done?

I looked around.

He could have walked away. There are several roads out of the park, including the one we'd come in on, the one we'd be leaving on, and one more, cutting straight through the park at a diagonal.

Or he could have left a car parked here, the way mine was parked now. In one of the parking spaces. But that would mean the murder had been planned, and he'd known he'd be coming here and would need a ride home.

And if he'd left his car here, how had he made it to Brentwood and the nursing home?

If he'd driven Julia's car here, had he left his own vehicle in Brentwood for the duration? So had he gone back there, then, from here?

Or had he taken a cab to the nursing home for the midnight rendezvous, because he knew he'd have to drive Julia's car here? That would mean he not only planned Julia's murder, but her disposal, and knew enough about her to know her car would be available.

I wandered back to the car in deep thoughts. Mrs. Jenkins looked sleepy. When I started the car and we drove away, she leaned back in her seat and closed her eyes.

SEVEN

When we got back home, I parked Mrs. Jenkins in front of the TV again. She probably needed some distraction and a nap, and I needed to visit the bathroom. That done, I picked up the phone.

I thought about calling Rafe, but decided it would be better if I could just take care of this minor detail myself. So I called the nursing home directly.

The woman who answered the phone must have been discombobulated, because it took her several rings to pick up, and when she did, she didn't respond with the name of the place and a question about how she could help me. Instead, she just gave me a breathless, "Hello?"

"Hi," I said brightly. "I'm sorry to bother you. I just wanted to know if you could tell me when the funeral for Beverly Bristol is?"

There was a pause. I thought I sensed suspicion wafting down the line, so I added, "My grandmother-in-law was a friend of Beverly's. We know that she lived at your place when she died. So we thought you might have some information. If it hasn't taken place already, my grandmother-in-law would like to go."

The thought had struck me in the FinBar earlier, when I'd seen Kenny Grimes and been reminded of the last funeral I'd gone to. Not that I expected a brawl to break out at Beverly's funeral. Not unless she'd had a lot of money and her heirs were competing for it. That was always a possibility. But I sincerely thought that Mrs. J might want to go. She'd seemed sad when she told us that Beverly Bristol died. And it would be something for us to do together.

Unless the funeral had already taken place, of course. It might have. She'd passed on last week. Her family might have gotten her into the ground already.

The woman on the other end of the line—whom I didn't know who was, since she hadn't introduced herself—must have decided to trust me, even though she didn't know who I was, either. Or maybe she just figured she'd let the Bristol family deal with me, and no sweat off her nose.

"It's tomorrow. Ten o'clock. The Phillips-Robinson Funeral Home. It's... um..." I heard the flapping of papers on the other end of the line.

"I know where it is," I said quickly.

I did. I'd been there before. Starting with Brenda Puckett's memorial service in August last year. And culminating with the knock-down, drag-out fight literally on top of Virgil Wright's coffin this summer.

Anyway, it was a few minutes away. Just a mile or two as the crow flew from where I was sitting. Maybe Beverly Bristol had lived in this area before she ended up in care in Brentwood. Or maybe one or more of her family members did.

I thanked the staff member politely, and looked up the phone number for Phillips-Robinson to double check the information. They informed me that yes, there was indeed a visitation for Beverly Bristol scheduled for ten AM tomorrow, and I was welcome to attend.

"In fact," the funeral home receptionist told me, her voice lowered in confidentiality, "I don't think we're expecting a big crowd. The visitation is in the smallest viewing room."

Good to know. I thanked her, and hung up. Mrs. Jenkins

was still in the parlor, in front of the TV, and I joined her. Pretty soon we were both napping.

Rafe came home around dinnertime, and brought Grimaldi with him. I had made enchiladas—the baby liked spicy foods, although my heartburn didn't—and as we sat around the kitchen table, they filled us in. Or at least they filled me in; I wasn't sure how much Mrs. Jenkins understood.

"Julia Poole did show up for work Saturday night," Grimaldi said, around bites of enchilada. "She clocked in at a few minutes before seven. And—"

She gave me a look, and I closed my mouth again.

"—two staff-members who were clocking out at seven and leaving for the night, talked to her."

So she'd actually been there. No one else had stamped her timecard for her.

"She performed the bed check," Grimaldi added, "starting at nine. All the residents were checked off, including your grandmother."

My grandmother-in-law. "Not to be picky," I said, "but if she checked off Rafe's grandmother as being in bed," when she clearly hadn't been, at least not later, "how can you trust that anyone else were where they were supposed to be? How can you even know that it was Julia who did the bed check?"

"A couple of the residents confirmed it," Grimaldi said. "Moving on: Once all the residents are in bed, she pretty much just spends the night reading and watching TV and trying to stay awake, in case anyone needs her. Most of the time no one does, but occasionally there's an emergency."

Like Ms. Bristol falling down the stairs. Or like Julia getting her throat cut.

Or for that matter like Mrs. Jenkins escaping, although no one had noticed that. It had been Julia's job, and Julia had been otherwise occupied.

"Any idea when she left the building? She wasn't killed inside, I assume?"

Rafe shook his head. His mouth was full of enchilada.

"It's a gated facility," Grimaldi said.

It was. I'd been there, and knew that there was a tall fence surrounding the property on all sides, and an electronic gate that stayed closed at all times. Just in case someone—like Mrs. Jenkins—managed to make it out of the building and halfway to freedom, I guess.

This makes it sound like a prison. It's not, I swear. It's a very nice, homey sort of place with good food and walking paths and caring, competent staff.

Julia Poole notwithstanding.

"The gate was opened a few minutes before midnight," Grimaldi said. "Whoever opened it had the code."

So someone who had been there before. Someone who worked there. Or someone who had been given the code by someone who worked there. Like Julia.

"I don't suppose there's a camera at the gate?"

Like I said, I'd been there. But I couldn't remember every detail.

"There's a camera," Grimaldi said, "so whoever's inside can see whoever's outside. But there's no film."

What's the point of a camera with no film in it? "So you don't know who arrived." I looked from one to the other of them.

"Nobody admitted it," Grimaldi said. "It doesn't seem to have been anyone on a legitimate errand."

It was a little late in the day to be visiting a loved one. Although I supposed, in emergencies, they might have ambulances and such arriving in the middle of the night.

"We did find the murder scene," Rafe said. He sounded like he was trying to cheer me up.

"Where was she killed?"

"There's a little gazebo near the river. Folks can sit there and look at the view."

On the other side of the seven-foot fence with the spikes on top. I nodded. "I remember. Seems like a nice place for a rendezvous."

Almost romantic. If you disregarded the rain that had swept through Middle Tennessee on Saturday night. The weather hadn't been conducive at all to romance. At least not outside.

Then again, there's nothing romantic about murder.

"The rain washed away a lot of the blood," Grimaldi said. "There was some left in the protected area under the roof, but even there, the rain had hit most of it. But there was enough left to determine that the murder had taken place there."

"I don't suppose you found the murder weapon?"

She shook her head. "He must have taken it with him. The ME determined a very sharp, smooth blade."

"Like a scalpel." Or straight razor. The kind of thing that had cut Brenda Puckett's throat in August a year ago.

We sat in silence for a moment.

"Beverly Bristol's funeral is tomorrow morning," I said. "I thought I might take Mrs. Jenkins to it."

I guess I was looking for approval, or permission. Or some reason, if one existed, why I shouldn't.

Rafe nodded. ""She'd like that."

If she remembered who Beverly Bristol was tomorrow morning. I wasn't sure she would.

But she might appreciate it even if she didn't remember Beverly. And it would give us something to do, and a change of pace.

I glanced at Grimaldi. "Sounds like a good idea," she said.

OK, then. "So what happens now? With the investigation, I mean?"

The two of them exchanged a glance. "Since it wasn't easy,"

Grimaldi said, and clarified, "since we couldn't determine who she met in the gazebo at midnight, we'll have to rely on good, old-fashioned police work to figure it out. I'll have to talk to her family and friends, her neighbors, to see if they knew who she was seeing. Someone she'd leave her job in the middle of the night, in the rain, to meet."

I nodded.

"We'll have to dig through her house and look at her cell phone records and that sort of thing. Boring routine."

"You don't need me for that," Rafe said. It was just as much statement as question. He's no more fond of boring routine than anyone else.

Although he was right: Grimaldi probably didn't need him for it, and it wasn't the kind of thing the TBI would normally get involved in. He was only involved now because of Mrs. Jenkins.

Grimaldi shook her head. "I can handle it on my own. I might call you if I find another link to the nursing home. But if the only connection is that she happened to be murdered there, by someone who came from the outside, it's none of your concern."

"Will you let us know how it goes?" I asked. I would have preferred for Rafe to stay in the investigation, to be honest, so we'd know what was going on. Just in case Grimaldi discovered that the person who had entered the property at midnight had been there on a legitimate errand and hadn't killed Julia Poole. I still didn't think Mrs. Jenkins had done it, but I didn't want Grimaldi to get the idea that she might have. The fact that Mrs. Jenkins wouldn't, or more likely couldn't, point the finger at someone else was a bit disturbing.

"I'll let you know," Grimaldi said. She glanced at her watch. "I should probably get going. I have some reports to write up before I'm done for the day."

She pushed her chair back. "Thanks for dinner."

I did the same. "You're always welcome. Thanks for staying to let us know what happened today."

I walked her to the door with Rafe right behind. We stood on the porch and waved until the sedan had disappeared down the road.

"Anything I should know about?" I asked him, as we headed down the hallway toward the kitchen again.

He shook his head.

"Did you hear back from the TBI lab about your grandmother's dress?"

He winced. "Yeah."

"I guess it was Julia Poole's blood?" Not very likely it would be anyone else's, after all. But we hadn't known about Julia when he dropped the dress off at the lab this morning.

He nodded. "Yeah."

"Did you tell Grimaldi?"

He gave me a look. "No."

So we were still keeping the blood from the police. The look said, very clearly, that I was expected to keep my mouth shut about it, too.

"I really don't think your grandmother is in any danger from Grimaldi," I said. "She knows that Mrs. Jenkins wouldn't hurt anyone."

Rafe didn't answer.

"And anyway, someone arrived at the nursing home at midnight. That had to be whoever killed Julia. Right?"

Rafe shrugged.

"Well, who else could it be?"

"Mighta been nobody," Rafe said.

"So who opened the gate? Someone did."

He glanced over his shoulder at the opening to the kitchen. We'd stopped halfway down the hall to finish the conversation. "Coulda been my grandma."

"That doesn't make any sense," I said.

He arched a brow.

"Fine," I said. "Explain it to me."

He lowered his voice another degree. "Imagine my grandma getting out of her room. Somehow. And imagine Julia Poole realizing it, and going after her. That was her job, right? And imagine the two of'em finding each other in the gazebo."

"OK," I said. I could imagine it so far.

"Imagine my grandma being confused. And imagine Julia trying to grab her and take her back to her room. And imagine my grandma lashing out with the knife."

I could imagine that, too. Except for a few details.

"What knife? Where would your grandmother have gotten hold of a knife? Especially one sharp enough to cut a throat in one slash? It's not like they'd leave that kind of thing lying around for the residents to find."

He had no answer for that.

"And anyway, what happened then? Your grandmother weighs less than a hundred pounds soaking wet." And she'd been soaking wet that night. "I haven't seen Julia Poole, or her body, but she would have had to have been even smaller than that for your grandmother to have carried her to the car. That's not likely. Most people are bigger than your grandmother. If she'd dragged Julia, you would have seen drag marks. If she'd driven the car to the gazebo, you would have seen tire tracks. And does your grandmother even know how to drive?"

"Yes," Rafe said. "And someone did drive the car to the gazebo."

Really? "Grimaldi didn't mention that."

"I guess she thought you wouldn't care," Rafe said.

She'd thought wrong. But of course she'd had no way of knowing that.

"So someone killed Julia in the gazebo—not your grandmother; whoever she had her midnight rendezvous with, obviously someone who brought the sharp knife with him, since I don't think Julia would have brought it—and then that person left her there while he went to get her car, since he didn't want to carry her from the gazebo to the parking lot. It's a bit of a walk, as I recall."

Far enough that anyone sane would opt for the car over carrying the body the distance. And anyway, it was a lot safer for the murderer to leave the body behind while he got the car. Staggering around with Julia's bloody body in his arms might be a bit hard to explain if anyone happened to see him.

"And while he was getting the car, your grandmother got to the gazebo and found Julia. And tried to help her, because Julia was hurt. And when the murderer came back, he found them both. And loaded them both into the car and drove them to Shelby Park. And pushed them into the water."

Rafe didn't say anything.

"You do realize he was trying to kill your grandmother, right? Or at least he was hoping that she'd drown, or die of hypothermia or something, so she couldn't testify against him."

"She can't testify against him anyway," Rafe said. "She don't know who he is."

Or didn't remember him, if she did.

"We could hypnotize her," I suggested. "Maybe if she was hypnotized, she'd be less confused."

"Or more." He shook his head. "Just keep it quiet about the blood for now. I don't want Tammy getting any ideas."

He put a palm against my stomach. "How's the baby?"

The baby—awake at this time of day—immediately noticed and kicked at it.

"Alive and well," I said.

"No problems?"

I shook my head. "I feel fine. I took a nap in front of the TV with your grandmother earlier. And I have a little heartburn from the spicy food, but nothing worth mentioning." No sense of impending doom, or impending labor. Everything was just as normal.

He nodded, and bent to brush his lips over mine. “I’m gonna go take a shower.”

“I’ll clean up after dinner,” I said, “and get your grandmother situated. I’ll meet you in front of the TV.”

He headed up the stairs, and I went to prepare for another slow evening at home.

EIGHT

The Phillips-Robinson funeral home consists of a couple of big, white, Southern-style buildings on Gallatin Road in Inglewood. There's a Mexican restaurant across the street, a Smoothie King on the next corner, and a big pine tree on the lawn in front of the funeral home. It wasn't decorated for the holidays yet, but a sign advertised a Christmas Tree Lighting Ceremony the first week in December. By now, we were two days away from Thanksgiving, so the holidays were coming up quickly.

When I'd been here last year for Brenda Puckett's funeral, the parking lot had been bumper to bumper, including vans from all the major networks. Brenda's murder had been headline news.

Today, it was quiet. Half a dozen cars in the parking lot, nothing more. I pulled the Volvo into a space between a muscular truck with a trailer hitch and a bumper sticker that said *"I'd rather be fishing,"* and a late model BMW convertible with the roof up in spite of the bright sunshine.

"Ready?" I asked Mrs. Jenkins. She nodded.

I'd tried to make her look as presentable as possible for the occasion. Since she insisted on wearing one of her new housecoats, and since we had a limited number of them—and they don't tend to come in mourning colors—I'd done the best I could under the circumstances. The housecoat was navy blue, with sprigs of white flowers. I had paired it with white socks and Keds, and the coat we'd bought yesterday. She looked... if not put together, at least clean and maintained.

The smallest viewing room wasn't hard to find. It was the only one in use at the moment, and in spite of the small crowd, there was enough noise to point us in the right direction as soon as we came through the front doors into the building.

"This way." I took hold of Mrs. Jenkins elbow. Not because she couldn't find her own way—I assumed she could, since she wasn't deaf—but the place was big, with lots of doors that all looked the same, and I didn't want to lose her. Who knew: with her luck, she'd probably end up in the embalming room, or somewhere like that.

The small viewing room held less people than I would have expected from the noise. The half dozen cars in the parking lot had resulted in maybe eight people in the small room, and a couple of them were conversing loudly. Under other circumstances, I might even say they were arguing, but since I'd been here before, and had witnessed an actual screaming match over the coffin, I'll give them the benefit of the doubt and just say they were talking loudly. They were certainly nowhere near as loud as Kenny and Stacy had been on that other occasion.

"...lucky we don't sue!" one man proclaimed.

He was almost as tall as Rafe, and ten years ago, might have been as muscular. Now, he was just big, with a few extra pounds around the middle, straining the buttons of the blue shirt he wore under a navy blazer.

In a weird sort of optical illusion, another man stood behind him, contributing his own two cents along the same lines. He looked something like a pale copy, or maybe a shadow. Same face, approximately twenty pounds lighter, and dressed in a gray jacket with a paler gray shirt under it.

Twins. Angry twins.

The man they were yelling at, on our side of the casket, was shorter, slighter, and older, with a head full of salt-and-pepper hair. And a nicely modulated voice with an educated, clipped accent that held more than a hint of annoyance. "I wouldn't recommend it. After all, who knows what might come out?"

When we walked in, they all turned to look at us. For a second, nobody said anything. The florid guy in the blue jacket, his color high, looked from me to Mrs. Jenkins and back, and his brother did the same.

However, it was salt-and-pepper who looked like he'd had the rug yanked out from under him. He flushed, and his mouth opened for a second before he hiked up his jaw again.

"I'm sorry to intrude," I said, since my mother taught me to be polite in all circumstances, even when other people aren't. "Is this the Bristol memorial?"

Nobody said anything, but a few people nodded.

"My grandmother-in-law was a friend," I said, gesturing to Mrs. J. "She would like to pay her respects."

They all stepped back from the casket. We stepped forward.

There wasn't much to see. The coffin was white, and pretty plain. Someone either had simple tastes, or not much money. Or maybe hadn't liked Beverly Bristol much.

The coffin was closed. I had thought maybe I'd get a look at Ms. Bristol, but I guess after a week, decomposition had probably started, and she might not have been a pleasant sight. The smell of lilies hung heavy in the air, masking—pretty well—the odor of anything else.

For a second or two, nothing happened. Then the guy with the salt-and-pepper hair murmured an "Excuse me," and brushed past us. He headed out the door, and I heard the hard soles of his dressy shoes slap against the floor in the hallway. A second later, the front door opened and closed.

It was like the rest of the room took a breath, and the guy in the gray jacket and shirt, less florid than his brother, managed a smile that looked more like a grimace. "Sorry about that."

I smiled back. "Family get-togethers can be fraught."

His brother, in the blue jacket, muttered something, and Gray Jacket gave him a warning glance before turning back to me. "I'm afraid I didn't catch your name."

That would be because I hadn't mentioned it. Of course I didn't say so. "I'm sorry. I'm Savannah Martin. Collier. This is my grandmother-in-law, Mrs. Jenkins. She knew your grandmother."

"Aunt," Gray Jacket said.

"I'm sorry. Your Aunt Beverly."

I smiled again. He didn't.

It was awkward. Weird and awkward. I'm sure they didn't mind us being here—why would they? They didn't know us, and that's what a memorial is for, isn't it? But I also got the distinct impression that we weren't welcome. Maybe they'd hoped to keep it to just the family. Or maybe they didn't like strangers.

Maybe we made them feel as uncomfortable as they made us feel.

I felt like they were all looking at us, just waiting for us to vacate the room.

I glanced at Mrs. Jenkins. She was looking around curiously, her black eyes birdlike in her little, brown face. If she felt any discomfort, or any lack of welcome, it wasn't apparent.

Maybe I was just imagining things. But it didn't feel that way.

I took a step back, keeping my hand on Mrs. J's arm. "I'm sorry for your loss. We'll let you get on with it."

Nobody said anything. Nobody asked why we were leaving so soon, or wondered why we weren't staying longer.

I pulled Mrs. Jenkins out of the small visiting room and down the hall toward the front door. And I admit I held my breath until we reached the door to the outside and pushed it open. When it swung shut behind us, I felt like I could take the first full breath of air since I'd walked into the funeral home. "That was weird."

Mrs. J didn't say anything, just smiled at me.

"Did you get a chance to say goodbye to Ms. Bristol?" That's why we'd come, and now I'd ruined it for her by yanking her out of there after just two minutes. Who knew, she might not have felt any discomfort at all. She might have wanted to stay. To commune further with the dead.

"Yes, baby." She patted my arm.

"OK. Good." I looked around the parking lot. It was still early. Too early for lunch. "Let's go get some ice cream."

It's never too early for ice cream.

Mrs. Jenkins beamed, and trotted next to me toward the Volvo.

I'm not entirely sure what happened next. One second we were on our way across the parking lot. The next, we had to jump out of the way as the fancy BMW parked next to us zoomed backwards out of its slot and straight at us.

I shoved Mrs. Jenkins to the side while I did my best to scramble to safety myself. We both ended up on the cold blacktop. Mrs. Jenkins skidded and skinned her knees. I watched the rear of the BMW come closer and closer, absolutely sure it was going to hit me... but just before it did, it came to a halt, and then sped forward. It belched a cloud of exhaust that made my eyes water, and I wasn't able to clear my vision again until the car had exited the parking lot and taken off south on Gallatin Road with a roar of the powerful engine.

Clearly the driver was upset.

I turned over on all fours and crawled the couple of feet to Mrs. Jenkins, who was looking dazed, bleeding from both knees. "Oh, my goodness. I'm so sorry."

It was my fault, or at least to a degree. I'd pushed her out of the way of the car, and she'd fallen and hurt herself.

On the other hand, if we'd stayed where we were, the car

would have hit us and we'd probably be hurt worse, so I couldn't feel too bad about it.

I'd managed to land on my butt. I'm reasonably well padded there, so I figured I was OK, maybe except for some bruises. And the baby wasn't hurt, which was the main thing. The stomach was absolutely fine.

Mrs. J's knees weren't. It was a good thing she was small and light, or I might not have been able to haul her to her feet. "Let me help you to the car."

I put my arm around her and supported her as we hobbled toward the Volvo. "There's a drugstore just down the street." The BMW was probably passing it just about now. "We'll stop there and get some Band Aids and Neosporin and get you fixed up. Then we'll go find some ice cream. That'll make you feel better."

She patted my arm after I loaded her into the car and made sure her seatbelt was fastened. I figured she was just offering comfort. She did that. But when I looked at her, it turned out she had something to say. "Fesmire."

I blinked. "Excuse me?" It sounded like something out of Harry Potter. Maybe some sort of healing spell.

Although it did sound familiar. It took me a few seconds to place it. "Doctor Fesmire? Alton Fesmire? From where you live?" Or used to live.

She nodded.

"In the BMW?"

She looked blank at that. Maybe she didn't know what a BMW looked like. "In the car? The one that ran us down?"

Mrs. Jenkins nodded.

Interesting. I chewed on it as I closed her door and made my way around the hood of the Volvo to the driver's side door. "Are you sure?"

She shrugged. So maybe she wasn't sure. Or maybe she just didn't want to talk about it.

I started the car and rolled out of the parking lot. Two minutes later, we parked in front of the drugstore and headed in. I would have left Mrs. J in the car—her knees had to be painful, and she didn't need to be there for me to buy Band Aids and Neosporin—but I was afraid I'd come back out and find her gone. So I made her come inside with me. There were chairs in the pharmacy waiting area, so I used one of those to smear a generous layer of cream across each knee before I covered them with the biggest Band Aids I could find.

As a side note, the Band Aid industry hasn't graduated to skin-coordinated products yet. The pale Band Aids stood out distinctly against Mrs. Jenkins's brown skin. Although when she stood up, the bottom of the blue housecoat fell to cover her knees, so I guess it was OK. Still, someone should go into business making Band Aids for people who aren't pale peach.

I paid for the products I'd used, and we hobbled back out. "Ice cream next," I told Mrs. Jenkins, and she beamed at me from the passenger seat.

There's a place a bit farther north into Inglewood that has homemade ice cream, so we headed there. And while we drove, I pulled out my phone and called my husband. "Tell me about Doctor Fesmire."

"Scuse me?"

"Doctor Fesmire," I said. "Alton Fesmire. The guy from the nursing home. What does he look like?"

There was a moment of silence. "You looking to leave me for a doctor, darlin'?"

"No," I said. "Your grandmother mentioned him. After someone tried to run us over in the parking lot of the funeral home."

The silence this time was fraught. I sighed. "How about I start from the beginning?"

"How about you do." His voice was dangerous.

"I'm not sure it was deliberate. But I don't know that it

wasn't, either. Anyway, we went there. For Beverly Bristol's funeral. The visitation started at ten. We got there maybe a quarter after. It was a small crowd." I told him about parking next to the BMW. "When we went inside, a couple of people were arguing. This big, burly guy whose suit was too tight. His brother, who looks just like him, except he weighs less. And this older guy with salt-and-pepper hair."

"Fesmire has gray hair," Rafe said.

"Dark, going gray and white?"

He made a noise that sounded like agreement.

"Small, spare guy? Well dressed? Drives a navy BMW?"

"I can call the DMV and find out what he drives," Rafe said. I opened my mouth, but he was already gone. I put the phone on speaker and dropped it in my lap, and concentrated on driving.

He came back on a minute later. "BMW convertible." He rattled off the license plate number. A couple of digits sounded familiar.

"I was too busy getting out of the way to remember it all," I told him, as I kept a steady course toward the coffee shop with the homemade ice cream. By now we were so close I could practically taste it. "But that sounds right. And it was definitely a navy blue BMW convertible with an older man with gray hair inside." Or at least it was a reasonable conclusion. The man with the gray hair had left the funeral home, and the BMW had started moving a minute or two later. I hadn't gotten a good look at the driver—too busy scrambling—but the guy with the gray hair hadn't been anywhere else that I'd seen. And it made sense that he might have sat in the car for a minute gathering himself before he started the engine. He'd seemed rattled when he left. "Your grandmother mentioned Doctor Fesmire."

"Then I'm sure she saw him," Rafe said. "You both all right?"

I saw the revolving sign of the coffee shop up ahead.

"We're fine. I have some bruising on my rear end, but at least I didn't land on my stomach. And your grandmother skinned both her knees. We stopped at the drugstore and fixed her up. Now we're having ice cream."

I flipped on my turn signal and waited for a break in traffic before pulling the car into the parking lot next to a small, red Mazda Miata. It looked familiar.

"Everything is fine," I added. "He probably didn't even realize we were there. He was upset. Beverly Bristol's nephews had just threatened to sue him for negligence. He was probably too angry to pay attention."

"That's no excuse," Rafe told me, but he sounded a little calmer. "Where are you?"

I told him where we were. The coffee shop is literally just three minutes from the TBI building. "You can come down here if you want. I think Alexandra Puckett's here, too. At least there's a car like hers in the lot." And she lived just a few minutes up the street and down on the other side. "Are she and Jamal still together?"

Jamal's one of the TBI recruits Rafe's training. He and the late Brenda Puckett's daughter had hooked up at Rafe's and my wedding back in June. I hadn't seen Alexandra for a few months, though, so I wasn't sure whether that was over by now or not.

Rafe made some sort of non-committal noise. "Stay there."

I had no plans of moving again until I'd devoured a triple-scoop of ice cream to settle my nerves, and told him so. He had plenty of time to throw himself on the bike or into a car and make it down here.

"Ready?" I asked Mrs. Jenkins.

She nodded, already smacking her lips in anticipation. We'd been here before, and it was obvious she recognized it.

So we climbed out of the car, careful of our cuts and bruises, and headed into the mid-century building with the checkerboard of black and white stone walls.

It used to be a bank. They use the old vault to make the ice cream now, and the drive-through window—for the coffee—is where people used to deposit and withdraw money. A heavy, old safe sits right inside the door, with a succulent garden on top of it.

While Mrs. Jenkins zeroed in on the ice cream counter, I looked around the room, at the dozen or so tables and chairs ranged where the banker's cubicles used to be. It didn't come as a surprise to see Alexandra Puckett's jet-black hair bent over a cell phone a few tables away.

She was alone. Could be deliberate, or she could be waiting for someone.

I peeled my eyes, but wasn't able to X-ray vision my way through the tabletop to determine whether she was still pregnant. Unless she'd done something about it, she should be, but that didn't mean anything.

"What can I get you?" the barista's voice interrupted my train of thought, and I turned back to the ice cream counter. Mrs. Jenkins ordered her triple scoop of chocolate, chocolate chip, and coffee, and the barista got busy scooping.

"What about you?" she asked me.

I hesitated, but only a moment. "Double mocha chocolate chunk." The delicious odor of coffee hung heavy in the air, and since I couldn't have any, I needed something to take my mind off it.

And anyway, dairy. Good for the baby.

Clutching our ice cream—Mrs. Jenkins was already digging into hers—we crossed the floor toward the tables. And toward Alexandra. She didn't notice me until I said her name, and then she looked up with a guilty start.

"Oh," she said after a second. "It's you."

It was me. "Who were you expecting?" After a second, I added, "Are you supposed to be in school?"

She rolled her eyes. She wore less makeup now than when I'd first met her a year ago, right after Brenda's murder, but her eyes were still heavily outlined in black. "Are you my mother?"

I wasn't. "Just concerned," I said.

"Well, I'm not supposed to be in school. We're off this week. For Thanksgiving."

Nice work if you can get it. When I went to school, we didn't get the whole week of Thanksgiving off. But then my parents had kept us in public school, while Alexandra went to a very exclusive girls' school—and by exclusive I mean expensive—where maybe a lot of the families traveled for Thanksgiving and needed a little extra time.

Anyway, it was apparently OK for her to be here at eleven on a Tuesday in November.

"You remember Rafe's grandmother?" I nodded to Mrs. Jenkins, who was busy spooning up chocolate chip. "Here. Have a seat."

I pulled out the chair at the table next to Alexandra's. They were small two-tops, suitable for romantic tête-à-têtes, but not bigger groups. Mrs. Jenkins dropped down and put her ice cream on the table.

"You look nice," Alexandra said, looking me up and down.

Since I hadn't been able to make Mrs. Jenkins as presentable as I would have liked, I'd gone out of my way to look presentable myself. Black wrap dress, black boots. Very somber. "Thank you," I said. "Funeral."

Alexandra's lips turned down. "I'm sorry. Were you close?"

"A friend of Mrs. Jenkins'," I said. "I didn't know her. She fell down the stairs at the nursing home last week and broke her neck."

"That's horrible."

I guess it was. Not as horrible as Julia Poole getting her throat cut, but I didn't bring that up, since I didn't want to remind Alexandra of her mother's death.

"Anyway," I said, "we decided to treat ourselves to some ice cream after the visitation."

Alexandra nodded.

"Is that coffee?" I glanced at the cup in front of her. It was orange, waxed cardboard, and had her name scrawled on it in black marker.

She looked like she wanted to roll her eyes again, but thought better of it. One hand closed around it, sort of protectively; the nails painted black. Maybe she was afraid I'd try to take it from her. "No. Hot chocolate."

Then she might still be pregnant.

Another second, and she confirmed it. "I'm off coffee. Remember?"

"I wasn't sure," I said. "I can't see below the table."

She scooted out of the bench and stood up to reveal a distinct baby bump under a tight, black turtleneck. Twisting back and forth to give me the full, left-to-right view, she told me, "Five months."

"Good for you. Everything OK?"

She nodded, and fitted herself into the bench again. "Everything's fine. I had an ultrasound last week. They think it's a boy."

"Nice to know ahead of time."

She looked at my stomach. "Don't you know?" The implication was that since she did, I certainly should.

"The baby wasn't cooperative," I said. "I guess we'll be surprised."

I put my hand on the back of the empty chair across from her. "Are you waiting for someone?"

She shook her head. "Have a seat."

I did. "Rafe's on his way. We had a small accident in the parking lot of the funeral home—a car didn't see us, and knocked us down—and he wants to stop by and make sure we're both—all three—all right."

"Always nice to see your husband," Alexandra said with a grin. Like Tim, she's had a crush on Rafe since she first met him, shortly after her mother was killed last fall.

I dug my spoon into the ice cream and looked at her from under my lashes. "Are you and Jamal still... um...?"

Her face closed. "He's been coming to some of the doctor's appointments. He was there for the ultrasound last week."

"So you're keeping him up to date on what's going on."

"It's his baby, too," Alexandra said. "I don't know whether he's going to want anything to do with the baby once he's born. Or with me. But I let him know what's going on. Once the baby's born, he can decide whether he wants any part of being a father or not. If not, he can sign away his rights, as far as I'm concerned."

As far as I was concerned, too. If he wasn't going to step up from the beginning, I wouldn't want him coming back three—or ten, or twenty—years later, trying to lay a claim.

Then again, Jamal was only twenty-one or so. Young. And immature. I guess, even if he didn't feel mature enough to be a father right now, he should still have the right to change his mind later.

On the other hand, Alexandra didn't have a choice. She had to dredge up that maturity from somewhere, whether she wanted to or not. And it sounded like she had.

"It sounds like you've worked things out," I said.

She shrugged. "The baby's coming in April. I'll have enough time to graduate with my class in May. I hope. And next year, I'll go to college somewhere around here, so the baby can go to daycare while I take classes. My dad said he'd help out."

That was good to know. Not that I'd had any doubt. Steven Puckett loved Alexandra and her brother Austin, and I'd never doubted that he'd step up and support her, no matter what she decided to do.

The front door opened, and Alexandra glanced in that direction. "Here's your husband."

Then her voice changed. "And he brought a friend."

He had. Jamal, to be specific. Who looked just as uncomfortable about unexpectedly coming face to face with Alexandra as she looked about coming face to face with him.

For a second, I thought he was going to turn around and run. Then he visibly squared his shoulders. And across the table, Alexandra braced herself.

I looked at my husband. He arched a brow back before saying a few words to Jamal. Jamal beelined for the coffee counter, while Rafe sauntered across the floor to us.

"Darlin'." He slipped a hand down the back of my hair to curl around my neck before he bent and gave me a lingering kiss. I could hear Alexandra sigh on the other side of the table. And then I didn't hear anything else until he stopped and the hand dropped from my neck.

"Hi." I smiled up at him, still dazzled after all this time.

He winked at Alexandra, and then he went down on one knee in front of his grandmother. "You all right?"

She nodded, and patted him on the cheek. "You're a good boy, worrying about your mama."

He was Tyrell today, it seemed. I guess that made me LaDonna. I wondered who Mrs. Jenkins though Alexandra was. Or whether she was even aware of Alexandra.

"Savannah said you hurt your knees."

Mrs. J nodded and pulled her housedress up to show him. "We went to the doctor."

We hadn't, but it amounted to the same thing, I guess. "It isn't bad," I told him. "She skinned her knees when she fell. I landed on my butt. You can check that later."

"Don't think I won't." He got to his feet and pulled an empty chair over from a nearby table, and straddled it. "That looks good."

He was looking at my ice cream.

"It is," I said.

He grinned. "You ain't gonna share?"

"You're seriously going to take ice cream out of your pregnant wife's mouth?"

But I handed the cup over, and watched him scoop a couple of spoonfuls into his mouth before he handed it back. "Thanks, darlin'."

"No problem," I said. "You really didn't have to stop doing whatever you were doing to come check on us, you know. I told you we were fine."

"We needed some coffee," Rafe said, with a look at Jamal, who was waiting patiently at the counter. He had a cardboard container with two cups in front of him. And he must have ordered more, because he was still standing there. "Tell me again what happened at the funeral home."

"Not much. We arrived. They were arguing. One of Beverly Bristol's nephews told Fesmire he was lucky they didn't sue. The nursing home, I guess. I can see their point. I mean, she was supposed to be safe there. Someone was supposed to make sure she didn't hurt herself. And then she fell down the stairs and broke her neck."

Rafe nodded. "And Fesmire said...?"

"Something about that maybe not being a good idea. Then he turned around and saw us. And stared at your grandmother for a moment before he left. We stayed another minute, but it was awkward, so we left again, too. When we got halfway across the parking lot, the BMW backed out of the parking space and clipped us."

"And he didn't stop."

I shook my head. "He drove away. Chances are he didn't even see us. I mean, he's a doctor, right? If he thought someone was hurt, don't you think he'd stop and check?"

"Unless he was trying to run you down," Alexandra

contributed from the other side of the table. She was very carefully not looking in Jamal's direction. At all.

"But if he was trying to run us down, don't you think he'd stop and make sure he had?"

Alexandra shrugged. "Maybe he wanted to scare you, and he wanted you to think it might have been an accident but it wasn't."

Maybe. Maybe not. It was all very confusing. And I found it very hard to believe that a respected medical doctor—and I had to assume he was respected; he was still licensed, right?—would go around running people down.

"Are you going to talk to him?" I asked Rafe.

"Eventually. Right now I'm just keeping an eye on him."

From here?

Who he was keeping an eye on, was Jamal. A third cup of coffee appeared in the cardboard container, and Rafe got to his feet. "Time to go."

"Only three cups?" I said, as Jamal picked up the cardboard container with a smile for the barista. She was young and pretty, and Alexandra watched with a stony face.

"José and Clayton are sitting on Fesmire," Rafe explained.

José and Clayton are the other two rookies. The last coffee must be for Wendell, who keeps them all—including Rafe—in check.

"What are you afraid he's going to do?"

"No idea," Rafe said, as he pushed the other chair back under the other table, "but if he tried to run into you on purpose, he could be doing something."

He could. Although he'd probably just go to work and spend the rest of the day there.

Rafe nodded when I said so. "Long day for Clayton, then."

Clayton must be sitting on the nursing home. I guess that meant José was hanging out outside—and maybe inside—Fesmire's home.

"Where does he live?"

Rafe contemplated me in silence for a moment. "Not sure I should be telling you that."

"I'm not going there," I said.

He arched a brow.

"I'm not!" I was extremely pregnant, and babysitting his grandmother. It wasn't like I'd risk either of them by doing a spot of breaking and entering on Doctor Fesmire's place. Especially if Rafe had already sent José to do just that.

"He has a house in Franklin," Rafe said. "José's on his way there. Clayton's on his way to Brentwood. They'll both check in when they get there. Should be another five minutes for Clayton and maybe fifteen for José."

"Let me know if they discover anything interesting."

Rafe said he would. "What're you three up to?"

I glanced at Alexandra. "We'll stay here a little longer and talk. Then I guess we'll go home and watch more TV."

My life was becoming about food and TV. I almost wished I could go to Franklin and break into Doctor Fesmire's house just for something to do.

Although if José was there, I wasn't likely to get within three feet of the door anyway.

"I'll check in later." Rafe dropped a kiss on my lips, another on the top of his grandmother's head, and winked at Alexandra across the table. "Be good."

She sighed as he sauntered off. "Why can't all guys be like that?"

"I have no idea," I said, as Jamal gave her a tentative nod as they headed for the door, and she gave him a grimace back. It might have been mistaken for a smile if you felt charitable. "But I don't think Jamal's a bad guy. He signed on for law enforcement. That says something. He wants to keep people safe."

Alexandra shrugged. But I noticed she watched him until

they had gotten inside the white TBI van parked outside—Rafe was driving—and had peeled out of the parking lot. Doctor Fesmire had nothing on my husband. I hoped the lids were on the coffee cups, or Jamal was likely to arrive back at the TBI building drenched in coffee.

NINE

They took off in the direction of the TBI building—I had a feeling Jamal was cursing Rafe as hot coffee soaked his jeans—and then it was just the three of us again.

"So what are you up to today?" I asked Alexandra.

She shrugged. "Dinner with my dad and Austin. Until then, I'm just hanging out."

"No plans with friends?" Maybe they'd all gone on vacation.

"I'm pregnant," Alexandra said. "Most of my friends—or the girls I go to school with—think I'm contagious. The rest think I'm stupid for not getting rid of it."

Ouch. "What about..." I searched through my memory banks for the name, "—Lynne?" She'd been Alexandra's best friend, as far as I'd been able to make out last fall. Or at least she'd been the excuse Alexandra had used when she'd wanted to spend the night with her then-boyfriend, Maurice.

Alexandra grimaced. "Switzerland with her family."

"I'm sorry. Are you still good friends?"

Alexandra shrugged. There was a lot of non-verbal communication going on. I wondered whether I'd done the same when I was seventeen, and whether my mother had found it as irritating as I did. "I'm having a baby. She's talking about which Seven Sisters colleges to apply to next year."

After a second, she added, "We still get along. We're just in different places. Lynne would never be stupid enough to get herself knocked up."

"Things happen the way they're supposed to happen," I said, since that's what I believe. And since I figured she needed to hear something like that. "Rafe's mother was young when he was born. Younger than you. David's mother was about your age."

In addition to being Rafe's son, David is also Austin Puckett's friend from school. Alexandra knows him.

She shrugged again. "His mother gave him up for adoption."

Not willingly. He'd been taken away from her and given to someone else, and it had taken her years to find him again. But that brought up another point. "You could do the same, you know. Just because you carry the baby to term, doesn't mean you have to keep it. There are lots of people who want to adopt newborns. You might even talk to the Flannerys. They might be happy to have another baby."

"They're old," Alexandra said. "David's thirteen."

And they might be past the point where they'd be willing to take on a newborn. But maybe not. "It can't hurt to ask. I can give them a call if you want."

"I'll do it," Alexandra said. "If I decide I don't want the baby."

"It's up to you, of course. I'm just reminding you that you have options."

And if she didn't want to take on the responsibility of a baby before she'd even graduated high school, adoption was an excellent choice.

Alexandra shrugged. In a way that I recognized put an end to this particular discussion. "You're welcome to hang out with us," I told her, returning to the previous topic of conversation. "We're probably just going to go home and vegetate in front of the TV. Mrs. Jenkins likes HGTV. And I rest a lot."

Alexandra bent to peek under the table. "Are your feet swollen?"

It was my turn to grimace. "And how. The only good thing is that my stomach is now too big for me to see them."

"I can't wait," Alexandra said, which made it sound like maybe adoption wasn't such a good option after all, since it sounded like she'd made up her mind that she was going to keep the baby, high school or not.

"I can't, either. In something like three weeks, I'll have a baby. And won't look like a small hippopotamus anymore."

"You look great," Alexandra told me. "All glowy. I still puke every morning." She made a face.

"I did, too, into the second trimester. You'll probably stop soon."

The conversation devolved into comparing pregnancies. At one point, even Mrs. Jenkins roused to talk about what it had been like when she'd been pregnant with Tyrell. Since that was something like fifty years ago now, her experience had been very different from ours. And yet, exactly the same.

"He was the most beautiful baby in the world. Looked just like his daddy."

If my baby ended up looking like his daddy, it wouldn't be a bad thing. Rafe's quite good-looking, in case you'd missed that part. And he probably looked like Tyrell's daddy, too, because there was very little resemblance between my husband and his grandmother.

We sat there a while longer, and then headed home. Alexandra chose not to take advantage of the scintillating offer of HGTV and a nap on the sofa, so she went off in the other direction, toward Winding Way and home. Mrs. Jenkins and I piled into the Volvo and headed home.

I got Mrs. Jenkins situated on the sofa, and then I made lunch.

Yes, I know we'd both had ice cream, but that was an hour

ago. It was time for something more substantial. So I fell back on bowls of soup and sandwiches—while Mrs. J ate anything I put in front of her, I'd noticed she preferred old-fashioned food to newfangled stuff like enchiladas.

We ate in front of the TV. I fully expected to spend the rest of the afternoon there, as well, so it came as a sort of pleasant surprise when, an hour or so later, the phone rang.

The number was local, but unfamiliar. I picked up the phone. "This is Savannah. How can I help you?"

There was a moment's silence, and then a woman's voice said, "You're a real estate agent, right?"

I was, indeed. Not a very good one, and not one that sold many properties, but I was licensed. And maybe my luck was about to change.

"That's right," I said brightly. "Are you interested in buying something?" Or selling something? Or both?

Both would be nice.

"There's this house," the lady said.

"Yes?"

She rattled off the address. I nodded, not that she could see me. "I'm familiar with it."

I was. Not because I'd been inside it or anything like that. At least not since it was renovated. But it was pretty close to where we lived. Two blocks down and four over, something like that. Five minutes away, at most. I'd driven by it every so often while they were working on it. I'd even stopped once to introduce myself and give them a business card, just in case they didn't have a realtor to help them list the house once it was done.

As it happened, the owner-and-renovator also had a real estate license, so he could sell his own properties and not have to pay anyone else to do it—that happens a lot—but I knew which house she was talking about. And knew that it was on the market now. "Would you like to see it?"

"Yes, ma'am," the caller said.

"What would be a good time for you?"

"I'm sitting outside it right now."

Oh.

"Oh," I echoed.

"Can you come and show it to me?"

I hesitated. I should. New clients—or potential clients—don't come my way very often, and when they do, I usually jump at the chance to help them. You never know when they might decide to buy something, and actually turn into money in the bank.

But there was Mrs. Jenkins. I was supposed to take care of her.

I glanced in her direction. She was asleep with her head against the back of the sofa, and her mouth open. She snuffled.

What I should do, was wake her up and take her with me. I wasn't supposed to leave her alone.

On the other hand, dragging my grandmother-in-law along on a business appointment wouldn't look very professional. And I wanted to look professional.

So maybe if I just left quickly and came back, she wouldn't realize I'd been gone. I could be at the house in five minutes. It would probably only take fifteen minutes or so to walk through; maybe less. I'd be back here in less than thirty minutes. Mrs. J might sleep through the whole thing. And if she did, and stayed right here on the sofa, she'd be perfectly safe.

"I can call someone else," the lady on the phone said, and I made up my mind.

"That's not necessary. I'm just a few minutes away. I can be there in less than five minutes. Just let me call and set up the appointment, and I'll see you then."

"I'll be here," the lady said.

I was out the door two minutes later, after arranging the appointment with the showing center and visiting the bathroom. Mrs. Jenkins was still asleep on the sofa. I shut the front door softly and double checked that I'd locked it before I folded myself into the Volvo and took off down the driveway with a spurt of gravel.

Less than three minutes later, I turned the corner of Ulm Street and pulled up in front of the renovated craftsman bungalow.

It looked like a nice little house. Very small compared to our—or Mrs. Jenkins's—three story Victorian, but it probably had sixteen hundred square feet, or something like that. And the renovator had done a good job of restoration. I'd seen the house before they'd started working on it, and the brick foundation had been painted a virulent blue, while the wood siding had been covered by aluminum. The front porch had been encompassed—sometime in the 1970s, at a guess—and not in an attractive way.

The workers had taken down the aluminum siding and replaced the rotted wood with fresh. There were cedar shingles on the porch overhang, and yes, the porch was back and the hideous addition gone. Everything was painted a nice, style-appropriate sage green with blue and saffron accents. The brick skirt—the foundation, the part between the wood and the ground—was even back to a lovely red brick.

When I got closer, I saw that it was in fact paint, but they probably hadn't been able to strip the old bricks. Sometimes, they can crumble if you powerwash them too hard.

And from a distance, anyway, everything looked great.

I climbed the steps to the front porch and looked around. I had expected my caller, my potential client, to be waiting. But I didn't see anyone.

There was a car parked across the street. Green with tinted windows. I squinted, but I couldn't see anyone inside.

Tentatively, I lifted a hand and waved. Maybe she needed encouragement to come out.

Or maybe she wasn't there. The car door remained stubbornly closed.

I turned to contemplate the front door. It was closed, and had a gray lockbox hanging from the handle. The box was also closed.

In August last year, something very like this had happened to me. I'd received a call from a man who told me he'd been stood up by my colleague Brenda Puckett, and since she hadn't shown up, would I come and show him the house?

I'd rushed over to Mrs. J's house and found Rafe waiting outside. I'd also found a compromised lockbox, an open front door, and Brenda dead inside.

I'll admit that my heart was beating a little extra fast when I reached out and tried the doorknob. Gingerly, like I expected it to be hot.

It wasn't. And while it turned, the door didn't open. So it didn't seem as if anyone had gone inside.

Maybe my potential client had parked on the other side of the house? Sometimes they do, if there's an alley and off-street parking. Anyone interested in buying would want to check out the parking situation.

I contemplated the yard. The ground was muddy, from the rain we'd gotten over the past couple of days. I might as well walk through the house. If she was back there, I'd have to open the door for her anyway.

The lockbox yielded to my secret code, just as it was designed to do. It bleepety-bleeped and opened. I dug out the key and stuck it in the lock. The door opened and I stepped through and inside.

And closed and locked the door behind me before I raised my voice. "Hello?"

There was no answer. I hadn't expected one, so that was perfectly OK.

The door opened directly into the living room of the house.

Big stone fireplace on the left, flanked by casement windows and built-in bookcases. Gleaming hardwood floors. The dining room was to the right, with a very nice—reproduction, I'm sure—Tiffany chandelier above the dining room table.

There was furniture, so it looked like they'd gone to the extra expense of staging the place before they put it on the market. And the renovation was top notch. If I didn't already have a place to live, I'd love to live here.

The kitchen was behind the dining room, through a swinging butler door. It was pinned back at the moment, with an iron dachshund in front of it. And beyond was a gorgeously updated kitchen, with all new cabinets and appliances, and marble counters, but in the true craftsman style.

Yes, I could definitely live here.

The kitchen ended in a door with a big window in the top half. I peered through, onto a nice deck, stained dark, and beyond, a parking area inside a tall privacy fence. The gate was open, but there were no cars parked in the yard.

I didn't bother to go out, just made sure the door was locked before I retraced my steps. Maybe my caller had decided to go get a bottle of soda while she waited?

I'd told her I'd only be a few minutes, but maybe she'd thought I was underestimating. I suppose I might have—or someone might have—if I knew it would take a while for me to get there, but I didn't want her to know how long she'd have to wait.

In this case, though, I'd literally been here in five minutes. And anyway, the nearest gas station wasn't very far away. Another couple of blocks to the west and south. If she'd gone there, she should be coming back soon.

I went back to the front of the house and looked out. There was no change outside. The green car was still parked in front of the house across the street. It hadn't moved. Nor had anything else.

I wandered in the other direction, just for something to do. When she showed up I'd have to take her around the house, so I might as well know what was here.

The master suite was behind the living room. A nice size bedroom with a big bath and a walk-in closet, and double French doors out to the deck. All brand, spanking new, but with the same craftsman feel as the kitchen.

A staircase in the middle of the house led up to a second half-story with two bedrooms and a shared Jack-and-Jill bath. It was as empty as the rest of the house. I surveyed the street from up high, and still didn't see anyone move around anywhere.

By the time I got downstairs again, I'd started to become worried. And annoyed. First, of course, I wondered whether I'd misunderstood something. Maybe I was at the wrong house, or at the wrong time.

But the description matched. I'd known exactly which house she was talking about as soon as she described it, and she'd said she was sitting outside. So where was she?

I decided to give her ten minutes to show up, and then I'd leave. And I counted them standing at the window. Three cars drove by. Neither stopped.

When the ten minutes were up, I pulled out my phone. And redialed the number she'd called me from.

A few seconds passed. Then the phone was answered. "Pay phone."

"Pay phone?" I didn't think they existed anymore.

"Yeah. Listen, lady, I got other things to do than stand here on a street corner talking to you. Whaddaya want?"

"Which corner?"

I could hear the eyeroll. The boy sounded like he might be twelve or so, and I was probably keeping him from his skateboard or his drug deal or whatever twelve-year-olds in this part of town did when they were supposed to be in school in the middle of the afternoon. "Dresden and Ulm."

Three blocks south of where I was standing.

"Thank you," I said. "Did you see anyone use the phone?"

But he hadn't. "I just got here, lady. I was walking by when the phone rang. And now I gotta go."

He hung up before I had the chance to say anything else.

I shut down my own phone a bit more slowly. My thoughts were, to say it politely, scattered. As I locked the front door and made my way down the steps to the car, I tried to reason things out in my head.

The lady who called me, had called from a payphone on the corner of Dresden and Ulm.

Maybe so I wouldn't have her cell phone number? Most people have cell phones these days, so it was hard to imagine that she didn't. And anyway, she'd lied. She'd told me she was calling from right outside the house, not from the payphone on the corner three blocks away.

By now, I'd been standing here for at least fifteen minutes, and she hadn't shown up.

She clearly wasn't interested in the house.

So what was she interested in? What was the point of calling me to meet her here, if not so I could show her the craftsman?

I unlocked the door of the Volvo and fitted myself inside. The answer to my question was depressingly obvious. She'd been trying to get me out of, and away from, my own house.

Or maybe that was just paranoia rearing its head. As I turned the key in the ignition and pulled away from the curb, I tried to think about it calmly and logically.

Maybe she didn't have a cell phone. Maybe she'd really wanted to see the craftsman bungalow, but something had prevented her. Maybe her car had broken down between here and the payphone, or she'd been in a fender bender. Maybe she'd gotten a call that her child had been taken to the hospital, and she'd had to run.

But no. She'd have to have had a phone for that. Never mind.

I didn't break any laws on the way home. I stopped—mostly—at every stop sign, and didn't speed through the residential streets. At least not by much. It wouldn't make much of a difference anyway, after all. I was just a few minutes from home. And a few seconds more or less wouldn't make any difference.

I sped up once I hit Potsdam Street. It's long and wide, a major street, and there are no stop signs. But my heart was beating double-time as I screeched into the driveway with a spurt of stones and stepped on the gas up to the house.

Everything looked normal. There were no flames shooting out of the third-story windows, and no black-clad commandos hiding behind the trees in the yard, automatic weapons trained on the porch. It all looked just as it should.

It wasn't until I came closer that I saw the front door hanging wide open.

TEN

I was out of the car as quickly as a nine-months-pregnant woman can move. Out of the car and up the stairs to the porch, and to that open door.

"Mrs. Jenkins!"

The TV was still on in the parlor, droning softly, but there was no sign of Mrs. J. She wasn't on the sofa where I'd left her. The blanket I had spread over her before I left, was tossed on the floor. Most likely she had just woken up and pushed it off, as there were no other signs of a struggle. The sofa pillows were still tucked in the corners of the sofa, and everything was in its proper place, including the TV remote.

I used it to turn off the TV. Blessed silence ensued. I opened my mouth again. "Mrs. Jenkins!"

This time there was a noise. Or at least I thought I heard something. From farther inside the house. Kitchen, maybe?

I left the parlor and hurried down the hallway.

The dining room was empty. I took the time to stick my head in.

So was the library, where we had found Brenda Puckett's butchered body once before. Nobody was dead in front of the fireplace this time.

I continued into the kitchen.

Everything looked normal there, too. With one exception.

The door next to the refrigerator gaped open, into the blackness of the basement. A cold draft emanated from down there.

I walked over to it. "Mrs. Jenkins?"

My voice sort of disappeared, like it was swallowed up by the blackness. But I distinctly heard a noise, something like a scraping, from downstairs.

Hell. I mean... heck. I guess there was nothing for it but to go down.

I hit the light switch beside the door. The rickety wood staircase descending into the jaws of hell winked into view. I took a deep breath and started down.

Slowly. With one hand clutching the railing. The stairs are steep and shallow, and I was front heavy. "Mrs. Jenkins? Are you down here?"

I could count on one hand the times I'd been down in this basement since I moved in with Rafe. It's disgusting. A hard dirt floor, a little wet in places, with half dirt, half brick walls that end in a four or five foot ledge. At the far end of the ledge, here and there, there are small, dirty windows. Dirty, because we can't reach them to clean them. Basically, we're talking about a hole in the ground under the house. I know there are spiders. I'm sure there are other types of bugs. I wouldn't be surprised if there was worse than that.

The place gives me the creeps. I never go down here unless I absolutely have to.

And no sooner had I made my way off the staircase onto the dirt floor, than I heard a rush of feet upstairs. The door slammed. The key turned. And the next second, the basement plunged into stygian blackness.

"No!"

I don't like the dark. We've already established that I didn't like the basement. I certainly didn't want to be locked in it while who knows who did who knows what upstairs.

Had Mrs. Jenkins shut me in the basement? Or had

someone else still been in the house?

For the first few seconds after the door slammed and the lights went out, everything was pitch black. I couldn't see anything. My eyes were open, but everything around me was dark.

I could hear, though. The pounding of my heartbeat in my ears was so loud it drowned out pretty much anything else, but I did hear the pounding of feet overhead. Running, in the direction of the front door, unless I was mistaken.

Yep, a second later, the door slammed. Hard enough that the house shook. Something—hopefully just old dust—fell from the ceiling onto my head.

So that answered that question. Someone else had been in the house. Those footsteps had been both too heavy and too fast to belong to Mrs. Jenkins.

So where was she?

If I went up to the top of the stairs and started yelling, would she hear me and come open the door?

I guess this might be a good time to mention that I'd left my handbag with my phone outside in the car. If Mrs. Jenkins wasn't around, or didn't hear me, I'd have to sit down here, in the company of the spiders and beetles, until Rafe came home from work. Which could take some time. He doesn't exactly keep regular business hours. And with José and Clayton staking out Doctor Fesmire's home and business, Rafe might decide to check in with them before he came home. I could be down here until eight o'clock.

I put my head back and opened my mouth. "Mrs. Jenkins!"

The basement was still dark, although my eyes were becoming more used to it. Pale gray light filtered in through the dirty windows in the foundation.

They were minuscule. A-foot-and-a-half square, maybe. I wouldn't have been able to fit through one even before I got pregnant. And in my current condition, I wouldn't be able to make my way up to one anyway. But the light helped a little bit. While I couldn't quite see my hand in front of my face down here in the middle of the basement, I could see the outline of the windows, and I knew there was daylight somewhere.

I opened my mouth again. "Mrs. Jenkins! Can you hear me?"

She hadn't responded the first time I yelled, so chances were she couldn't hear me. But I had to do something. And yelling was all I had left.

"Mrs. Jenkins!"

And then came what was almost the worst part of the whole thing. While I stood there, in the dark in the middle of the basement, I heard a sound. The kind of sound you associate with ghost stories and old houses like this one.

A creak. A long, drawn-out creak, as from the opening of a door where the hinges hadn't been oiled in a hundred years.

Followed by the sound of fabric brushing dirt. Like the edge of a long skirt touching the ground.

The hairs on the back of my neck and my arms stood up, and I don't like to admit how close I came to losing control of my bladder. If there'd been anywhere to run, I'd have run. But I couldn't see the staircase. And the last thing I wanted, was to fall and maybe hurt the baby.

So I gritted my teeth and stayed where I was as the sound of dragging footsteps filled the air.

The only thing missing was the clanking of chains.

Something brushed my arm, and almost sent me into a heart attack. My blood was rushing so hard in my ears it was a miracle I could hear anything else at all.

And then I jumped when something clawlike clamped around my forearm.

"Baby!" a voice said.

It was familiar. I knew it. It's a testament to how freaked

out I was that it took me several seconds to recognize Mrs. Jenkins.

"Oh, my God!" I wrapped my arms around her. She was warm and alive. "Oh, my God. You're here." I wasn't alone.

And there were no ghosts.

And whoever had been here hadn't found Mrs. Jenkins and taken her.

Everything was OK.

Well, except for the fact that we were still locked in the basement while my purse and my phone were on the front seat of my car—if they were even there anymore—and we had no way to call Rafe, or anyone else, for help.

But we were alive and well and together and as long as I didn't go into labor, we'd survive.

Even so, I clung to Mrs. Jenkins for a lot longer than necessary. It was nice not to be alone in the dark. Eventually, though, she twitched away from me. She'd never been all that touchy-feely, really.

"What happened?" I asked.

"The bad man came," Mrs. Jenkins said.

"What bad man? Do you know him?"

"He hurt Julia," Mrs. Jenkins said.

Julia Poole's killer had been here?

Whoever it was must have realized that Mrs. Jenkins had survived her trip into the Cumberland River, then.

Actually, he'd probably realized that sooner than this. It would have been on the news if she hadn't. But now he'd figured out where she was. And had come to take care of the problem. He'd left her alive Saturday night, probably hoping the cold water would take care of the job for him, and now that it hadn't, he had to get rid of her before she could spill the beans on him.

Except... what made him think she hadn't already told someone everything she knew? Anyone sane would.

"C'mon, baby," Mrs. Jenkins said, and derailed my train of thought.

Come on? Where?

But when she took my arm and pulled me away from the bottom of the staircase, I went with her. I couldn't see where I was going—her night vision must be a lot better than mine; I knew Rafe's was, so maybe he had inherited it from his grandmother—but I stumbled along beside her. Until she stopped.

"Wait."

That I could do. And did.

Mrs. Jenkins let go of my arm and disappeared. I heard some shuffling, and a squeak, and some more noises I couldn't exactly place. And then her voice, disembodied and sort of hollow, somewhere in the vicinity of my knees.

"C'mon, baby."

"Come on where?"

"In the tunnel," Mrs. Jenkins said.

Tunnel? There was a tunnel?

I'd lived here for almost a year, and I'd never seen a tunnel. I'd be willing to bet everything I owned that Rafe hadn't, either. If he'd known there was a way into the house through the basement, that way would be nailed shut before you could blink.

Although Mrs. Jenkins had lived here for donkey's years before either Rafe or I had set eyes on the place, so if she said there was a tunnel, most likely there was one. And most likely it was close to the ground.

I reached out and braced one hand against the cold dirt. Slowly, I squatted. It wasn't easy, but I made it. "Mrs. J?"

"Here, baby."

Her voice came from in front of me. I reached out and felt around.

Yes, there it was. The outline of an opening in the dirt wall.

How could we have missed this?

The answer presented itself the next second, when my hand encountered wood. A post or pillar, crumbly and old.

The entrance to the tunnel was under the stairs. The stairs that were held up by wooden beams and planks. Some of which must swing in and out to cover and uncover this hole in the ground.

The tunnel emitted a sort of a cold breeze, even colder than the basement air already was. I could hear Mrs. Jenkins scrabbling in front of me.

"Am I going to fit?"

She didn't answer. I'm not sure whether it was because she didn't hear me, or because she didn't know the answer.

"Dear God, please let me fit."

He didn't make any promises, either. I swallowed my fear and pushed inside the dank hole.

I won't bore you with an inch by inch description of the trip through the ground. It was uncomfortable, and felt like it took hours. I had a couple of smallish panic attacks when I thought about the tunnel collapsing on top of us, and Rafe never realizing what happened. I had to force myself to think about something else. The air got worse the further in we went, and then I started worrying about passing out, and about brain damage. To me and to the baby. Mrs. Jenkins would be stuck ahead of me, and wouldn't be able to get around me to get back, and also wouldn't be able to move my much larger body.

I had to force myself onward from that thought, too.

And then there was the size of the tunnel. Small. The dirt roof brushed my head, and the sides brushed my shoulders. It was easy for Mrs. J. She was small. I wasn't.

Moving along on my hands and knees hurt. My hands and knees as well as my back, which had to carry the weight of the baby.

By the time we reached the end of the tunnel—a narrow shaft going up—I was crying. Silently, but crying. Big, fat tears rolling down my face. I was afraid, I was tired, and I needed to pee. I wanted it to be over.

And then it was. I ran my head into two thin twigs, which turned out to be Mrs. Jenkins's legs.

It took a second for the correlation to sink in. She was standing up. The tunnel had ended.

A second later, one of the legs moved. And then the other. She was climbing.

I moved forward, into the shaft, where I could get off my hands and knees and sit up. I didn't dare stand, not quite yet, since I didn't want to knock Mrs. Jenkins off whatever she was hanging onto, and I also didn't want to hit my head on anything else. I had no idea how tall the shaft was, after all.

About fifteen feet, as it turned out. There was a screech up above, from yet another tortured soul, and then a square of light opened up. Into what looked like heaven. Blue sky. Pale sunlight.

I took my first deep breath since I'd entered the tunnel. It made me cough.

Over my head, Mrs. Jenkins scrambled out of the shaft and into the world. After a moment, her head appeared again. I couldn't see her face, just the outline of it. Her hair was sticking out every which way, like a halo. The pins I had put in it this morning must have fallen out.

That was OK. I'd fix it later. And at the moment, she deserved the halo. She deserved a whole lot more, too.

"C'mon, baby."

I got to my feet, wincing. My knees hurt. And the shaft looked narrow. Too narrow for me to fit.

But if I could stand in it down here, chances were I could fit up there. The narrowness must be an optical illusion. Just like the thought that it looked like there was a long way up. There couldn't be. We'd started out at basement level. And I didn't think we'd gone down, so we must still be at basement level. We were also—I assumed—somewhere in the backyard. It wasn't likely that the tunnel extended onto someone else's property, and while it felt like it had taken hours to get here, I didn't think we'd traveled quite far enough for that, either.

The way out was lined with wood. Old wood. With a makeshift ladder running up one side. Just more wood—horizontal this time—nailed to the vertical boards lining the shaft.

I reached up, experimentally, and took hold of a plank. The surface was rough. I'd probably end up with splinters.

But since the alternative was to crawl back down the tunnel, into the dark basement, and to wait there until Mrs. Jenkins had made her way into the house to unlock the basement door—if she even remembered at that point what it was she was supposed to do—I decided that the splinters would be worth it. There was daylight and fresh air up above. And my house and my sofa and my fridge. And my husband, when he came home. And a shower and clean clothes.

Yes, the splinters would definitely be worth it. Hopefully the old wood was strong enough to hold my weight—and the baby's—as I made my way up.

I started climbing. The old planks were scratchy under my hands, and they groaned under my feet. I could feel old nails give way when I put my weight on them, and as every foot got me closer to the top, I got more and more worried about something giving way and dropping me—dropping us—back to the bottom.

So I wrapped my fingers around the old planks, and ignored the splinters digging into my skin. I could whine about them later. The only thing that mattered now was holding on until I got to the top.

And then I was there. My head rose above the opening of

the shaft, into blinding sunlight.

It was actually largely overcast, but after being in the dark so long, even that felt like blinding sun.

I blinked a couple of times while I oriented myself.

Yes, definitely still on the property. I was facing the back of the house. There was an expanse of dry grass and some brush and dead stalks of flowers between us, but there was no question I was still in the yard.

"The gazebo."

Mrs. Jenkins nodded. She was standing next to me, toeing her hands. "C'mon, baby."

I gathered myself for a final feat of strength, and crawled the last few feet up the ladder and out of the shaft, onto the floor of the gazebo. And just lay there for a minute, on my side, catching my breath.

Yes, we have a gazebo, too. Not as big as the one where Julia Poole breathed her last. That's the kind of gazebo where you can put a string quartet or a small marching band and stand around and watch them play. Ours is more of a two-person gazebo, the kind of place where, in the old days, a gentleman would escort his beloved for the purpose of some privacy. To steal a kiss or to propose, say.

And for some reason, it had a secret tunnel from the basement. Or into it.

But now was not the time to worry about that. I could figure that part out later.

I pushed myself upright. Or half upright. To a sitting position. "We have to call Rafe."

Mrs. Jenkins nodded.

"And Detective Grimaldi."

After this, even Rafe had to agree. Someone was after Mrs. Jenkins. Surely that proved someone else had killed Julia Poole.

Of course, we'd always known that. But after this, surely even Grimaldi couldn't think that Mrs. J had had anything to do with Julia's murder.

I shook my head. Getting bogged down in surelies wasn't going to help.

"Let's go." I got to my feet and stood for a second, finding my equilibrium. Everything seemed all right in the vicinity of the stomach. The baby didn't appear to have taken any damage from the trip through the ground.

I grabbed Mrs. Jenkins's arm—as much for support as to support her—and we staggered down the steps from the gazebo and across the dead lawn toward the front of the house.

ELEVEN

When Rafe burst through the door thirty minutes later, Mrs. J and I were sitting in the kitchen having ice cream.

Yes, again.

If there was ever a day for two rounds of ice cream, it was today.

The Volvo had still been parked in the driveway when we came around the corner. I had been a little worried that our unknown burglar had driven off in it, but either he didn't know how to hotwire a car—the keys were in my pocket—or he'd had a ride waiting.

Most likely the latter.

And even better: my purse with my cell phone was still on the front seat, so he hadn't taken the time to grab it. Or hadn't wanted it. Or just wanted to get away as quickly as possible and hadn't even realized it was there.

I grabbed the bag and phone on our way past, and dialed Rafe even as we made our slow way up the steps to the porch. "Something's happened. You have to come home."

"You all right?"

I wasn't sure whether he meant me, or me and Mrs. Jenkins, or me and the baby, or all three of us, but I replied in the affirmative. "We're fine. All of us. Someone broke in."

He didn't say anything, but I could feel a cold blast of

anger.

"Nothing's broken or missing, that I know of. He was after your grandmother."

The anger intensified.

"Just get here," I told him. "And so you know, I'm calling Grimaldi when I get off the phone with you. We can't have people breaking in and trying to kill us without letting the police know."

He didn't say anything about that, so I guess he agreed with me. Or at least was resigned to it. "I'll be there in thirty. I'm in Brentwood."

"At the nursing home?"

He made an affirmative sound.

"Is Fesmire there?" If he was, at least that was one suspect we could take off the list.

"No," Rafe said grimly. "I'm on my way."

He hung up. I dialed Grimaldi, as I closed and locked and bolted the front door behind us.

The detective's voice came on. "Savannah."

"I need you to come to my house," I said.

There was a beat. "What's wrong?"

"Nothing now. Someone broke in. They were after Mrs. Jenkins. Long story. If you come over, I'll tell you."

There was an infinitesimal pause. I imagined her checking the time. "Twenty minutes."

"Make it thirty," I said. "Rafe has to get here from Brentwood." And Mrs. Jenkins and I needed a shower. Each.

"I'll see you then." Grimaldi hung up, without wasting time with any more questions.

I wiggled out of my coat and dropped it on the floor in the hallway. I hadn't taken it off when I ran in earlier, and after the trip through the underground, it needed to be dry-cleaned.

Mrs. Jenkins hadn't been wearing one, but had—I assumed—run into the basement in her housedress. It looked as bad as the coat: dirty and crumpled. The little white socks I had put on her this morning were a lost cause by now. Good thing I'd bought a big pack of them.

"I'll fill the tub for you," I told her, as I nudged her toward the stairs. "We'll both feel better once we're clean."

And so it was that when Rafe burst in, we were sitting at the kitchen table eating ice cream, while the washing machine was humming away in the laundry room.

He stopped in the doorway and arched a brow.

"Pregnancy comfort," I told him, and was happy to see a corner of his mouth quirk.

"You sure you're all right?"

"We're fine. Did you know there's a tunnel from the basement to that old, overgrown gazebo in the backyard?"

This time both eyebrows went up. "No."

We hadn't spent a whole lot of time on the yard. It had been a busy summer, between getting married and going on the honeymoon—and Rafe going missing—and everything else that had happened. Not to mention being pregnant. I hadn't wanted to mess around outside in the heat. And Rafe had had other things on his mind.

"There is," I said. "Under the staircase in the basement."

He glanced at the basement door.

"Feel free to go look. We didn't close the door behind us, so I don't think you can miss it. And by the time you come back upstairs, Grimaldi will probably be here, and then we can talk."

He didn't need another invitation, just headed across the kitchen floor to the basement door and turned the key in the lock.

"Don't go into it," I told him. "I'm not sure you'll fit. And I don't want to spend the time having to dig you out. Not today."

He gave me a look, but headed down the stairs without comment. I heard his footsteps on the wood, and then heard them disappear as he reached the dirt floor. I went back to my cold comfort.

He came back up three minutes later. There were cobwebs stuck to the top of his hair. "I never saw that before."

"I haven't, either. But your grandmother knew where it was."

She gave him a grin, and he grinned back. "You all right?"

She nodded. "We did good."

Yes, we did. Or at least she did. I was the one who was snookered by the lure of a new real estate client, into leaving her alone here. If I hadn't, none of this would have happened.

"Or he'd'a killed both of you," Rafe said, when I said so out loud.

I shook my head. "I don't think so. When I came home, he hid until I'd gone down into the basement, and then he locked me in. If he'd wanted to hurt me, he had plenty of time to do it." And lots of kitchen knives available for the job, in case he hadn't brought something of his own for the purpose.

The doorbell rang, and Rafe glanced over his shoulder, his eyes narrowing.

"Probably Grimaldi," I said.

"I'll get it." He headed down the hallway toward the front door. Hopefully it really was Grimaldi, because anyone else was likely to run screaming from the look on his face.

It was Grimaldi, and since Mrs. Jenkins and I had finished our ice cream, and since the other two declined to partake, we took the party into the dining room. The table was a bit bigger than the one in the kitchen, and the chairs a bit more comfortable, with padding. And unlike the parlor, there was no TV to distract Mrs. Jenkins from answering Grimaldi's questions.

I laid it all out, from Mrs. Jenkins's bloodstained arrival in the early hours of Sunday morning, to crawling through the tunnel and emerging through the floor of the backyard gazebo this afternoon. Grimaldi looked grimmer and grimmer as I went along, but she kept scribbling notes until the bitter end, and didn't start asking questions until I was all the way finished.

"So Mrs. Jenkins was covered with blood on Sunday morning?"

"I wouldn't say covered..." I glanced at Rafe. He rolled his eyes.

Grimaldi looked up. "That's what you said. 'Covered with blood.'"

"She wasn't covered. OK? But there was a lot." I looked at Mrs. Jenkins, who was sitting on the other side of the table with a beatific look on her face. She didn't seem to feel any need to interrupt, or defend herself. I'm not sure she had any idea what we were talking about. Down in the basement, she'd seemed alert and aware and with it. Now, she'd slipped back into this vague, not-quite-here state she seemed to be inhabiting most of the time. "At first we worried that it was her blood. When we realized it wasn't, we knew something must have happened to someone. The problem was that Mrs. Jenkins couldn't tell us who."

"So you had the dress analyzed."

Rafe nodded.

"When were you going to tell me the results?"

"I wasn't," Rafe said. "If this hadn't happened, I wouldna told you nothing."

Grimaldi didn't seem surprised. I guess she'd expected it. "But it was Julia Poole's blood?"

"Lab confirmed it yesterday. Human blood and river water. I had'em check for that, too."

Smart move. I'd already guessed Mrs. J had been in the car when it went into the river, but it was nice to have it confirmed. Especially since it made it less likely that she was the one who had killed Julia.

Grimaldi made a note. "Tell me about the funeral again."

I told her about the funeral again. About the—very truncated—argument over the coffin and about Doctor Fesmire almost running us down in the parking lot. "He sounded like he wasn't afraid they were going to sue. Or that they'd win if they did. But Beverly Bristol probably really shouldn't have been out and about walking around at that time of night, should she? Someone should have been there to take care of her if she needed something, right?"

Grimaldi nodded.

"Let me guess. Julia Poole?"

"She was on the schedule for that night," Grimaldi said. In a voice that said nothing at all, yet managed to convey a whole lot.

"So... bear with me for a minute here, but let's say that this wasn't the first time the Bristols, or whatever their names are..."

"All sorts of things," Grimaldi said. "Beverly Bristol was a spinster. Never been married. But she had an older brother—dead now—who had a couple of daughters. They're married, and have different names. And there was a sister, who had twin boys, who of course have their father's name. None of them are named Bristol."

Whatever. "So let's say that at some point prior to this morning, someone in the Bristol family had floated the idea of suing the nursing home. In Doctor Fesmire's hearing."

Grimaldi nodded. So did Rafe. Mrs. Jenkins looked like she wasn't listening.

"And let's say that Doctor Fesmire knew that if they did, they might win. That's not how he sounded this morning, but if Julia Poole was out of the building on the night Beverly Bristol fell—the way she was on the night she died—and he knew or suspected that she was, and that's the reason Beverly Bristol died..."

I had to stop because I ran out of breath. Grimaldi nodded.

Rafe's lips were twitching. I gave him a quelling look before I finished my thought, and the sentence. "Then is it possible that he might have killed Julia? I know that sounds crazy, but if he knew she was responsible for Beverly Bristol's death—or if not exactly responsible, she was negligent—and the Bristol family is thinking of suing, and the nursing home's reputation—and his reputation along with it—would be dragged through the dirt... do you think he might have killed Julia in a fit of rage?"

"Anything's possible," Grimaldi said.

"It would explain why he didn't kill Mrs. Jenkins. He wouldn't want the death of another resident to reflect badly on the nursing home."

"Safer to take her back inside and convince her she'd been wrong about Julia," Rafe said. "Keep her medicated. Tell her Julia's in the hospital and is coming back. And in a week or two, put her to sleep. Gently."

I glanced at Mrs. Jenkins. She was humming. I lowered my voice anyway. "He'd probably be signing the death certificate, so I guess that could work. Although he did try to run her down this morning."

"Careless of him not to stick around and make sure the job was done, though."

It had been.

"So go over what happened this afternoon," Grimaldi said, yanking the conversation back on track. "You got a call?"

I nodded. "From the payphone on Ulm and Dresden. Although I didn't know that until later. When I tried to call back and some kid picked up."

"The caller was a woman?"

I had thought it was. "I don't think I would have gone if it had been a man. You have to be careful in this business."

Grimaldi glanced at Rafe. "Isn't that how she met you?"

A corner of his mouth turned up, and he nodded.

"That was a lucky break," I said. "And frankly, it didn't

seem like one at the time. You both scared me to death."

Rafe chuckled. "And now look at us. Your husband and your maid of honor. And you barefoot and pregnant."

I was barefoot and pregnant. And a cliché. "So it worked out that time. Realtors go to meet clients sometimes, and end up dead. Look at that nutcase in North Carolina." Or maybe it was South Carolina.

"I think he was the realtor in that case," Grimaldi said, but abandoned the subject. "So you think it was a woman. Any chance you could be wrong?"

I'm sure I could be. "It sounded like a woman. But some men sound like women. Especially when they try. So I guess it could have been a man throwing his voice."

"Fesmire?" Rafe suggested.

I thought back. I hadn't heard him say much at the funeral. Just a few words. He hadn't had a deep voice. I mean, there was no way I could mistake Rafe for a woman, even on the phone. In that first phone call, more than a year ago, he'd been oozing testosterone down the line.

He smiled when I said so. Not that last part; the one about him not being mistaken for a woman. "Thank you, darlin'."

"No problem. I guess it's possible it could have been Fesmire. If he was trying. It wasn't a long conversation. Or he could have gotten someone to call for him. Is he not at the nursing home?"

Rafe shook his head. "Both José and Clayton came up empty. He hasn't been home or at work since you saw him this morning."

So he could have been here in the house trying to silence Mrs. Jenkins. Once he realized that Mrs. Jenkins was alive and well, and after he heard me introduce myself, it wouldn't have been hard to figure out that she was staying with me, with us, and where we lived. All he had to do was call the nursing home and have someone look up the records. Rafe's in there as next of kin, with phone number and address and everything nice, and since we got married, I'm sure so am I.

So it could have been Fesmire. Or let's say I couldn't rule him out.

"He drives a pretty distinctive car. At least for this neighborhood. If he was parked around here somewhere, someone may have noticed it."

Grimaldi nodded. "We'll talk to some of the neighbors. So you didn't get a look at him?"

I shook my head. "There was nobody at the other house. Nobody parked outside or anywhere nearby. A green car parked across the street. It was there when I came and still there when I left. It didn't move the whole time I was there. And I didn't see anyone inside."

"And when you came back?"

"I was too preoccupied to look around much. There was no car in the driveway. Nothing parked on the street—although you can't really park on Potsdam, anyway."

Rafe shook his head.

"I didn't check any of the nearby driveways. I'm sorry. I just got here as fast as I could. But if there was a convertible BMW parked anywhere nearby, I didn't see it."

Grimaldi nodded. "And when you came inside?"

"The door was open. I figured the house was empty. That whoever had called to get me out of the house, had taken her." And it had been scary. And the reason why I hadn't been more careful when I burst in. "I called her name. And I heard a sound from back in the kitchen, so I ran down that way. The basement door stood open, and I thought Mrs. Jenkins might be down there."

"And she was," Grimaldi said.

I nodded. "I guess the bad guy must have been waiting on the back porch for me. As soon as I was at the bottom of the stairs, he slammed the door and shut off the light. I could hear him running away, but I couldn't see a thing. I never saw him. But..."

Something struck me, and I tilted my head sideways as I thought about it. "I heard Doctor Fesmire hurry out of the funeral home this morning. He was wearing dress shoes with hard soles. They slapped against the marble floor in the foyer."

Grimaldi nodded.

"This didn't sound the same. Heavier treads. Heavier soles."

"The footsteps might sound different because they were above you," Grimaldi said.

"And he mighta been carrying a pair of boots," Rafe added.

I tried to imagine Alton Fesmire in his nice suit and heavy boots, and couldn't. Although if he'd been carrying a change of footwear, he might have been carrying a change of clothes, too.

"I can't identify him one way or the other, anyway. I didn't see him. And when we got up above ground again, there was no one around."

Grimaldi nodded and closed her notebook. "I'll have a crime scene crew stop by and get some fingerprints. Stay away from the light switch to the basement and anything on the back porch."

No problem. "We'll probably just spend the rest of the day in front of the TV."

It wasn't exciting, but it was safe.

Grimaldi turned to Rafe. "I'm going to call in a squad car to help us do a door-to-door, just in case someone saw something. It's too much for just you and me."

"I can call the boys in," Rafe offered, "unless you want'em sitting on Fesmire's work and home for now."

Grimaldi hesitated. "Keep them there. Between us, you and I and two officers can handle the knocking on doors."

Rafe pushed his chair back. "Prob'ly won't be many folks home, anyway, in the middle of the day."

Probably not. Most people work for a living. But it had to be done. And it might lead somewhere.

He turned to me. "I think you oughta leave, darlin'."

"Excuse me?"

He elaborated. "We were gonna go to Sweetwater for Thanksgiving anyway, right?"

We were, but not until Thursday morning. Now it was Tuesday afternoon. And I hadn't counted on Mrs. Jenkins coming along, although I probably should have. It wasn't like we could leave her here. Especially after this.

I just hadn't had time to think much about Thanksgiving since she showed up. I'd had other things on my mind.

"I think the two of you oughta pack a couple bags and go now," Rafe said. "Spend the day tomorrow helping your mama, or stay outta her way, or whatever she wants you to do. But somebody's already come after you once. I don't want'em to do it again."

It was nice of him to include me in the concern, since nobody had really come after me. It was Mrs. Jenkins who was in the bull's eye. Although it was certainly possible I might be hit by a stray bullet, if I stood next to her. And anyway, if I'd gone into labor down in that basement earlier, with no phone and no way out, and something had gone wrong, something really bad could have happened.

However— "Surely he won't come back here. Not after this."

"Probably not," Grimaldi agreed. Just as I was starting to feel better, she added, "But there are plenty of other places he can go and things he can do. You can't barricade yourselves in the house forever, after all."

Hopefully it wouldn't be forever. But I saw her point. What would keep him from waiting until we were all asleep, and then setting fire to the house?

But if I took Mrs. Jenkins to Sweetwater early, it might give

Rafe and Grimaldi time to work things out before we came back. I hadn't planned to drive back until Friday afternoon. Surely by then, they'd have the culprit in custody.

"I'll go pack," I said.

Grimaldi nodded. And turned to Mrs. J. "Did you know the man who came here?"

I lingered in the doorway for a second to hear what she said. "He hurt Julia."

"Did you see Julia leave the house? Did you follow her?"

Mrs. Jenkins looked sly.

"It's all right," Rafe told her. "You can tell."

She nodded.

"Did you see the man who hurt Julia?"

"He said Julia got hurt," Mrs. Jenkins said. "We have to help Julia."

I headed off down the hallway and up the stairs. They were going in circles in there. The chances of Mrs. Jenkins being able to tell them anything definitely were slim to none in my estimation, and I had packing to do.

By the time I came downstairs with the two bags—one with Mrs. Jenkins's meager wardrobe, one with my own cherry-picked clothes, they had given up.

"I'll call in the crime scene crew," Grimaldi was telling Rafe. "Maybe we'll get lucky and get a print off a doorjamb or the light switch. Meanwhile, we should start knocking on doors."

Rafe nodded. "Just let me see my wife off first."

Grimaldi had no problem with that. "Have a good trip," she told me.

"Have fun working on Thanksgiving," I retorted. "Would you like me to take a message to Dix?"

Her face closed. "No."

I gave her a closer look. "You two are all right, aren't you?"

"We're fine." Her expression dared me to disagree.

"If you say so. But don't think I won't ask Dix when I'm

there."

"Ask away," Grimaldi said, in a tone that said something different.

I tilted my head to look at her. "What's wrong?"

She scowled back. "Nothing."

And then she relented. "It's been a year since your sister-in-law died. Your brother's having a hard time with the anniversary. The last time we spoke, he told me he was feeling guilty."

"For?"

She shrugged. "For not grieving, I guess. For getting on with his life." After a second, she added, "It's normal."

I'm sure it was. "I'll talk to him," I said. "And I know you said you're working. But if you change your mind, you're always welcome. It doesn't have to be as Dix's date. You can just come as our friend."

Rafe nodded. He'd been watching the conversation with his lips curved. I guess he thought the girl/relationship talk was funny. "You're still coming," I asked him, "right?"

He looked innocent. "Course, darlin'."

"You won't use this—this break-in, the situation—as an excuse to avoid my mother?"

"I love your mama," Rafe told me, as he gestured me toward the door. "I'll be there for dinner on Thursday. Promise."

"I'll call you tonight," I told him as we wandered toward the front door. He had appropriated the two bags and was carrying them, leaving me to herd Mrs. Jenkins in front of me. Grimaldi stayed in the dining room, either so she could make the phone call to the crime scene crew, or to give us privacy for our goodbyes. It was probably the former, since with Mrs. Jenkins there, it wasn't like we'd be engaging in any kind of passionate farewell. And anyway, if I knew my husband, he'd hustle both me and his grandmother into the car just as quickly as he could, while using himself as a shield between us and any potential danger.

He nodded.

"And probably tomorrow morning, to make sure you made it through the night."

He nodded, opening the front door.

"And tomorrow night, to see what you've found out."

He nodded, scanning the yard.

"And maybe on Thursday morning, to find out when you're coming."

"For dinner," Rafe said. "C'mon."

He headed out onto the porch. "Stay behind me."

I stayed behind him, and made sure to keep Mrs. Jenkins in front of me, so she was covered on both sides. She was the one at risk here, not either of us.

He loaded her into the car, and then walked around to my side. "Drive carefully."

"I always do," I said, squeezing myself behind the wheel. "And I meant it about the phone calls."

He leaned down to kiss me. His lips were warm and lingered for a second. "I wanna hear from you. I wanna know you're all safe."

"You don't think this person's going to follow us, do you?"

Rafe straightened. "If I thought that, I wouldn't send you somewhere where I can't protect you. But it wouldn't hurt you to keep an eye out. You remember how to look for a tail?"

I remembered. "Don't worry," I told him. "If something happens, you'll be the first to know."

"Drive carefully." He shut my door and stepped back. His lips were still moving.

I rolled down the window. "What?"

"Love you."

"I love you, too," I said, as I felt all gooey inside. "I'll call you later."

He nodded and lifted a hand. I put the car in gear and rolled down the driveway and onto Potsdam Street.

TWELVE

The Martin Mansion sits above the Columbia Road on the way to Pulaski, about an hour, hour-and-a-half south of Nashville.

The time it takes to get there depends on who's behind the wheel. When it's Rafe, it's less than an hour. When it's me, it takes longer. On top of that, I'd been distracted by the fact that I had to keep an eye in the rearview mirror to make sure we weren't followed, and with the extra traffic, it wasn't easy. We'd gotten caught in the beginning of rush hour, and had driven south in a sea of other cars, also headed home to the suburbs. They started peeling off in Brentwood, then Franklin, then Spring Hill, and by the time we got to Columbia we were pretty well alone on the road. The only other car that got off with us—a silver sedan—turned west toward Columbia while we headed south in the direction of Sweetwater and, if we kept going, Pulaski and the Alabama border, so they clearly weren't interested in us.

"Have you ever been here?" I asked Mrs. Jenkins. And then changed it to, "I know you came down for the wedding. But I meant other than that. On your own, or with Rafe, to look around."

This was where her grandchild had been born and raised, after all. And where his mother had been born and raised, and died.

She shook her head.

"Maybe tomorrow we can take a drive and look around. The Bog—that's the trailer park where Rafe grew up, and where LaDonna and Big Jim lived—it's gone now. This guy named Ronnie Burke bought it last year, and was going to develop it into a subdivision. But that didn't work out. It's a long story. Anyway, there's nothing there anymore. But I can show you where it used to be. And we can go the cemetery on Oak Street, where LaDonna is buried, and put some flowers on her grave. I know you didn't know her, but she was Rafe's mother. And Tyrell's girlfriend. And there's a nice little café on the square in downtown where we can have lunch."

"Ice cream?" Mrs. Jenkins asked hopefully.

I grinned at her. "I'm sure we can find ice cream somewhere." Dix or Catherine would know where to go. They both have young children.

And I should probably make sure that ice cream was on the menu for Thanksgiving, too. Not everyone likes pumpkin pie. Although Mrs. Jenkins probably did. I hadn't fed her anything yet, that she'd refused to eat.

"There it is," Mrs. Jenkins pointed.

I nodded. There it was. The Martin Mansion. Squatting above the road like a large, red brick toadstool.

Although I have to admit I was a little surprised that she remembered. She'd only been here once.

Then again, the place makes an impression. Big—almost twice the size of Mrs. J's Victorian, which is a big house in its own right—and with tall, two-story white pillars across the front. A true Southern antebellum mansion of the old-fashioned type. Big double doors in the front, and a wide staircase flanked by urns going up to it.

I see it mainly as my childhood home. But since I met Rafe, I've learned that other people see it differently. He calls it the mausoleum on the hill, and I guess it has a certain fusty old elegance to it. I think he probably also called it that as a remark on my family, and my ancestry, and Southern history in general, and a whole lot of other things. We won't go into it.

As we drove up to the door, it occurred to me that I should perhaps have called and warned my mother we were coming.

Not that she would turn me away. She never has before. Except for that one time she told me to leave because I was trying to stop her from drowning her sorrows in brandy, but there were mitigating circumstances. She never has before. Or since. Not even when I brought Rafe into the house and up to my bedroom and made love to him under my mother's roof. I wouldn't have been surprised if she'd tried to then, but she didn't. So I didn't think she'd turn us away now, either.

But I should probably have called and told her I was coming. A day early. And that Mrs. J was with me.

Oh, well. Too late now. I pulled the Volvo to a stop in front of the wide staircase and cut the engine. "Here we are."

Mrs. Jenkins nodded.

"I'll come open the door for you."

I walked around the car and opened the passenger side door. Just as the front door to the mansion opened. My mother stood in the opening. "Savannah? What are you—?"

And that's as far as she got, because a pale gray blur shot past her and down the steps, barking threateningly.

Mrs. Jenkins shrieked. I froze. I think my mother said a bad word, but I couldn't swear to it. "Pearl!"

Pearl stopped halfway between the steps and me. If that doesn't sound so bad, like maybe she was far enough away not to be scary, I could feel her hot dog breath on my calves.

"Hello, Pearl," I said. My voice shook, but Pearl must have recognized it, because she tilted her head to look at me. "How are you?"

The last time Rafe and I were in Sweetwater, Rafe was helping Sheriff Satterfield with a case. A bunch of members of the same family had been shot, in their beds, all within an hour or so of each other. Pearl had belonged to one of them. We'd found her guarding a trailer up in the foothills by the Devil's Backbone, a range of hills west of Columbia, and for some reason she had taken to me. I'd ended up bringing her here, where she had bonded with my mother. At the end of the case, I had planned to take her home to Nashville with me, but she had indicated her desire to stay here, so Mother had taken her in instead.

I'd forgotten... not Pearl, but how scary she could be.

Pearl wagged her stub of a tail tentatively, her tongue lolling. She has a broad face with a big mouth (and strong jaws), and at the moment she looked like she was smiling.

I extended a hand, carefully. The last thing I wanted was for her to think I was making a threatening move.

She took a step forward to sniff my fingertips. After a second, her tail wagged again, and kept wagging. I deduced she had recognized me.

"Hi, sweetheart," I told her. "It's good to see you. I need you to meet Mrs. Jenkins, OK? And be gentle with her."

I know it sounds sort of crazy to talk to the dog like she'd understand. Robbie Skinner certainly hadn't. He'd kept her chained under his trailer like an animal. But I swear she understood me. Somehow.

"It's OK," I told Mrs. Jenkins. "She won't hurt you."

Mrs. J looked a little fearful, but when I took her arm to help her out of the car, she didn't resist. "This is Pearl," I told her. "My mother named her." After a Chihuahua she'd had as a girl. "Rafe and I found her last month. She's been living with my mother since."

Pearl gave Mrs. Jenkins a quick sniff, but seemed to realize that Mrs. J was apprehensive and would need some time to get used to her, because she kept her distance after that, and didn't push. Instead she bounded up the stairs to my mother, who was still standing in the open door.

We followed, a lot more slowly. As we approached the door, I gave my mother a bright smile. "I should have called and let you know we were coming a day early. Sorry."

"That's all right," Mother said, in a tone of voice that told me, eloquently, that it wasn't. At all.

I lowered my voice. I'm not sure why, when Mrs. Jenkins was standing right next to me. "She's my husband's grandmother. My grandmother-in-law. And someone's trying to kill her. Surely you can spare one of the five bedrooms for a night."

Mother looked at me down the length of her nose. Considering that she's a couple of inches shorter than me, it was quite a feat. So was her tone of voice. "Of course." The two words dripped with ice cubes, and made me feel guilty for ever entertaining the thought that she wouldn't be gracious.

She dismissed me with the flick of an eyelash, and turned to Mrs. J. And turned on the charm. "It's so good to see you again. I'm sorry to hear you're having problems."

Only my mother would call being hunted by a murderer 'having problems.' But since she was being nice to Mrs. Jenkins, I rolled my eyes very quietly. And didn't complain when she detached Mrs. J from my arm with years of practice—I'd learned to do that too, in finishing school. Of course, the target then hadn't been a wrinkled old lady, but a personable young man you wanted to get away from another young lady who had sunk her claws into him.

I let her get away with it, even though I'd also been taught how to hold my own should I be the one originally in possession of the gentleman. They walked into the house, and I headed back to the car to bring in the overnight bags. Pearl dithered, not quite sure whether to stay with me or follow them. After a second's contemplation, she followed Mother. There was more chance of a snack inside the house than outside, I assumed.

I grabbed the bags and hauled them up to the door. And took a quick look around. Nobody was hiding in the bushes with a pair of binoculars. There were no cars driving slowly by on the road. I didn't think anyone had followed us. If they had, they'd stayed so far back that I hadn't seen them. But just in case, maybe I should pull the car around to the back, and the old carriage house that now serves as the garage.

I dumped the bags on the floor inside the door, and made sure the door was shut. Pearl must have followed Mom and Mrs. J up the stairs, because she wasn't anywhere to be seen, but I didn't want to risk leaving the door open and having her run off. I shut it behind me and went back to the car.

It took a couple of minutes to park and return. By the time I had, Mother and Mrs. J had returned from the second floor to greet me, along with Pearl.

Mother gave me a look.

"Sorry," I said. "I didn't want to leave the car in plain view, in case someone drove by who shouldn't see it."

"Let's go to the kitchen," Mother said firmly. "You can tell me everything."

I gestured. "The bags..."

"You can take them up later," Mother said. "Right now, I think we could all use some tea."

She headed down the hall toward the kitchen, her heels clicking decisively on the wood floors. Pearl's nails clicked, too, more softly, as she followed. I'm sure she had figured out that the kitchen was where the food was. And the treats.

I smiled at Mrs. Jenkins. "Shall we?"

She nodded. We followed Mother down the hall.

She makes tea the old-fashioned way, by boiling water in a kettle on the stove. Then she pours it into a proper teapot, where it steeps. Once it's ready, she serves it in paper thin china cups on saucers, with silver tea spoons, and a proper sugar and creamer set, and cloth napkins. The only incongruous thing this time was the fact that we were all sitting around the kitchen island, instead of properly around the table in the parlor, balancing the cups on our knees as befits Southern ladies.

I watched like a hawk, but unless Mother had laced the cream jug with brandy, she didn't spike her tea with anything. For a while after she'd found out about Audrey and Dad, there was a lot of spiked tea flowing. Along with mimosas for breakfast and milk with rum for bedtime.

But not today.

"Tell me everything." She fixed me with a steady stare over the rim of the flower-painted cup, pinky elegantly extended.

I filled her in, much as I had done Grimaldi a couple of hours ago. Everything from waking up at three in the morning on Sunday to pee, and seeing Mrs. Jenkins under a tree in the yard, until we'd crawled out of a hole in the backyard this afternoon.

"Dear me," my mother said when I was done. That's her version of something more expletive. "Are you all right?"

She included Mrs. Jenkins in the glance.

I nodded. "We're fine. But Rafe and Detective Grimaldi thought it would be a good idea for us to get out of town a little earlier than planned, so they can focus on the investigation. They have a pretty good idea who the bad guy is."

At least it seemed that way to me. Doctor Fesmire had known Julia Poole. He had something to lose—like his cushy job—if it came out that Beverly Bristol had died because Julia had been negligent. That gave him reason to kill Julia. And if he'd killed Julia, and had tried to kill Mrs. Jenkins, on Saturday, he had every reason to want to eliminate Mrs. Jenkins now. The fact that he was in the wind—not at work, not at home, when José and Clayton looked for him earlier today—was an additional indication that he might be guilty. At least if you asked me.

Mother didn't, though. She just took my word for it and

moved on. "Rafael will be coming down for dinner on Thursday, I hope?"

My mother is the only person in the world, with the exception of Tim, who calls Rafe by his full name. And where she had a real problem with him before we got married, now she adores him as much as I do, if not more.

"He's planning to," I said. "Unless something goes wrong, I'm sure he will."

Mother smiled, pleased. "And you don't think anyone followed you here?"

"I didn't see anyone. And I looked." I glanced at Pearl, who was lying on the floor watching the proceedings. In case something should happen to fall like manna from Heaven, I guess. "If anyone shows up, I'm sure Pearl will let us know."

Mother glanced at her, too. "I've been meaning to talk to you," she said.

My heart sank. "You don't want to get rid of her, do you? She seems happy. Although I can take her home with me, if you insist."

"No, darling," Mother said. Unlike Rafe, she pronounces the G at the end. "I love Pearl. She's wonderful. Very gentle."

"Good." She hadn't been so gentle with a small, stuffed toy I'd bought her just after we got her, so I hoped Mother was keeping small animals away from her. "Have the children interacted with her? Abigail and Hannah and Catherine's three?"

Abigail and Hannah belong to my brother Dix. Catherine's children are Cole, Robert, and Annie.

"She's very patient with them," Mother nodded. "Of course, I'm careful. But she doesn't seem to mind at all. She sits perfectly still while the girls tie ribbons around her neck and decorate her ears."

I looked at Pearl and tried to imagine her with decorated ears. It didn't quite compute, but good for her on sitting still for it.

"And the boys roughhouse," Mother added, "and she doesn't seem to mind that, either."

Excellent. Of course, Robbie had had a daughter—twelve year old Kayla—and I'm sure he would have made Pearl feel it if she'd done anything to her. So she might have learned to be nice to children the hard way.

"You're a good girl," I told her. She slapped her tail against the floor a couple of times, and smiled at me.

"I'd like to have her fixed," Mother said.

Fixed? As far as I could tell, she wasn't broken.

"Oh. You mean spayed. Robbie didn't do that?"

"She isn't very old," Mother said. "Maybe he was planning to breed her."

I wouldn't put it past him. "Yes, I think that would be a good idea. Does she have a tendency to run off?"

And maybe hook up with a handsome mongrel from the wrong side of town?

"She hasn't yet," Mother said. "But if she does, I'd rather make sure I won't end up with a litter of puppies."

I didn't blame her. I liked Pearl, but I didn't want five of her. Or more. "Sounds good. Why are you asking me?"

"Because she's technically yours," Mother said. "You found her."

"I gave her to you. That makes her yours."

"You didn't give her to me," Mother said. "She chose to stay here."

"That makes her even more yours." I shook my head. "Do whatever you want. Just make sure she's healthy and happy."

Mother nodded. She took a sip of tea and avoided my eyes. "What plans did you have for this evening?"

I arched my brows. "We didn't really have any. Are you going somewhere?"

"I made plans to have dinner with Bob," my mother said.

She's been dating the Sweetwater sheriff for a while now. A couple of years, maybe? Or maybe more. It took me a while to catch on, to be honest. My brother and sister, who live here in Sweetwater, might have known before me, but I think Mother and the sheriff kept it pretty quiet.

"Of course. Don't let us cramp your style. Mrs. Jenkins sleeps pretty well, and I don't wake up until someone stands over me and shakes me these days." Or until I have to pee. Whichever comes first.

Mother flushed. "If we're planning to do anything like that, we'll go to Bob's."

I guess 'anything like that' probably meant sex. I hadn't mentioned sex, and I didn't plan to. "Isn't Todd there?"

"He spends a lot of time with Marley," Mother said primly.

Todd—the assistant DA for the county—tried to prosecute Marley Cartwright for murdering her baby once. Around this time last year. It's very nice of her to overlook that, I think. Although she has her baby back now—he must be around three at this point—so I guess she can afford to be magnanimous. And I'm happy for them. I like Marley. And for a while, I was afraid Todd was never going to move on from asking me to marry him.

"They don't live together, do they?"

Mother shook her head. "He comes home every night. But they do spend a lot of time together."

"How does Bob feel about that?"

"Now that we all know that Marley didn't do anything to that sweet baby," Mother said, "I don't think anyone minds."

Good to know. "Sure," I said, "go to dinner with Bob. Stay out as late as you want. Is there anything to eat here?"

If not, we could always order a pizza. Or maybe not. In the movies, the bad guy often pretends to be a pizza delivery person.

Not that there was a bad guy. Not here in Sweetwater.

Nobody had followed us.

"The fridge is full," Mother said. "Don't eat the turkey."

As if I would. "Any ice cream?"

"Help yourselves," Mother said, and slipped off the stool. "I should go get ready. I gave Mrs. Jenkins your sister's room."

"That'll work." I got up, too. "We'll take the bags upstairs and get situated. And figure out something to eat. And we'll probably end up watching TV for the rest of the night. You have cable, right?"

"Of course," Mother said.

"HGTV?"

"Of course," Mother said.

"Then we're all set. Don't be surprised if you come home and find us both asleep in the parlor."

Mother said she wouldn't, and we all headed out of the kitchen and down the hall with Pearl's nails clicking on the hardwoods behind us. I snagged the two overnight bags from beside the door, and carried them upstairs. Mother disappeared down the hall toward the master bedroom, and I dropped my own bag next to the door to my room, and carried Mrs. Jenkins's over to Catherine's old room. "Would you like some help unpacking?"

"No thanks, baby." She patted my arm.

"I'll just go wash up and put away my own things. I'll see you downstairs in a few minutes, I guess. The bathroom's across the hall, if you need it." I pointed to the door. Mrs. J nodded. "Once Mother leaves, we'll take a look at what's in the fridge and see what we can do about dinner."

While the tea had filled the empty spot inside, it wasn't going to be long before I needed something more solid. Mrs. Jenkins must be hungry too, because she looked cheered at the prospect.

So I left her bag on the bed, and went into my own room and put away my own clothes. My back hurt, so I curled up on the bed for a few minutes—on my left side—to see if I could get it to go away, but it didn't. Too much time sitting in the car, maybe, on top of crawling through the tunnel earlier. It had been a long and exhausting day.

I was almost asleep by the time I heard Mother clicking down the hall on her high heels, followed by the softer clicking of Pearl's nails. Forcing myself awake, I got myself upright and padded downstairs after her.

She was standing in the middle of the foyer putting on her coat, with Pearl sitting at her feet gazing adoringly up.

My mother is pushing sixty, and looks great for her age. She's a little shorter than me, and at the moment at least, a lot smaller around. Like the rest of the Georgia Calverts, she has blond hair and blue eyes. Dix and I do, too, while Catherine has inherited our father's dark hair and more sallow skin. So has Darcy, to even more of a degree. Darcy's coloring is really more like Rafe's than any of ours. Of course, Audrey also has jet black hair, but I don't know how much of it owes its hue to nurture versus nature. I imagine she was born with very dark hair, and as she's gotten older, she's chosen to keep it dark. Same with Mother. I can't imagine her hair is quite so naturally blond anymore. But I've never even seen a hint of gray.

"You look wonderful," I said.

"Thank you, darling." She finished tightening her belt around her waist. Unlike me, she still has one. "We'll be at the Wayside Inn, if you need me."

"I figured." The Wayside Inn is the nicest restaurant in town, and my mother's favorite. "I doubt we'll need you, though. We're just going to find something to eat and then crash in front of the TV. We'll be fine."

"I'll take the dog out when I get home," Mother said. "Or make Bob do it."

It would probably be 'make Bob do it.' "I don't mind," I began.

"Bob doesn't, either."

Sure. "How about we just figure it out later."

"I won't be late," Mother said, just as a pair of headlights flashed across the wall in the foyer. Tires crunched their way up to the door.

"Stay as long as you want. We're both adults. And I'll make sure the dog is walked and the doors are locked if you're not home at a decent hour. Does Pearl have the run of the house at night?"

She did. She had a bed in the master suite, and a bed downstairs. She could choose to sleep in either. Or on the sofa, if she preferred. Or anywhere else her little doggie heart desired.

"If I'm not here," Mother said as she opened the door, "she'll probably choose to be downstairs to wait for me. That way she can keep an eye on the door."

And keep a look out in case someone other than Mother should show up, too. Not that we have a lot of crime in Sweetwater. The mansion isn't a target of burglars very often. But I won't say it hasn't happened.

Mother made her elegant way down the stairs toward Bob's truck. I gave him a wave from the open door. "Evening, Sheriff."

"Evening, darlin'. I didn't know you were gonna be here tonight."

"Change of plans," I said. "Mrs. Jenkins and I came down a day early. Mother can fill you in. It'll give you something to talk about over dinner."

"We always have something to talk about over dinner." He opened the door for Mother and helped her up into the seat before closing the door behind him and giving me a wink. "Don't wait up."

"I wasn't planning to," I told him, and stood on the porch and waved until they'd navigated the long driveway. Once I couldn't see them anymore, I went inside and locked the door and looked around for Mrs. Jenkins.

THIRTEEN

She wasn't in the foyer. I had assumed, when she heard my mother go downstairs, she'd follow, the way I had done. But she hadn't. Maybe she'd fallen asleep.

I headed back up the stairs, with Pearl keeping pace. She looked worried. Maybe I wasn't moving fast enough for her. My back still hurt, and climbing stairs was getting more and more difficult every day.

"Mrs. Jenkins?"

I entered the second floor stairwell and headed toward the back of the house. Past my open door to Mrs. Jenkins's—formerly Catherine's—room.

The door was open there, too. It only took a second to see that the room was empty. The overnight bag was still on the bed where I'd left it. And it didn't look like Mrs. Jenkins had laid down for a rest the way I had.

"Mrs. J?"

I turned toward the bathroom. The door stood open there, too. Not much chance anyone was inside, but I peered in anyway.

It was empty. The shower curtain was pulled to the side, and no one was hiding in the tub.

"Mrs. J?"

Dix's old room is on the same side of the hallway as the bathroom. I stuck my head inside. Empty, of course.

She must have waited until my mother left, and then gone into the master suite. I headed that way.

"Mrs. Jenkins?"

There was no answer.

If you've ever watched HGTV—and I had watched a lot of it this week—you'll have noticed that one recurring phenomenon is potential homebuyers walking into the master suite, doing a half turn, and then saying, "I don't think it's big enough," or words to that effect. "I'm not sure our furniture is going to fit in here." Usually, the master bedroom in new construction is huge. In old houses, like this one, not so much. Back in 1840, people didn't think of a master bedroom as a retreat the way we do today. It was just somewhere you went to crash after a long day of hard work.

Mother's room was a little bit bigger than mine, but it wasn't huge. The attached bath—not 1840s vintage—wasn't, either. It took me less than twenty seconds to look through it all and determine that once again, Mrs. Jenkins wasn't here.

I put my hands on my hips and did that HGTV half-turn. So where the hell—excuse me, heck—was she?

I'd been awake the whole time we'd been upstairs. I would have heard her if she went past my door and down to the first floor. I'd heard Mother. I'd followed Mother. Mrs. Jenkins hadn't been between us, and hadn't come down while we'd been standing in the foyer.

"Mrs. J?"

There was no answer. I headed for the back of the house and the narrow staircase down to the kitchen.

And that's where I found her. In the kitchen. With three burners going on the stove—gas, of course; Mother wouldn't consider cooking with anything but gas—and the island afloat with food stuffs. When I walked into the room, she was mincing something green, super fast, with a knife as long as her arm. Knowing my mother, I'm sure the knife was lethally sharp. And she was humming.

"There you are," I said, too relived to have found her to yell at her for scaring me. "What are you cooking?"

"Fried chicken," Mrs. Jenkins said, "mac'n cheese, and collard greens. And biscuits."

Lovely. Sounded like we were in for a feast. My stomach rejoiced, even as my arteries whimpered.

Another very nice thing, was that she sounded completely lucid. A lot of the time, she sounds a little vague, like she's not entirely sure where she is, who you are, and maybe even who she is.

Not so now. She was cooking from scratch, humming as she dredged chicken pieces in flour and some sort of crunchy mixture. Bread crumbs, or Corn Flakes, or maybe potato chips.

"Need any help?"

I know how to cook, sort of. Soul food isn't a strength, though, so I was relieved when she told me, "No, baby. You just sit down and watch."

I sat down and watched. Kept my eye on the sharp knives and the gas flames on the oven, to make sure she didn't hurt herself. And on Pearl, whom I had to tell to go lie down in the corner, since her position, on the floor between the island and the stove, might cause Mrs. Jenkins to stumble over her and fall. Pearl grumbled, but went.

An hour later, we had fried chicken and macaroni and cheese—from scratch—and biscuits—ditto—and collard greens. I didn't like the greens that much. They were wilted and sort of greasy. But everything else tasted like heaven. When we were finished, it was all I could do to stagger into the parlor and collapse in front of the television. "HGTV?"

Mrs. Jenkins nodded. She didn't look as full as I felt. And she'd eaten as much as I had.

Of course, she didn't have an almost-full-term baby pushing on all her internal organs, either.

I fell asleep over *Property Brothers*. Mrs. Jenkins patted me and told me she'd stay with me. I grunted something and fell asleep again, and didn't wake up until Mother came home. By then it was after ten o'clock and time to go to bed. And I was alone.

"Damn. I mean..." I pushed upright and looked around, frantically. "Where is Mrs. Jenkins?"

"She went up to bed," Mother said calmly, unbuttoning her coat. "Where you should be, too."

I should. But before I could, I had to call Rafe. I had told him I would, and if I didn't, he'd worry. So after dragging myself upstairs and brushing my teeth, I forced my gluey eyelids to stay open long enough to call my husband.

He sounded disgustingly alert. Although, considering that it was only about ten-thirty, maybe it wasn't surprising. "Evening, darlin'."

"Ugh," I said.

His voice turned sympathetic. "Rough night?"

"Rough day. Right from the beginning." I took a breath, carefully, and added. "The evening was actually pretty peaceful. Mother went out with Bob Satterfield, and we just stayed here. Your grandmother cooked. I ate too much. And fell asleep in front of the TV."

"Sorry, darlin'." I could hear amusement lacing through his voice.

"I feel like a beached whale."

"I know." The sympathy was back, along with the amusement. "It'll be over soon."

It would. And then I'd probably wish I could stuff the screaming, inconsolable, small poop-machine back inside for a while so I wouldn't have to deal with it. "We're going sightseeing tomorrow," I said. "I'm showing your grandmother around. And tomorrow afternoon, we'll probably help Mother prepare for Thanksgiving. You're still planning to come, right?"

"Course."

"Mother asked. She's looking forward to seeing you."

"I'm looking forward to seeing her, too," Rafe said, which had to be a lie. Or maybe not. "So no problems getting there?"

"None at all. Nobody followed us that I could see. Is there anything new where you are?"

He grunted. Annoyed. "We did the door-to-door. Nobody saw nobody at the house. Nobody saw nobody using the payphone. Nobody noticed any strange cars. Nobody noticed a BMW. It was all sedans and trucks and the usual stuff."

"So we can't put Fesmire at the house."

"No," Rafe said. "And we can't put him nowhere else, neither. I told José and Clayton to go home at ten."

"They haven't seen Fesmire all day?"

Apparently they hadn't. "He didn't show up at home or at work so far."

"So where is he?"

"God knows," Rafe said. "For all we know, he ran off to Vegas with his mistress."

"Does he have one?" Had her name been Julia Poole? "Is he married?"

He was.

"He probably doesn't have a girlfriend, then," I said.

"You never know," Rafe answered. "Wealthy doctor like that might look good to some gold-digger twenty-year-old."

Maybe so. "But you don't know where he is. Or where she is, if she exists." Maybe it was Fesmire's girlfriend who had called and gotten me out of the house earlier.

"No," Rafe said. "If he ain't home or at work by tomorrow morning, Tammy'll put out a BOLO and see if anybody's seen him. Until then we wait."

"You'll wait carefully, right? Just in case he decides to come back in the middle of the night?"

"I'm sleeping on the sofa," Rafe said. "With a gun on the

coffee table."

Good. "I'll let you get to it. And I'll call you tomorrow morning. Do your best to stay alive so you can answer the phone."

My husband assured me he would. "Sleep well, darlin'."

"You, too," I told him. "I miss you."

"Miss you, too. But I'm glad you ain't here."

I was, too, if it came to that. This afternoon had been scary. I was perfectly happy to stay out of the way until they caught the bad guy, be it Alton Fesmire or someone else. "I'll talk to you tomorrow."

"Love you." He hung up, and saved me the trouble of doing so. I plugged the phone in to charge next to my bed, and crawled underneath the covers.

When I woke up again, it was morning. Bright sunlight slanted through the curtains, and I could smell coffee and hear voices from downstairs. Mother must be up, and she either had company, or was talking to Mrs. Jenkins.

A quick look at the phone showed me that it was close to nine. I swung my legs over the edge of the bed, and groaned. My back still hurt. Too much activity followed by too much sitting around yesterday, probably, and then falling asleep on Great-Aunt Ida's uncomfortable loveseat.

Rafe hadn't called, and that was a little worrisome, since he should certainly be up by now. But when I called him, he answered immediately. "Morning, darlin'."

"Good morning. Did anything happen overnight?"

I imagined him shaking his head. "Nothing. I slept like a baby."

Funny. According to Catherine, babies don't sleep well at all. At least not for the first eight months or so.

"Any news?"

"Nothing so far. Everything's quiet. José and Clayton have

gone south." To Brentwood and Franklin, I assumed; both of which are south of Nashville. "We're just keeping on keeping on."

"You do that," I said. "I'm going to grab some breakfast and then show your grandmother around. Call me if there's anything I need to know. Otherwise, I'll talk to you again tonight."

Rafe said he would. We made kissy noises at each other, and then I hung up and headed downstairs.

Mrs. Jenkins's door stood open, and I found her in the kitchen with Mother. They seemed to be getting along all right. I have to admit I'd been a little worried about Mother doing the Lady of the Manor act with poor Mrs. J. My mother, not to put too fine a point on it, was brought up with some old Southern mores she hasn't been entirely successful in eradicating.

I'm not sure she's ever felt it necessary to eradicate them, to be honest. At least not until I brought Rafe into our midst, and she came face-to-face with her prejudices. She's doing a lot better than she was, but I know I can't expect miracles, so I'd made my way down the stairs concerned that the atmosphere in the kitchen was tense.

It wasn't. They were sitting at the island having coffee together. Mother was doing most of the talking, but that wasn't unusual. Mrs. Jenkins never had a whole lot to say, and as she's gotten more confused over the past year, she's said less and less. But she looked clean and comfortable, in one of her housedresses—not the same one she'd been wearing yesterday—and a pair of clean, white socks.

"We should get you a new dress for tomorrow," I said, as I headed for the fridge and the bottle of milk. The coffee smelled good, but I couldn't have any. "For Thanksgiving dinner."

Mother nodded.

"Would you like to come with us?" I offered. "Later, I mean? I need something to eat first. But we were going to do the grand tour of Sweetwater. I was going to show Mrs. Jenkins the Bog, and the cemetery where LaDonna's buried, and I thought we might have some lunch at the café, maybe."

"That's all right," Mother said pleasantly. "I have things to do here."

I looked at her. "You and Audrey still aren't talking?"

"She slept with my husband," Mother said.

"Before he was your husband. Before he even knew you. And he broke it off with her as soon as the two of you met."

Mother looked stubborn.

"We've been over this before," I told her, as I dipped a spoon into a cup of yogurt I'd found in the fridge. "There's no point in rehashing it again."

And then I proceeded to rehash it anyway. "She's been your best friend since before Catherine was born. There are good reasons why she didn't tell you she had Dad's baby and gave it up for adoption. You're being silly."

Mother looked mulish.

"Fine," I said. "Don't come with us. But you're going to have to deal with this sooner or later. Darcy is my sister. And Audrey's her mother. Neither of them is going away. Dix and Catherine and I want a relationship with Darcy. And we love Audrey. I understand that you're hurt—anyone would understand why you're hurt—but holding on to your feelings doesn't help anybody. All it does, is leave you without your best friend. When you need her most."

Mother's mouth opened, probably to tell me it would be a cold day in hell when she needed Audrey for anything. I continued. "Audrey's all right. She has her daughter back. I'm sure she misses you, but she gained something from this. All you gained, was a step-daughter you didn't want."

I waited a second. She didn't deny it.

"But nobody did any of this to hurt you. And the person you're punishing the most, is yourself."

Mother didn't have a response to that.

"I'm going to go upstairs and get ready," I said, as much to my mother as to Mrs. Jenkins. "I need to wash and put on real clothes." Since I'd come down in my bathrobe. "I'll be back in a few minutes. And then we can go."

Neither of them said anything. I padded down the hallway and upstairs.

When I came down twenty minutes later, Mrs. Jenkins was sitting on the bottom step of the staircase talking to Pearl. My mother was nowhere to be seen. I assumed she was sulking, so I didn't push it. "Ready?" I asked Mrs. Jenkins instead.

She nodded.

"You'll need your coat. Is it upstairs?"

She nodded.

"I'll get it." I was pregnant, but she was old. And moving might be good for me. I still had that niggling lower backache.

I found Mrs. J's coat tossed over a chair in her—or Catherine's—room, and brought it back down. I helped her into it, and we headed out. Since I didn't know where Mother was—inside or out—I made sure I locked the door behind us. And while I wasn't unmoved by Pearl's forlorn expression and sad puppy eyes, we couldn't take her with us. "I'm sorry, baby," I told her. "But we're going to Audrey's, and she wouldn't appreciate you in her store. The folks at the Café on the Square wouldn't be happy to see you, either. And I don't want to leave you in the car. You'll be better off here. I promise. I'm sure Mother's around somewhere..."

Pearl dropped her tail and her ears, but she didn't try to follow us out. I felt horribly guilty, though.

Once in the car, I was able to shake it off. The dog wasn't being abandoned, after all. She had food and water and was well taken care of. She had doggie beds and furniture to lie on, and we were only going to be gone a few hours. Maybe I could take her for a walk when we got home. A walk might help my back, as well.

"Where would you like to start?" I asked Mrs. Jenkins.

But of course she didn't know, since she hadn't been here before. I decided to head toward the Bog. It was the farthest away, on the south side of town. We could make our way back from there.

While we drove, I gave her a little history.

"When I was growing up, the Bog was a trailer park. Rafe lived there with his mother and grandfather. I didn't know him, though. Not until I started high school. Although I'd heard of him..."

We'd all heard of him. LaDonna Collier's good-for-nothing colored boy, who was always getting in trouble.

I didn't realize at the time that some of that trouble wasn't of his own making. Plenty was. But whenever something—anything—went wrong in Sweetwater, Rafe was the usual suspect. And he wasn't always guilty.

"Old Jim died when Rafe was twelve. The sheriff always thought Rafe and LaDonna had something to do with it, but Rafe says no. That his grandfather was drunk and fell into the river one night, and that they didn't find him until later. That they were just happy he wasn't inside the trailer giving them a hard time, and they weren't about to put themselves out to go look for him."

Mrs. Jenkins didn't answer. When I gave her a sideways look, her expression was peaceful. Could have been a couple of different reasons for that. She might not be listening to me. She might not have any idea who Rafe and Old Jim were. Sometimes she didn't. Or—seeing as Old Jim shot her son Tyrell in retaliation for Tyrell's knocking up LaDonna—she might be just fine with the idea of Old Jim staggering out of the trailer, dead drunk, and falling headfirst into the Duck River. Nobody else had mourned for him, so it seemed fitting.

"Rafe and I met in high school. That was the first time I

went to the Bog."

After a second, I added, honestly, "Not that I went to see him, or anything. We weren't on those terms. But we found him in Columbia once. I was there with my brother and some friends to see a movie, and Rafe had been beaten up. He was sitting on the curb just down from the movie theatre. We loaded him in the car and drove him home."

Much against Todd's wishes. It was his car, and it was brand new. He didn't appreciate Rafe bleeding on the leather upholstery. And it totally destroyed Dix's plans of necking with Charlotte in the backseat on the way home. Instead of having the backseat to themselves, they had to share it with me, squeezed in like sardines in the small sports car, while Todd kept shooting hostile glances at Rafe.

Mrs. Jenkins smiled.

"After that, I didn't see him again for twelve years. Until he called the real estate office and asked me to meet him outside your house last year. He knew who I was as soon as he heard my name on the phone." He'd double-checked, I remembered. "I didn't recognize him at first. I knew there was something familiar about him, but twelve years is a long time. He didn't look the same."

And when I did realize who he was, I'd been scared. I remembered taking a step back. *"I thought you went to prison."*

And that purring answer, *"That was twelve years ago, darlin'. I got out."*

Now it seemed crazy that I could ever have been afraid of him. Not that he can't be plenty scary. And plenty dangerous. But not to me.

Never to me.

"I think I fell for him almost from the second I set eyes on him. Even though it took me a long time to admit it." Especially to myself. Other people had known long before I had.

He'd probably known long before I had. Although I think

he'd been a bit afraid I'd never admit it. And that I'd marry Todd instead, because my mother wanted me to, and because it was what a properly brought-up Southern Belle was supposed to do. Not shack up with the bad boy from the trailer park on the wrong side of town, and get pregnant out of wedlock.

"Here's the turnoff." I took a right, and the Volvo bumped and scraped down the rutted path toward what had been the Bog up until a year and a half ago. "The first time I came here was last fall. A couple of days after I met Rafe again. I wanted to see where he'd grown up."

Of course, I'd told my mother and myself something different. LaDonna Collier had died a few weeks ago, and Brenda Puckett had died a few days ago, both of them with a connection to Rafe. I had put forth the theory that he'd had something to do with both deaths. I'd been sleuthing, basically. But I'd also wanted to see where he'd grown up. Even if I hadn't been willing to admit it.

"There were a couple of clapboard shacks down here, then. And a couple of abandoned mobile homes. Ronnie Burke had already bought the land, and most of the people who lived here had moved out. LaDonna was the last holdout." Until she died. "It was the most depressing place I'd ever seen."

And while I'd been sneaking around, peering through windows—trying to identify the Colliers' trailer—Rafe had snuck up behind me and damn near scared a couple of years off my life.

It looked different now. All the houses had been leveled and the debris hauled away, and the mobile homes had been towed off, too. The singlewide trailer where Rafe had spent his formative years was on a scrap heap somewhere, no doubt. It hadn't been good for anything else.

Ronnie had started staking out building plots before he went to prison. Most of what he'd done was gone by now, six months later, but here and there, a piece of plastic flapped forlornly at the end of a wooden stake driven into the ground. And he hadn't been able to do much more before the whole business venture had blown up in his face.

It was still one of the most depressing places I'd seen.

"Let's get out of here." I put the car in reverse and made my way up the track. When we were on the road and headed back to town, I added, "So that's the Bog. What did you think?"

Mrs. Jenkins shrugged.

Yeah, not a whole lot to say about it, really.

"How did Tyrell come to know LaDonna, anyway?" I asked. An African-American eighteen-year-old from the urban core of Nashville would have had no reason to come to Sweetwater. And while LaDonna might conceivably have gone to the city for something, I couldn't imagine what. The Colliers hadn't been big on culture, and we had doctors in Maury County. A school trip, maybe? To see the State Capitol or something like that?

"Dunno," Mrs. Jenkins said.

"He never told you?"

She shook her head.

Could be true, or could be one of those many misplaced details. It's tough, trying to get information out of someone who can't remember who you are from day to day, and not much of anything else, either.

We drove to the Oak Street Cemetery next. It's on the outskirts of town, about halfway between the square and the mansion, and for the past hundred years or more, all the Martins have been interred there. Before the public cemetery was established, we had our own, in the woods behind the mansion. It's still there, but we're not allowed to bury anyone there anymore. Mrs. Jenkins might be interested in seeing it, though. Or maybe not. It wasn't a very pleasant time of year to go stomping through the woods.

Everyone else in town is also buried at Oak Street, so

naturally LaDonna was there. So, I assumed, were Old Jim and Wanda, his wife, and maybe Bubba, LaDonna's brother, but I'd never looked for their graves. I did know where LaDonna's was, though, so I guided Mrs. Jenkins there.

Rafe had arranged for the stone. From Memphis, the sheriff had told me. Rafe had been in Nashville at that time, actually, as far as I knew. But the stone was his doing. It had an arched top with an engraving of a cross. *LaDonna Jean Collier. In loving memory.*

We stood for a moment and looked at it. Mrs. Jenkins didn't say anything. I didn't, either. I wondered what she was thinking. Would she have liked to have met LaDonna? Or didn't she really care?

She loved Rafe, so she might have liked to have known him growing up. And I'm sure she'd have given anything to have had Tyrell be alive and well, instead of dead.

FOURTEEN

After the cemetery, we drove into town and parked on the square. It was a little early for lunch, so I contemplated stopping by Audrey's first. But the yogurt hadn't quite done the job this morning, and the baby felt like it was gnawing on my insides. I might as well suggest it.

"Lunch?" I asked Mrs. Jenkins.

She brightened. "Sure, baby."

We headed for the café. And had barely ordered our food when the door opened again, and Darcy walked in.

She's pretty, my sister. Doesn't look anything like me, which I guess makes sense, since Dix and I take after Mother and the Georgia Calverts. Although Darcy doesn't look much like the Martins, either. Her skin's a little darker than Catherine's, and so is her hair. She keeps it short, but unlike Catherine's, it's straight, like a sleek cap around her head. And unlike Catherine, who's short and round, Darcy has Audrey's build, with dramatic cheekbones, long legs, and a lot of height. All in all, she looks more like Rafe's sister than either of ours, but of course she isn't.

She turned when I called her name, and flashed a smile. "Savannah." She has a great smile, too. It lights up her face, which is already pretty to begin with.

I made to get to my feet, and she shook her head. "Stay. You look ready to pop."

I felt ready to pop, and told her so, when she leaned down to put her cheek to mine. "You remember Mrs. Jenkins? Rafe's grandmother?"

"Of course." Darcy smiled at Mrs. Jenkins. Mrs. J gave her a toothless smile back, but didn't say anything. "I didn't realize you'd be here already."

"We came down a day early," I said, without going into the reasons for it. "Do you want to join us for lunch?"

"I'm picking up a salad. We're short-staffed today, because of the holiday. But I'll stay with you until it's ready." She pulled out one of the chairs and seated herself. "I'm glad you're here. It gives me a chance to see you."

I wrinkled my brows. "What do you mean? You're coming to dinner tomorrow, aren't you? Surely Mother invited you?"

The whole rest of the family was coming. Plus Bob. Maybe even Todd. Mother couldn't have neglected to invite Darcy. And even if she had, Dix and/or Catherine would have made sure to tell her she was invited.

"She mentioned it," Darcy said. "But you know as well as I do that my... that Audrey isn't going to be there. And I can't go to your house for Thanksgiving dinner and let my mother sit home by herself."

I guess she couldn't. "My mother's being a jerk."

"It's a lot to deal with," Darcy said, which I thought was pretty damn—darn—nice of her, everything considered. I'm not sure I'd have been as understanding under the circumstances. "Anyway, Patrick and I will be spending tomorrow with my mother."

Patrick is the boyfriend. Patrick Nolan, an officer with the Columbia PD. They'd met a couple of months ago—I'd been there—and Nolan still couldn't take his eyes off Darcy.

"That's nice," I said. "I mean, I wish you were all coming to us instead, but it's nice that you'll be together. You and Nolan and Audrey."

Darcy nodded.

"You two doing OK?"

"Me and Patrick? Or me and Audrey?" She didn't wait for me to answer. "Patrick and I are doing great. He's really nice, and he treats me well. Not at all like my ex."

I could relate. I had an ex, too, and he hadn't treated me well, either. For much the same reasons as Darcy's ex.

"He and Audrey get along well," Darcy continued, "and Audrey and I are working things out. We meet here for lunch a couple of times a week. Sometimes we have dinner together. We're doing all right."

Good to know. "Maybe, if we just give it time, Mother will come around, too."

"Let's hope so," Darcy said, but she didn't sound optimistic. I didn't blame her. I didn't feel optimistic myself. My mother doesn't have a habit of coming around.

Then again, if she'd changed her mind about Rafe, it was possible to change her mind about anything. But it might take another man with a gun and another threat to her life to do it.

Darcy glanced across the table at Mrs. Jenkins. "So what are you two up to today?"

"Sightseeing." I told her about the drive to the Bog and the stop at the cemetery. "After lunch, we're going to stop in at Audrey's, to look for a dress for Mrs. J. We left Nashville in sort of a hurry, and I didn't think to bring anything for her to wear to dinner tomorrow."

Not that she had anything suitable. Unless I wanted to make a trip to the nursing home where she'd been staying, all she had was the handful of housecoats I'd bought her.

"She'll enjoy that," Darcy said, and looked up when someone called her name. "That's my salad. If you're still around on Friday, maybe we can grab lunch then. The office is closed."

I thought that sounded wonderful, and told her so. "We're

supposed to go back to Nashville on Friday. But I'm sure we can have lunch first. I'll call you Friday morning to touch base."

Darcy nodded. "I'll talk to you then. Have fun tomorrow."

She legged it toward the front counter, where she paid for her salad and left. A minute later, our food arrived, as well, and Mrs. J and I got busy eating.

The Café on the Square has some wonderful bread rolls, dripping with butter, and Mrs. Jenkins turned out to be as appreciative of them as I've always been. The rest of their food is also reliably good, and we ate hardy. At the end of it, I leaned back in my chair and smiled at Mrs. Jenkins across the table. "Good, huh?"

She nodded, and smiled back. And then she gave a sideways glance at the door. "Who's the girl?"

The girl?

"You mean Darcy? She's my sister. Half-sister. My father's daughter. You met her at my wedding, remember?" Although we hadn't known then that she was part of the family. She was there as Dix's receptionist and a friend of the family. "Her mother owns the store we're going to next. Audrey. My mother's best friend." Former best friend. At least temporarily.

Mrs. J nodded. She looked worried.

"Is something wrong?" I asked.

Her face cleared and she smiled. "No, baby."

"You sure?"

She nodded.

"Ready to go, then?"

She nodded. I pushed my chair back and planted my feet. It was getting harder and harder to get up.

I waddled to the door and outside. And had to stop once I got out on the sidewalk to put a hand against my lower back.

It was Mrs. Jenkins's turn to inquire, "Something wrong, baby?"

I managed a smile. "My back hurts. The baby's heavy."

And the chairs at the Café on the Square, while elegant and spindly, aren't all that comfortable.

She nodded. "Wanna hold my arm?"

"I'm all right," I said. Truth be told, I could have used a strong arm for support, but I wasn't about to rely on Mrs. Jenkins's. She was stronger than she looked, but she was also a head shorter than me, about fifty pounds lighter, and almost as many years older. If I fell and dragged her down with me, she was liable to break something. Like her hip. And I didn't want that on my conscience.

So I made my own way toward Audrey's. Waddling like a duck. While Mrs. Jenkins trotted behind. I don't know if she was planning to catch me if I fell—I suspected she was, although I'd squash her flat if she tried—but it was moot. I wasn't falling.

And didn't fall. I made it to the door under my own steam, turned the knob, and went inside. And held the door for Mrs. J to do the same.

While she looked around, her face concerned, Audrey appeared, like a genie from a bottle, between the racks of clothing. "Savannah!"

I managed a smile. "Hi, Audrey."

"My goodness, you look ready to drop. Come over here and sit down." She took my arm and dragged me over to an elegant little French chair that looked like its legs would splay if I attempted to lower my bulk on it.

"I don't think that's going to work," I said, eyeing it.

"Don't be silly. Sit." She put a hand on my shoulder and pushed me down. The chair hesitated, but held. I tried to make myself as light as possible, but it wasn't easy. "What can I do for you?"

"I brought Mrs. Jenkins," I said, gesturing toward the front of the boutique. "Rafe's grandmother. We're down early for Mother's Thanksgiving dinner."

And then I remembered that Audrey wasn't coming, after having Thanksgiving dinner with us for twenty years, and wished I'd just kept my big mouth shut.

Audrey winced, but tried to hide it.

"I'd like to get Mrs. Jenkins something to wear," I added. "We left Nashville in a bit of a hurry. All she has are a bunch of housecoats. I doubt my mother will approve."

Audrey nodded. She knows my mother well. And doesn't have any illusions about her. Especially after the past couple of months.

"Something nice, but not too fancy. I don't think she'd like that. Mrs. Jenkins, I mean." I wanted her to be able to wear it again. "And hopefully not too expensive?" Since I was paying.

"We'll see what we can do," Audrey said. "Just let me find your grandmother-in-law."

She straightened and looked around, hands on her hips.

Like her daughter, Audrey is tall. A couple of inches taller than me, and the heels put her over six feet.

However, Mrs. Jenkins is so short she didn't show above the clothing racks. Audrey frowned.

She's an attractive woman. Like my mother, she's pushing sixty but looks younger. Unlike Mother, who looks soft and pretty, Audrey is angular and striking. Tall, with prominent cheekbones and dramatic coloring. Her skin is pale and her eyes blue, but her hair is jet black, cut in a severe wedge with straight bangs above black brows. And she always wears bright, primary colors—like the emerald green dress she had on today—and bright red lipstick.

I raised my voice. "Mrs. Jenkins?"

There was a giggle from somewhere. It sounded little-girlish, and I felt a chill creep down my spine. It was eerie.

"Come and find me, Oneida!"

Her voice sounded younger, too. Like a girl playing hide and seek.

I braced my feet to get up, but Audrey put a hand on my shoulder. "Stay."

"She's my responsibility," I protested.

"You're about ready to give birth. Just stay on the chair. I've got it."

"Come on, Oneida!" Mrs. Jenkins called. "Come and find me!"

"Who's Oneida?"

Audrey didn't answer. I wasn't surprised. I didn't know, either. Why would she?

But she was willing to play the game. "Ready or not," she called, "here I come!"

She wandered off toward the front of the store.

It was a short game. The store isn't big, and there weren't many hiding places. Mrs. Jenkins ran around for a minute or so, easily tracked by her giggles, and then Audrey brought her back to where I was sitting. Mrs. Jenkins was hanging onto Audrey's hand, and she was grinning, her dark bird-eyes dancing.

"Here." Audrey pulled forward another chair. "Have a seat."

Mrs. Jenkins's face dropped. "Am I in trouble, Oneida?"

"No, Tondalia." Audrey's voice was gentle. "You're not in trouble. We're just going to talk."

Mrs. Jenkins grinned. "OK." She had to scoot up on the chair, and her feet didn't quite touch the ground.

"Who's Oneida?" I asked. I'd heard it before. It took a second before it came back to me: it was the name Mrs. Jenkins had told us she'd planned to use had she had a daughter instead of Tyrell.

Mrs. Jenkins pointed at Audrey.

I shook my head. "That's Audrey, Mrs. J. She's Darcy's mother. We spoke to Darcy in the café earlier, remember?"

Mrs. Jenkins looked confused, but I'm not sure whether it

was because she didn't remember Darcy, or because I'd told her that Audrey wasn't Oneida.

"I'm sorry," I told Audrey. "She gets like this sometimes. She doesn't always know whether I'm me or LaDonna. Or whether Rafe is himself or Tyrell."

Audrey nodded. She squatted in front of Mrs. Jenkins and put a hand on her knee. Her nails were painted the same bright red as her lips. "I'm not Oneida."

Mrs. Jenkins looked sad. Her lower lip trembled.

"Oneida was my mother," Audrey said.

Huh?

I straightened on the chair. My lower back protested, but I ignored it. "Who's Oneida?" And why had I never heard about her?

"My mother," Audrey said again.

"Yes, but..." I turned my head to look at Mrs. Jenkins. "How would Mrs. J know your mother?"

I remembered Audrey's mother, but only vaguely. She'd died when I was a girl, I didn't know from what. I could sort of remember Audrey being distraught and Mother making us go to the funeral. But my own grandparents had also died when I was a girl, so I wasn't sure I was keeping it all straight in my mind.

"Oneida was my mother," Audrey said. "And Tondalia's sister."

Excuse me?

"But you're..."

I stopped before I said 'white.'

It would have been accurate, though. Audrey was as pale as I am. Not exactly white—I don't know anyone who's white; we're all more of a pale pinkish, peachy color—but certainly not brown. Mrs. Jenkins was brown, with wrinkled raisin skin and black eyes.

"My mother was light-skinned," Audrey said, her voice

tight. "She could pass for white. So she did."

Someone walked by outside the window, and she added, with a glance that way, "Let's take this somewhere else. It's a long story, and I don't feel like getting interrupted by someone coming in to look for a party dress. It's the day before Thanksgiving. I probably wouldn't get much business anyway."

She looked at me. "You remember where I live?"

Of course I did. She'd lived there her whole life, in a small house she'd inherited from her parents. From her father and Tondalia Jenkins's sister.

"I'll see you there. It's better if we do this privately." She helped Mrs. Jenkins up. I could have used a hand, too, to be honest, but I made it to my feet under my own steam. Every time I sat down, it was harder and harder to get moving again.

We shuffled to the door, and Audrey let us out. I heard the door lock behind us, and watched her turn the *Open* sign to *Closed*. Then she flipped off the lights, and hurried toward the back of the store. I pointed to the car, and Mrs. J and I made our slow way toward it.

Audrey's house is just a few blocks from the square. We got there in two minutes, once we had the car running. She wasn't there yet, so I pulled up to the curb and cut the engine.

It's a cute little house. Not the kind of thing you'd expect Audrey to live in, though. Not judging by the way she looks. She'd have looked right occupying a penthouse apartment in the city, a garret in Paris, or some sort of ultra-modern collection of boxy shapes held together with steel and wood and corrugated metal.

Instead, she lives in a cottage. One of the symmetrical one-story Victorians—we have dozens of Victorian cottages around town—where the roof comes to a point and there's a porch across the full width of the front. With porch swings and rocking chairs.

I turned to Mrs. Jenkins. "Oneida was your sister?"

She nodded. "Yes, baby."

"And she lived here?"

Mrs. Jenkins shrugged. "Dunno."

Behind me, Audrey's car pulled up to the curb.

The car doesn't suit her any better than the house. She'd have looked right at home in Alexandra Puckett's fire-engine red Mazda Miata. Or even Alton Fesmire's BMW. Or the bright green car that had been parked across the street from the craftsman bungalow yesterday.

Instead, she drives a van. A plain gray van. It might be for function—moving merchandise or sales displays or whatever; those certainly wouldn't fit in the back of a Miata—but it's undeniably boring. Even more boring than my pale blue Volvo.

We walked up to the house together. Audrey unlocked the front door and waved us in. "I'll put on some tea."

She headed for the kitchen, and left us in the front room—the living room—to fend for ourselves.

The inside of the house looks more like Audrey than the outside. The walls are painted in jewel colors, as befits a true Victorian, and although I generally cringe whenever I see all that original dark woodwork painted white, in this case it was a nice contrast to the bright walls. There were a lot of black-and-white photographs everywhere—street scenes from Paris and somewhere in Italy, maybe Rome, in the living room.

I wondered why Audrey had never packed up and left. She hadn't married. Her parents were dead. She didn't have any other family, not after she'd given Darcy up for adoption. And she'd probably enjoy Paris or Rome.

We could hear her rooting around in the kitchen.

"Let me take your coat," I told Mrs. Jenkins. She wiggled out of it, and I hung it, along with mine, over the back of a chair. The furniture was black leather with chrome legs, which I thought was totally Audrey, and it also worked surprisingly well with the Victorian architecture.

"Let's have a seat." I nudged Mrs. J toward the sofa. She dropped down, and I followed suit. The cushions were a lot softer than I'd expected. It felt like the sofa was trying to swallow me. I struggled against it, but eventually had to admit defeat. Flopping around like a beached whale was so undignified. I'd have Audrey give me a hand up later. And in the meantime, I made myself as comfortable as I could and turned to Mrs. J. She was so small and light she just perched on top of the leather like a little bird. "So you had a sister named Oneida?"

Mrs. Jenkins nodded. "Yes, baby. My big sister."

"What happened to her?"

"Dunno," Mrs. J said, with a shake of her head. "She left. I didn't see her no more."

"How old were you?"

She thought back. "Maybe ten?"

Audrey came back into the living room in time to hear this part of the conversation. Like Mother, yesterday, she had put together a tray with cups and saucers, cream and sugar, a plate of little cookies, and cloth napkins. She put the whole thing down on the coffee table. "Oneida was the eldest daughter. There was one more, Eurelia, and a boy. And then Tondalia."

The kettle in the kitchen whistled, and she straightened. "I'll be back in a minute."

She walked out. I noticed she had kicked off the three-inch heels as soon as she came in, and was padding around barefoot. I usually do that, too. I've been taught to suffer for vanity, but I don't see the point in suffering if nobody's watching. Or nobody important, I should say.

She came back thirty seconds later with the teapot, and started filling cups. We all had a sip. Mrs. Jenkins grabbed a cookie. I wanted a cookie, but I couldn't reach them, being stuck in the clutches of the sofa, and it was probably just as well. I didn't need a cookie.

"So," I said, when the silence had gone on for a while, only interrupted by Mrs. J's munching. "Your mother's name was Oneida."

Audrey nodded. She wasn't eating a cookie, but she kept her mouth shut as if she were.

"And she was Mrs. Jenkins's sister."

Another nod.

"Oneida, Eurelia, a brother, and Tondalia."

Audrey nodded.

"How did Mrs. Jenkins's sister come to be your mother?" She didn't say anything, and I added, "I mean, that's a pretty big coincidence, isn't it?"

"Not really," Audrey said. "You're looking at it from the wrong perspective."

I was?

"Didn't you ever wonder how Tyrell Jenkins, an eighteen-year-old black kid from the city, even met a fourteen-year-old Sweetwater girl like LaDonna Collier?"

Of course I had. I had asked Mrs. Jenkins about it just an hour or two ago. And it wasn't the first time the question had crossed my mind. But so far, nobody I'd asked had had an answer.

"He was here to see you," I said, as light dawned.

Yes, that made a lot more sense. Mrs. Jenkins wasn't coincidentally related to Audrey; Mrs. Jenkins's son had been here in Sweetwater, and had met LaDonna Collier, *because* he was related to Audrey.

"He came to see my mother," Audrey said. "She was still alive then." She sighed and shook her head. "It didn't go well."

"Why not?"

"That will take a while," Audrey said and leaned back. She folded one long leg over the other. I struggled into a more comfortable position in the clutches of the sofa.

FIFTEEN

"My mother was born Oneida Jefferson," Audrey began. "She was born in the late 1930s. Before World War Two. Thirty years before the Civil Rights movement."

I nodded. I knew when the Civil Rights movement had taken place. I'd learned about it in school.

"It was hard to be black back then," Audrey said. "It isn't easy now—just ask your husband—but it was harder then. Did you know that in 1955, a fourteen-year-old black boy was lynched in Mississippi because a white woman said he'd whistled after her in a grocery store?"

I had heard of that. I had also heard that the woman later recanted and said the boy hadn't done anything inappropriate at all. But by then it was far too late, of course.

Audrey and my father and mother had been born into that time. Oneida Jefferson would have been a teenager when Emmett Till was murdered. Not much older than he'd been. Than he ever got to be.

"Here." Audrey got up from the chair and disappeared into the other room. A moment later she came back with a framed photograph she handed me.

It was a wedding photo. Black and white, in a silver frame.

The couple was young, maybe not even out of their teens. The man was tall, with that distinctive Elvis-look to his hair, and what looked like a carnation in the buttonhole of a dark suit. I could see Audrey in the cheekbones and jaw. The woman next to him was dressed in a lovely fifties-style dress, calf-length, with a wasp waist and a wide skirt. She was carrying a small bouquet of flowers, and had a white hat covering most of her hair, except for a few dark ringlets framing a face memorable mostly for a pair of cat's eye glasses.

She did not look black.

She didn't look much like Audrey, either. But I recognized some of Darcy's softer features, like the big, dark eyes.

"She could pass for white," Audrey said, as I handed the framed photo to Mrs. Jenkins. "So she did. She met my father and married him, and she moved to Sweetwater, and never told anyone that she wasn't as white as they were."

"He didn't know?" Her husband? Audrey's father?

"Not at first," Audrey said. "They got married at the courthouse. She didn't tell her family. My father never met them."

Wow. That took dedication. And a real desire to break free. Or to keep secrets.

Next to me, Tondalia Jenkins—born Jefferson—was looking at the picture of her sister with tears running down her wrinkled cheeks.

"Of course, then she got pregnant," Audrey said. "Birth control wasn't as readily available then as it is now. And that's when she told my father. So he could prepare himself for having a brown baby. So they could come up with a story, if the worst happened."

That conversation must have been fun. *"By the way, I never mentioned this, but..."*

"I hope he took it well," I said.

"He told her he loved her," Audrey answered, "and that he didn't care what color she was. And that they weren't going to talk about it again, since they could both go to prison."

Prison?

"Until 1967," Audrey said, "and the Supreme Court decision on *Loving v Virginia*, interracial marriage was illegal in Tennessee." She smiled. "I was ten when the Supreme Court decided. We had cake to celebrate."

It sounded like a worthy reason to have cake.

If I'd been born eighty years earlier, I realized, I couldn't have married Rafe. Or if I had, we both could have ended up in prison. Our marriage might not have been legal in the state where we lived.

And in high school, if he'd winked at me and said, "*Looking good, sugar,*" the way he'd been wont to do when we passed in the hallways back then, he could have been dragged out behind the bleachers and beaten to death. And those who did it, would have gotten away with it.

Yeah, *Loving v Virginia* seemed like an excellent reason to celebrate.

"So did your mother come out and admit she was black, then? After that?"

Audrey shook her head. "Everything continued just the way it had been. I imagine my parents may have been breathing a little easier, but nothing changed. The law might be different, but people's opinions weren't. And my mother was still afraid."

I guess that kind of thing doesn't go away overnight. It takes years, maybe decades, for attitudes to change. Maybe longer.

"So what happened with Tyrell?" I asked.

Audrey took a breath and let it out slowly. "That was much later. Another ten or fifteen years. I'd had Darcy, and had given her up for adoption." She hesitated a second before admitting, "I think my mother was happy about that. Darcy was darker-skinned than me. Than her. It would have been hard for her to explain how her daughter came to have a brown baby."

"It didn't just come from Oneida," I told her. "My great-

great-grandfather William was the son of one of the grooms during the Civil War. Great-great-great-grandma Caroline had an affair while her husband was off fighting the Damn Yankees."

"Margaret Anne never mentioned that," Audrey said.

"She didn't know until recently." Quite recently. Like, a month ago. "Aunt Regina told me last year. Because of Rafe. She and my father had been told by their father. But Dad never told Mother." And he obviously hadn't told Audrey, either. In all the time they'd known one another. "I'd been keeping it in reserve, just in case she crossed the line at some point. But then she ended up liking Rafe. So I told her about Caroline and William when I was down here last month."

"Oh," Audrey said. I could see the pieces of information sort of realigning themselves in her head. "That's interesting."

I shrugged. "I'm sure a lot of us have a mixture of races in us, and most of us don't even know it. I didn't, until Aunt Regina told me. I wouldn't be surprised if there's some long-hidden family secret in the ranks of the Georgia Calverts, too, that Mother either doesn't know about or hasn't shared with the rest of us. It's not important. Nobody cares anymore."

Not entirely true. Some people cared. Some people cared too much. But we're all getting better, generation by generation. If my mother could embrace Rafe, and David, and the new baby, and the rest of us given this new knowledge about our ancestors, there's hope for the rest of the planet, too.

I returned to what had happened years ago. "So Tyrell came to see your mother."

Audrey nodded. "He'd figured out where she was. Went to the courthouse and checked the marriage records, I guess, and found my father's name, and started looking. And ended up here."

"Was that the first time your mother had had any contact with her family since she got married?"

Mrs. Jenkins had wiped away her tears now, and was listening intently to the conversation, but she was still clutching the wedding photo of her sister in her lap, her small, brown hands tight around the frame.

"As far as I know," Audrey said, with a glance at her. "I don't remember another time."

Mrs. J shook her head. She might remember, or she might not, but either way it didn't really matter.

"She was terrified," Audrey said. "He came while my father was at work, so it was just her and me at home. She was afraid the neighbors would see him, so she got him inside as quickly as she could. And explained to him why she couldn't have anything to do with her family. That she'd built a life here in Sweetwater, and him being there was liable to ruin it for her."

She looked down at the hands she was twisting in her lap. "She pretty much ran him off. And not in a nice way. I went after him, to try to explain, but at that point he was angry with both of us. And I can't say I blame him."

"And that's when he met LaDonna?"

"Somewhere between our house and the bus station," Audrey said. "Or so I assume. I never spoke to him again. If he came back to Sweetwater, he didn't come to see me. Us. And six months later he was dead."

Because Old Jim Collier had figured out who had knocked his daughter up. Next to me on the sofa, Mrs. Jenkins's eyes filled with tears.

"So..." I counted on my fingers, "you and Tyrell were cousins."

Audrey nodded.

"Mrs. Jenkins is your aunt. You're her niece."

Audrey nodded, with a glance at Mrs. J, who seemed to be taking this in stride. The tears were going away as she listened.

"Darcy is Mrs. Jenkins's..."

"Great-niece," Audrey supplied.

That took care of that part of the family. Now onto the other part. "Rafe is Tyrell's son. So he's your cousin's child."

Audrey nodded. "Rafe is my first cousin once removed." Her voice shook a little when she said it. It might have been something she'd never said out loud before.

Although she'd obviously figured it out. These aren't relationships you know off-hand. Cousins to the first, second, and third degree are confusing.

"So Darcy is Rafe's second cousin once removed."

"Something like that," Audrey agreed.

Well, it explained why Darcy had always looked more like Rafe than like us, anyway. They'd gotten whatever it was from the Jeffersons.

"I guess you and I are related, too. Not just through Darcy, but through my marriage."

Audrey nodded.

"Just one big, happy family."

Audrey snorted. It was a wet snort, but more laughter than tears. "I can't wait until you tell your mother."

God, yes. Would my mother be able to handle one more blow on top of everything else she had to deal with?

Maybe it would be better if I kept this news to myself for a while. Or maybe it would be just what it would take to snap her out of her self-pity.

"I have to call Rafe," I said.

Audrey nodded. She turned to Mrs. J. "I have some other photographs of my mother. And some of her things. Would you like to see?"

Mrs. Jenkins indicated that she would. The two of them went off together, in the direction of the two bedrooms—like I said, a small house—and I pulled out my phone and dialed Rafe. "You'll never guess where I am!"

"Sweetwater," my husband said.

"Well, yes. That. But you'll never guess where in

Sweetwater I am!"

"Since I'll never guess, how about you just tell me?"

I made a face. "Fine." Since he really wouldn't be able to guess. "I'm having tea with your first cousin once removed. And your grandmother."

"No kidding." His voice was perfectly pleasant. "Anybody I know?"

"As a matter of fact she is. Did you know that your grandmother had a sister who lived in Sweetwater?"

"No," Rafe said.

"I'm not sure she did, either. Your grandmother, I mean. But she did. Have one. Her older sister Oneida."

"Just checking," Rafe said, "but you haven't been drinking, right?"

I sniffed. "Of course not. I haven't had a glass of wine in eight months."

"Like I said, just checking."

"I know it sounds crazy," I told him. "Out of the blue like this. But didn't you ever wonder how your mother and father met? Tyrell and LaDonna?"

"I knew they met in Sweetwater," Rafe said. "When I was little, I'd ask my mama a lot of questions about my daddy. Like, why didn't he live with us and where was he?"

"M-hm."

"She didn't like to talk about him. And Old Jim'd go ballistic if he heard. So she never said much. But she did tell me she met him in town. That he was on his way to the bus station."

"He'd been to see his aunt," I said. "His mother's sister. And her daughter. His cousin."

"She tell you that?"

I nodded. And then I realized he couldn't see me, and added, "Yes. He came to see his aunt. Oneida is dead now. But her daughter isn't."

"And you're having tea."

"At the moment, I'm the only one having tea. Audrey took your grandmother into the bedroom to look at pictures."

There was a beat. "Audrey," Rafe said.

I made a face. "So much for my big buildup."

I could hear the amusement in his voice. "You never were much good at keeping secrets, darlin'."

No, I wasn't. "Oneida was your grandmother's oldest sister. She met and married Audrey's father when your grandmother were around ten, and they settled in Sweetwater. She never told anyone she was black."

I thought for a second and added, "Not that she was black. I mean, she didn't look black. That's how she was able to pretend she was white."

He still sounded like he was smiling. "I figured."

"So Audrey's your cousin of some sort. So is Darcy. And Audrey is Mrs. Jenkins's niece."

"My family just keeps getting bigger all the time." His voice was dry.

"I know it's a lot to take in..." And since it was, I didn't push. He'd probably need some time to process what I'd told him.

We sat in silence a few seconds. I figured I'd just let him say something when he felt he was ready. Whatever he felt the need to say at that point.

"How's the baby?"

Changing the subject. OK, then.

"Still in there," I said. "Still moving around, but not as much."

"There ain't much room left to move."

No, there wasn't. "You're still planning to come down tomorrow, right? I promised Darcy we'd have lunch with her before we go home on Friday. We'll get Audrey to come with us, too. The three of you—or four of you, with Mrs. Jenkins—

can talk."

Rafe said he was still coming for Thanksgiving dinner tomorrow, and would be happy to have lunch with his new family members before going back to Nashville on Friday.

"Any news on your end?"

It probably couldn't compare with the bombshell I'd just dropped on him, but I figured I should be polite and ask.

"Fesmire turned up," Rafe said.

"Oh." I smiled. "That's good. I was starting to get a little worried about him."

"The water cops fished him out of the Cumberland River earlier."

Oh. Not good. "What happened?"

"He has a crack on the head," Rafe said. "Coulda happened when he jumped, or before."

"Did he jump?"

I imagined the shrug. "No telling. He was in the water. The usual ways are, you fall, you jump, or you're pushed."

True. "Was he drunk?" Shades of Old Jim Collier...

"Dunno," Rafe said. "The ME'll check."

No doubt. "What are the chances someone hit him over the head and dumped him in?"

"As good as any," Rafe said. "He didn't have no reason to wanna jump."

Maybe, maybe not.

I didn't realize I'd said it out loud before he asked me what I meant. "Oh. Sorry. I was just thinking earlier. What if he was having an affair with Julia Poole? You know, the work girlfriend? Didn't you say he had a wife?"

Rafe confirmed that he had.

"And she was probably his age. While Julia was a lot younger. And a nurse. She'd probably look up to a doctor. And he wasn't bad-looking, for a guy his age."

Rafe made a noise. It wasn't quite agreement, but it wasn't

disagreement, either. Maybe he'd laughed. Or objected to my noticing Fesmire's relative attractiveness. For his age.

"So he got adoration and a young woman willing to sleep with him," I said. "They probably had sex at the nursing home while she was working. After the bed check, she had all night free, pretty much. And there wasn't likely to be anyone else around. It would be easy for him to tell his wife that there was something wrong and he'd have to run in to work for an hour or two. She probably wouldn't think anything of it."

"Maybe not," Rafe agreed.

"So maybe Fesmire and Julia were... what's that expression you used once?—banging like hammers when Beverly Bristol woke up. And because Julia didn't answer the bell, Beverly got out of bed, and fell. And died."

"Uh-huh."

"And Julia felt bad, because she's been having sex with Fesmire when it happened. She'd been neglecting her job and banging a married man. So she cut him off. Or maybe she said she'd confess to the licensing board, or something like that. Nurses have a licensing board, don't they?"

"I'm sure they do," Rafe said.

"And doctors definitely do. Doctors can lose their license to practice medicine. Doctor Seaver did, when she went to prison."

"Uh-huh," Rafe said.

"So maybe Fesmire didn't want to lose his license, or his cushy job. He had to shut Julia up before she could spill the beans. So he arranged to meet her for a romantic tryst in the pavilion. And then he killed her. He's a doctor. He's probably had surgical training. He'd know how to cut a throat." He'd also have access to a scalpel.

"OK," Rafe said slowly.

"Maybe, at the funeral yesterday, before I came in and heard the tail end of the conversation, the Bristols—or whatever their names are—said something that made Fesmire think they knew what had happened. They were talking about suing. Maybe he felt threatened. Then we came in, and he recognized Mrs. Jenkins, and knew she'd seen him kill Julia. That was a bigger threat, or at least a more immediate one. So he had his wife, or maybe one of the nurses at the nursing home, call me and pretend to want to see the house on Ulm to get me away from home. And he tried for Mrs. Jenkins, but couldn't get her. And then he realized the jig was up, that the Bristols would sue and Mrs. Jenkins would rat him out, and he jumped in the river."

"Yeah..." Rafe said. Obviously I hadn't managed to convince him yet.

"Or how about this? Maybe Beverly Bristol didn't fall down the stairs and break her neck. Maybe she got out of bed when Julia didn't answer the summons, and she came upon Julia and Fesmire going at it. And Fesmire pushed her down the stairs. She was a frail old lady. Maybe he snapped her neck first, and then pushed her down the stairs to make it look like she'd fallen. Maybe that's why he had to kill Julia. Because she knew he'd killed Beverly Bristol."

"Uh-huh," Rafe said.

"They're good ideas, right? It would explain everything."

Rafe allowed as how it would. "I'll pass it on to Tammy. Maybe we'll go have a chat with the Bristols—or whatever they're called—in what's left of today. See what was said before you crashed the funeral. See if they were planning to sue."

"I'll give you a call tonight," I said, "to find out what happened."

"You do that, darlin'. Take care of my baby. And my grandma."

I promised I would. "I love you. You take care of yourself, too."

"If Fesmire's the murderer," Rafe said, "there's no danger.

All we gotta do, is tie up the loose ends."

Exactly so. "Thanks for letting me know what happened."

"Thanks for letting me know I have cousins. This is gonna take some getting used to."

"At least they're nice people," I said. "You're related to Denise Seaver, too, you know. On your mother's side of the family. It could have been worse."

He agreed that it could. "We'll figure it out. I better go close this case so I can come and have turkey tomorrow."

"You do that. I'll talk to you later." I disconnected, and fought my way out of the clutches of the sofa to go find Audrey and Mrs. Jenkins.

SIXTEEN

Mother had hired help for Thanksgiving. When we got back to the mansion, three women were busy setting the dining room table and loading prepped food into the large refrigerator in the kitchen, while a fourth was going over cooking temperatures and times with Mother. "If you're planning to eat at three, the turkey needs to go in the oven by nine. It's a big turkey, and it's stuffed, and you'll want some time for it to rest after it comes out. The green bean casserole..."

I gave Mother a quick wave and a gesture to indicate that I was going upstairs. My back was killing me, and so were my feet. I'd practically had to peel the booties off when I came in. My ankles were weeping with joy, not to mention spreading.

Mother nodded and held up a finger to silence the discourse on the green beans. "Where's your grandmother-in-law?"

"I put her in front of the TV," I said. "She'll probably take a nap, too. It's been a big day." A lot bigger than my mother realized.

Mother nodded. "I'll go in and sit with her when we're done here."

I told her I appreciated it. "I'll probably be down in an hour or so. I just need to get off my feet for a while."

I hobbled out and down the hallway, while Mother and the caterer returned to the food prep. In the parlor, Mrs. Jenkins's eyelids were already getting heavy.

"I'm going upstairs," I told her. "Mother's in the kitchen. She's coming in here as soon as she's finished talking to the caterer."

Mrs. J nodded. "You go on and lie down. Don't want nothing to happen to that baby."

No, we didn't.

Not that anything was likely to. It was my ankles that hurt, not my stomach. But I did need to take a break for a moment. It had been a big day for me, too.

By the time I came back downstairs, it had been a lot longer than I'd planned. While I'd only intended to put my feet up for a bit, I'd actually fallen asleep. And snoozed away a couple of hours, while God knew what was going on downstairs.

Although nothing much had gone on, I discovered when I descended the stairs. Mrs. Jenkins was still sitting in front of the TV. Mother had joined her. The caterers had left. And Pearl was curled up on a pillow in the corner, with her nose buried in her tangle of legs. When I left, she'd been following the catering staff around, trying to trip them up while they were carrying plates to the table, rumbling deep in her throat.

When I staggered into the parlor, Mother gave me a bright smile. "Feeling better, dear?"

I was, and told her so. "I'm so ready for this to be over. Just a few more weeks."

"I remember," Mother said sympathetically. "With Catherine, I felt like it took forever before she was born. With you and Dix I knew what to expect, so it was easier to be patient."

"I'm not sure I'm ever going to want to do this again," I told her, as I dropped onto the sofa next to Mrs. J. The old springs groaned and Mother frowned. Mrs. Jenkins bounced and then settled back down.

"Give it time," Mother said. "You might change your mind."

I might. But Rafe already had David. Now he'd have another child. He might think that was enough. And at the moment, I couldn't imagine putting myself through this again.

"Some people only have one child." Like LaDonna. And Audrey. And Oneida, who had probably been afraid she wouldn't get lucky the second time, and would have a darker-skinned baby that would give away her secret.

I turned to Mrs. J. "You only had Tyrell."

She nodded. "Yes, baby. He was my only one."

"Didn't you want any more?"

Mrs. Jenkins shrugged. "We were poor, baby. Better to feed one baby well, than more babies poorly."

Hard to argue with that. Rafe and I weren't all that well off, either. I didn't make much, and people in law enforcement are notoriously badly paid. But we lived cheaply, in Mrs. Jenkins's paid-off house that she'd bought a long time ago, when housing in that area was a lot more affordable than now. And we could probably afford to feed more than one baby. Whether we could afford to send more than one—or two, if David needed help—to college, was another story entirely.

"How about we just take it one baby at a time? Let's get this one to a year old, maybe two, and see how I feel?"

Catherine, Dix, and I are all more than a year apart, so that's what Mother must have done. She nodded. "What's this I hear about Audrey?"

Mrs. Jenkins must have told Mother about Oneida. No wonder my mother was confused. Even if Mrs. J had told the honest truth, with all the details available, it was still fairly unbelievable.

"Audrey's mother was Mrs. Jenkins's older sister," I said. "Oneida Jefferson."

Mother shook her head. "I remember Audrey's mother. She

wasn't..." She stopped, just as I had done earlier.

"Black," I said. "Actually, she was. Or the same amount black as Mrs. Jenkins. Or so I assume. Did you and Oneida have the same parents, Mrs. J?"

Mrs. Jenkins nodded. "Yes, baby. Same mama and daddy."

"Oneida was just lighter-skinned," I told my mother. "So she spent fifty years or so in Sweetwater pretending to be white." So people like Mother wouldn't treat her like a second class citizen.

Of course I didn't say that. Not only would Mother have had my hide for rudeness, and rightly so, but it would have been hurtful. She's changed. Maybe not as much as she could—or should—change, but she wasn't the same person she'd been a year ago, when I'd sat right here in the parlor and told her I loved Rafe and no matter how much she wanted me to, I was never going to marry Todd Satterfield. She hadn't taken it well. And now she loved Rafe, and was looking forward to being the grandmother of his baby.

So yes, she was changing.

"In other news," I told Mrs. Jenkins, "Doctor Fesmire is dead."

Her mouth dropped open.

"You remember Doctor Fesmire?"

I hadn't been sure she would. When we'd seen him at the funeral yesterday morning, it hadn't seemed as if she knew who he was. Although she'd known that it was him in the BMW, so who knew?

Really, trying to keep up with what Mrs. Jenkins remembered at any given time was a full-time job.

"How's he dead?"

"He drowned," I said.

She stuck her bottom lip out. "Like Julia."

Julia's COD—cause of death—had been the cut throat. But Mrs. Jenkins might not realize that.

"Did Doctor Fesmire hurt Julia?"

"Doctors don't hurt people," Mrs. Jenkins said. "Doctors help."

All right. "When Julia was hurt, did Doctor Fesmire try to help?"

Mrs. J looked blank.

"Remember?" I prompted. "You said you had to get help for Julia. That Julia was hurt. Did you go get Doctor Fesmire to help Julia?"

"Who's Julia?" my mother wanted to know.

I gave her a quick glance. "Night nurse at the home where Mrs. Jenkins has been living. She was killed last Saturday night."

Mother shuddered. Visibly. "I saw that on the news. A terrible shame. Such a young, pretty woman."

Was she? I hadn't even seen a picture of Julia, so I had no idea.

"But what did your grandmother-in-law have to do with it?" Mother wanted to know.

"Nothing, as far as we know." She'd better not. "But she was there. At the home that night. And she said that Julia was hurt. I'm trying to figure out who hurt Julia. And who went to get help for her."

I turned to Mrs. Jenkins. But it was obvious that we'd lost her attention during the aside between the two of us. She was looking at the TV screen and humming, her face peaceful.

"Maybe she's blocked it," Mother whispered. "It was too traumatic for her to remember, so she blocked the memory."

I wouldn't be surprised. I'd seen Brenda Puckett's cut throat more than a year ago, and I can't tell you how many times I'd wished I could block *that* memory.

"Mrs. Jenkins?" I tried one more time. "Was Doctor Fesmire there the night Julia was hurt? At the nursing home? Did you see him that night?"

"Julia drowned," Mrs. Jenkins said. "In the car. In the water."

"Do you remember who drove the car into the water?"

"Nobody drove the car," Mrs. Jenkins said. "The car drove itself."

Of course it had. I wanted to bang my head against the coffee table, but I refrained. I'd get a bruise, and anyway, I couldn't bend that far anymore. "Do you remember who drove the car to the river? With you and Julia inside?"

"We have to get help for Julia," Mrs. Jenkins said. "Julia's hurt."

I gave up. Mother gave me a sympathetic look and a *'what are you going to do?'* sort of shrug. I settled back into the sofa to watch HGTV.

"Your grandmother can't confirm that Alton Fesmire was there the night Julia Poole was killed," I told Rafe later that night. As I'd told him I would, I called him before bed to say goodnight and to hear anything else that had happened since we last spoke.

"His wife says he wasn't. That he was home all night. But she's figured out that we're looking at him for Julia Poole's murder, so it's in her best interest to lie."

"If he cheated on her," I said, "wouldn't she be more inclined to nail his hide to the wall?"

Excepting the fact that said hide was already on a slab in the medical examiner's office, of course. That might make a difference. She might be Southern, like me, and have been brought up not to speak ill of the dead.

Rafe sounded amused when I said so. "Under the circumstances, would you worry about speaking ill of the dead?"

"If you cheated on me," I said, "and murdered your girlfriend, I'd call Grimaldi myself."

"Good to know. To answer your question, we're not sure. Somebody got there around midnight. Someone who had the code to the gate. Fesmire had the code, and nobody woulda thought it was strange to see him there. Even at that time of night."

Right.

"And Mrs. Fesmire—her name's Mary Carole—might wanna avoid the notoriety of being married to a murderer. Double murderer, if you're right about Miz Bristol."

"Did you talk to the Bristols? Or whatever their names are?"

"Hammond," Rafe said. "If you're talking about the twins. There's a niece named Mrs. Roberts. And one named Mrs. Wilkerson. And yes, we've been all over town talking to them. From Madison to Bellevue to Hermitage and back."

From north to west to east, in other words. From one corner of Nashville to another.

"I guess the folks in Madison picked the funeral home." Madison's up the road from Inglewood and the Phillips-Robinson funeral home by a few miles. But a lot closer than either Bellevue or Hermitage. "Did any of them think it was likely that their relative was murdered?"

"They were shocked and appalled," Rafe said. "That's a direct quote. Why would anybody wanna murder poor Auntie Beverly?"

"Fesmire," I answered, "if she'd come across him and Julia having sex on his office desk."

Rafe made a humming, sort of '*don't be too sure*' noise. "You gotta remember it's a memory facility, darlin'. Miz Bristol had problems with reality, too."

"Your grandmother doesn't have problems with reality," I told him. "She just has more realities than we do."

"Yeah, well, Beverly Bristol had a few different realities, too. If she told somebody she'd seen Fesmire having sex with

Julia, I don't know that anybody woulda believed it."

"So that wouldn't have been a reason to kill her? Is that what you're saying?"

"Dunno," Rafe said. "Depends on whether Fesmire thought anybody woulda believed her or not. But he prob'ly had simpler ways of getting rid of a patient than breaking their neck and tossing them down the stairs. If he'd given her a pill or something, some random night, he coulda just pretended like she fell asleep and never woke up. The way old folks do sometimes. Nobody woulda thought anything of it. And he'd get to put natural causes on the death certificate."

Good point. I wasn't willing to give up on my idea quite yet, though. "Was there another reason to get rid of Ms. Bristol? Did she have money? Did the nursing home inherit any?"

"She had some money," Rafe said. "She had a good job back in the day, and no kids of her own to spend the money on. She died with almost a million dollars in her bank account."

"That's enough money to kill for."

"To some," Rafe said, "a twenty-dollar-bill is enough to kill for. But Fesmire ain't getting any of it. It goes to the family. Besides, Fesmire had more than that."

That didn't mean he wouldn't want more. "I don't suppose there's any chance his wife killed him? For the money, and because he'd cheated on her?"

"Anything's possible," Rafe said. "It's Tammy's case. I'm sure she'll figure it out."

She would. No question about it. "So what happens now?"

"Now I get some sleep," Rafe said. "And less'n something happens overnight—and I don't see what could, with Fesmire on a slab at the morgue—I get up in the morning and make my way to Sweetwater. We have dinner with your family and the next day, we have lunch with my family. And then we go home. And by then Tammy oughta have things tied up, so my grandma'll be safe again."

That sounded good to me. "How do you feel? About having family you didn't know about?"

"It's gonna take a little getting used to," Rafe said. "But at least they're nice people. Like you said, it coulda been worse."

"There might be others, you know. Family. Your grandmother had two other siblings. And your mother probably has relatives around here, too."

"If they ain't crawled outta the woodwork in thirty-one years," Rafe said, "they can stay there."

After a second he added, "I got you. And a baby on the way. And your family. And my grandma. And her family. And David. And the Flannerys. I got all I need."

Well, then. "I've got all I need, too," I told him, sniffing back a tear. "As long as I've got you, it's all I need."

I could hear the smile in his voice. "Thanks, darlin'."

"You're welcome." I sniffed again.

"Hormones?"

"Something like that." I did a last sniff and moved on. "So when should we expect you tomorrow?"

"I'll call you in the morning before I leave. Just to let you know I'm heading out."

Lovely. "I'll talk to you then," I said.

"Get some sleep, darlin'. Take care of my baby."

I promised him I would, and let him go. And crawled into bed and fell asleep.

I'm not sure what woke me, whether I heard a noise, or I just had to use the bathroom again.

I did have to use the bathroom. But there was also a noise in the hallway outside my room. One of the boards squeak—not unusual in house that's almost two hundred years old; there were squeaky boards in Mrs. Jenkins's house, too—and if you don't know where it is, it's hard to avoid.

I rolled out of bed, and I mean that in the literal sense. If I sharpened my ears, I could hear soft footsteps on the stairs.

It might have been Mother, going for a midnight—or three AM—snack. Or Mrs. Jenkins, ditto.

Or maybe the sheriff had shown up after I fell asleep, and he and Mother had spent the first part of the night together, and now he was on his way home.

Or maybe it was someone who wasn't supposed to be here.

I opened my door carefully. It squeaks, too, unless Mother oils it regularly. She must have done so recently, because the hinges stayed silent. I stepped out into the hallway.

Nothing moved. Quietly, I made my way to the top of the stairs and peered over the railing into the foyer. And caught my breath quickly when I caught sight of a small, white shape flitting down the last couple of steps and across the floor toward the door.

When I was younger, my brother Dix used to regale me with ghost stories. True ghost stories; the South is rife with them.

For some reason, there are no ghost stories associated with the mansion. You'd think there'd be, it being such an old house. But we don't have ghosts. I've never once experienced anything weird or creepy inside the house.

Of the supernatural variety, I mean.

The grounds are a different matter. I mentioned the old Martin graveyard in the woods behind the house. Rumor has it, one of the Martin daughters walks there. She died young, in the influenza pandemic of 1918. Her name was Marjorie, and she was eleven. I've never seen her, but Dix once said he did. He was much younger then, though, and probably just trying to scare me, and anyway, how would he have managed to be out in the woods in the middle of the night to see anything at all? It's not like Mother let any of us—even Dix—camp in the woods at night.

We also have an old slave cabin on the property. Restored

now, of course. The local school children come to see it as part of their American history class each year. It's an eerie little place, and I wouldn't be surprised if someone told me it was haunted, too.

But what I was looking at, was neither little Marjorie Martin, nor one of the slaves. As the apparition reached out a small, brown hand for the doorknob, I raised my voice. "Mrs. Jenkins!"

You're not supposed to wake sleepwalkers. But I wasn't sure she was sleepwalking, and anyway, I couldn't let her run outside in bare feet and just a thin nightgown. She'd already done that once this week—twice if you count the adventure on Monday morning—and besides, if she did, I'd have to run after her. And I didn't want to.

Mrs. Jenkins froze with her hand on the knob. And my voice must have woken Pearl, whose deep, threatening barks increased in volume as she came scrabbling down the hallway from the kitchen.

"No!" I screamed as I navigated the stairs as quickly as I dared. "Pearl, don't! No!"

Pearl burst through the opening from the hallway to the foyer. And she did try to stop. Her nails scrabbled ineffectually on the slick floors. It wasn't her fault. She didn't launch herself at Mrs. Jenkins. She slid into her. And they both crashed into the wall before landing in a heap on the floor.

SEVENTEEN

It took a little time to get things sorted out. Nobody was hurt, at least not badly, but Mrs. Jenkins was upset and so was Pearl. I tried to make her feel better, but I'd yelled at her earlier, and she felt bad about it. She slinked back to her doggie bed in the kitchen, stub of a tail tucked as far between her legs as she could reach, and although she deigned to accept a biscuit, she wasn't happy.

Mrs. J, meanwhile, couldn't tell me where she'd been going, in the middle of the night in bare feet and her nightgown. I thought there was something sort of sly in her expression, but it could have been my imagination. It was late—or early—and I wasn't thinking straight. My back hurt, I was tired, and my feet were cold.

And of course the ruckus woke up Mother, too. My mother doesn't like to be inconvenienced, and this definitely counted, so she let me know. Then she flounced back to bed, her lace-trimmed negligee quivering, and left me to clean things up.

I locked and bolted the door, and made sure it was secure. Then I got Mrs. Jenkins back to bed and tucked her in. Then I went to the bathroom—and none too soon, either. That done, I headed back to my own room. Before I crawled into bed, I went to the window and looked out. There was nothing to see. No people, no cars. A movement in the distance turned out to be something small moving across the dry grass; maybe an opossum or a raccoon. Or a stray dog or cat.

Whatever it was, Mrs. Jenkins hadn't gone out to meet it. And it didn't seem as if she'd been headed out to meet anyone else, either. So she'd probably just been sleepwalking. Or had found herself awake in the middle of the night, in a strange house, and she'd gotten confused.

I tucked my cold feet back under the comforter and closed my eyes.

When I woke up again, it was Thanksgiving. Mother was banging around in the kitchen, getting the turkey into the oven, and I could hear Mrs. Jenkins rustling in Catherine's room.

I let her have first dibs on the bathroom, since I wasn't in dire straits yet, due to the bathroom visit in the wee hours. Once I'd heard her flush and shuffle back to her own room, I made my own way across the hall and into the shower.

In all the excitement yesterday, we'd neglected to buy Mrs. Jenkins a nice outfit for Thanksgiving, so after squeezing myself into something—in just the two days I'd been here, I felt like my clothes were getting tighter—I padded into Catherine's room and made a beeline for the closet.

Of all my mother's children, Catherine was always the rebel. At least until last year. Now, after Rafe, I guess I've taken over that mantle. But Catherine married a Yankee—a law student from Boston she met at Vanderbilt Law School—and when she was younger, she was less inclined to let Mother fuss with her clothes and hair the way I let her fuss with mine.

In fact, I knew that in the back of Catherine's closet, there still hung a couple of dresses Mother had bought for her when she was a teenager—three babies ago—that Catherine had left there when she went off to college.

Fifteen years ago, my sister had been much more Mrs. Jenkins's size than I'd ever been. At least not since I was about twelve, and I had no clothes left from that time.

Mrs. J wasn't in her room. She must have headed

downstairs while I'd been in the bathroom. So I opened the closet doors and dug in.

Yes, just as I remembered. A sweet, little dress of navy eyelet, with little cap sleeves and a scalloped hem. It was a summer dress, but Mrs. J had a cardigan she could wear over it. And it would look all right with the white Keds.

I lifted it to my face. It smelled all right. Mother leaves lavender sachets here and there in drawers and closets, so there was a hint of that, but at least it didn't smell old and dusty. And I was certain Catherine wouldn't mind. She couldn't have stated her opinion of the dress and Mother's taste any more strongly than when she left it behind in the closet.

I put it on the bed along with the cardigan I found crumpled on the floor, and headed downstairs.

Mother and Mrs. Jenkins were in the kitchen. So was Pearl, who must have forgiven me for last night. She greeted me with a doggie grin and a couple of slaps of her stubby tail against the floor.

"Hi, baby." I bent and gave her a scratch between the ears. I had to brace myself with the other hand on the top of the island to do it, and it took effort to get myself straight again.

Mother watched me, her expression vaguely worried. "How do you feel, dear?"

"Fine," I said, because that's what you're supposed to say. You're not supposed to mention that your ankles hurt before ten in the morning, and that your lower back never stopped aching last night.

"How much longer?"

She didn't have to ask until which event. There was only one event on my horizon at the moment. Christmas and New Year be damned; it was all about giving birth.

"Two weeks and five days." Not that I was counting. At this point I didn't have to. I reminded myself every morning how much longer I had to wait. At home, I had a calendar where I marked off the days. If I could have, I'd have counted the hours and minutes, too.

"I think the baby's dropped," Mother said.

Dropped? Where?

I almost looked around before I realized what she was talking about. "It isn't time for that yet. That happens just before labor. I have more than two weeks to go."

"Sometimes the baby drops early," Mother said. "And sometimes the baby's born early, too."

Mine wouldn't be. I wouldn't be that lucky. I'd be going through every last interminable day and hour of my pregnancy. In fact, the baby would probably be born late.

"Do you have a backache?"

I did have a backache. And since she'd asked, it was all right for me to admit it.

"The baby's dropped," Mother said. "From now on, you'll be going to the bathroom every hour."

"I'm already going to the bathroom every hour." Or very near.

"And you'll probably get Braxton-Hicks contractions."

I'd heard of those. I'd even had a few. They hadn't lasted long, and hadn't been all that uncomfortable.

My mother chuckled. Evilly. "Just wait," she said.

We spent the morning fiddling with the food. The table was already set, and beautiful, so there was nothing to do there.

Rafe called just before eleven. "Sorry, darlin'."

"Don't tell me you aren't going to make it!"

"I'm gonna make it. I just had some stuff to do this morning. That's why I haven't left yet."

"Oh." I might have overreacted just a touch, then. "What happened?"

"We took another shot at Mary Carole Fesmire," Rafe said. "She recanted."

Doctor Fesmire's wife? "Recanted what?"

"Now she says he did go out on Saturday night. Just after eleven."

"How far from his house in Franklin to the nursing home?"

"Under thirty minutes," Rafe said, "but not too much under. He lives on the south side of Franklin. And he might have stopped for gas or a cup of coffee or something."

Or a scalpel. Although, being a doctor, he probably owned one of those already.

"So maybe it really was Fesmire who came through the front gate just before midnight."

"Maybe so. Tammy sent Spicer and Truman to knock on doors, just in case somebody'd been up and seen the car. On a Saturday night, people tend to stay up late. And come home late."

True. Someone might have seen Fesmire's car go by in the direction of the nursing home between eleven-thirty and midnight. It was a fairly distinctive car.

On the other hand, it had been raining pretty hard that night, so people might have stayed home. Although someone could have looked out the window and gotten lucky, I suppose. At any rate, Officers Spicer and Truman would find out. They're not the types to give up until they do.

"But you're still coming?"

"I'm throwing a change of underwear in a bag right now," Rafe said. "I'll head out in ten minutes. I'll see you around noon."

Of course he would. I couldn't have made it from Nashville to Sweetwater in the time that was left before noon, but I had no doubt he could.

"Drive carefully."

"Always," Rafe said, and hung up. I rolled my eyes and dropped the phone in my pocket.

It wasn't until I'd done that, that I remembered I hadn't told him about the events of last night, and how Mrs. Jenkins had been on her way out of the house. When he got here, we'd have to have a talk about it. Whether she'd done it on purpose or not, we couldn't have her walking around in the middle of the night unsupervised. One of these nights she was liable to disappear completely. We'd either have to find another facility for her—because I wasn't about to send her back to Fesmire's place after what had happened—or we'd have to figure out a way to dope her up every evening so we could be assured she'd sleep through the night. Her nocturnal wanderings had gotten her in enough trouble.

For a second, I thought about calling him back. But then I decided to just discuss it when he got here. If I didn't call him back now, he'd be able to hit the road and get here sooner. And I'd rather see him than talk to him on the phone. And anyway, we had hours and hours to go until it was nighttime again. Plenty of time to figure things out.

So I left the phone in my pocket and headed back downstairs to the kitchen. "Rafe will be here by noon."

"Wonderful," Mother said warmly. She was rotating pies in and out of the oven. Pumpkin, of course, sweet potato, and apple. The smells were delicious.

I looked around. "Where's Mrs. Jenkins?"

"In front of the TV," Mother said. "Didn't you see her when you came down?"

I hadn't. Now I went and checked, and yes indeed, she was there, just too short to show over the back of the sofa. On screen, some guy with tattoos all up and down his arms was reeling in a fish and talking about lures and bobbers and things I knew nothing about. I checked the channel logo on the bottom right on the screen. Looked like we'd moved on from HGTV to CMT, Country Music Television.

Mrs. J was watching the fishing show just as intently as she'd watched the renovating. I perched on the loveseat next to her. "Have you ever gone fishing?"

She nodded. "Yes, baby. It's cheap food."

I guess it was. I hadn't ever gone fishing myself—it had definitely been unsuitable for a Southern Belle—although Dix had. And I'm sure Rafe had fished whatever lived in the Duck River out when he was a boy.

I wondered whether his grandfather had taught him to fish. Or maybe LaDonna knew how. Living next to the river, the way they'd done, she probably had. And as Mrs. Jenkins had said, it was cheap—or free—dinner.

They say it's relaxing, but I have to say, I'd much rather buy my fish cleaned and filleted at the store. Or even better, grilled and plated in a restaurant, with a little butter and a thin lemon slice on top. You can call me privileged if you want—I'm sure I am—but I had no desire to try to catch my own dinner. And was grateful that I didn't have to.

"The river ran right past the nursing home, right?" You could see it from the pavilion where Julia Poole had died. I'm sure it was a romantic view by moonlight. If not so much in the driving rain.

Mrs. Jenkins nodded. "Yes, baby."

"But there's a fence." So the old folks wouldn't accidentally wander off and fall in and drown.

"Yes, baby."

"No fishing? Or boat trips?"

"Miz Bristol's family took her out on the river."

Had they? I guess the nephew—or maybe niece; let's not be sexist—whose truck had had the fishing bumper sticker, also had a boat. It made sense. There aren't that many places you can go fishing without one.

And—when I thought back to the morning of the funeral, and the truck—it had had one of those round balls in the back, that you can attach things to.

"That was nice of them."

Mrs. Jenkins shrugged scrawny shoulders inside the

housecoat.

"That reminds me," I said. About the housecoat, not the boat. "I found you a dress to wear for dinner. It's on the bed in your room. We didn't get around to finding one yesterday, remember? It used to belong to my sister Catherine." I described it. Mrs. Jenkins liked blue, so she perked right up when she heard that it was.

"It might be a little big on you," I warned, "but it'll fit better than anything of mine. And you'll look lovely. Would you like to come upstairs and see? And maybe change before Rafe gets here? He's on his way."

Mrs. J nodded eagerly. She definitely wanted to change, and look pretty, before Rafe got here. She might not always remember who he is, but she adores him.

So we headed upstairs, where I combed and pinned her hair, and helped her into the blue dress. As I'd expected, it was a bit too big. Not to put too fine a point on it, but it hung on her birdlike frame almost like on the hanger.

I found a white belt and cinched the waist. That helped a little. And made me wish, not for the first time, that I still had a waist of my own. I'd get it back after the baby was born—a few months after the baby was born, probably—but it would never be what it was.

And it hadn't been anything that exceptional to begin with. Now that I'd realized I'd never see my old figure again, I wished I hadn't been so critical of it when I'd had it.

Since we were upstairs anyway, and since I also wanted to look nice for Rafe, I changed into my party dress, as well. It was black—Mother likes to point out how slimming it is, so I figured I'd come down on the side of caution—and nicely streamlined. There was no way to streamline the baby bump, of course. But from the back, I looked pretty darned good, if I do say so myself. And the multi-strand necklace I draped around my neck drew the eye up and away from the stomach, and emphasized my décolletage, which is the only part of my body that's actually improved with pregnancy.

Mother even nodded approvingly when we came back downstairs. "Very nice. And slimming."

"Thank you," I said.

Mother turned to Mrs. Jenkins. And frowned. "That doesn't look like one of Audrey's."

It might have been. Fifteen years ago. "It's Catherine's," I said. "She left it in the closet when she left for college. I thought it might fit Mrs. Jenkins." And it wasn't like Catherine was ever going to wear it again. She hadn't liked it in the first place, and by now, she wouldn't be able to pull it up over her hips.

"I'm sure she won't mind," Mother said graciously. She smiled at Mrs. J. "You look very nice, Tondalia."

Mrs. Jenkins beamed back. "Thank you kindly."

"Rafe's almost here," I said, "or at least he should be, so we're going to sit in the parlor and wait."

Mother nodded. "I'll go upstairs and change, too. The others should start arriving soon, as well."

We went our separate ways. Mother upstairs to primp, and Mrs. J and I to the parlor and the TV.

It can't have been more than five minutes later than we heard the rumble of the Harley-Davidson outside. I left Mrs. J to the Property Brothers, and went outside to meet my husband.

We haven't spent a lot of nights apart in the time we've been married. And we haven't been married long enough yet that anything about being together is old hat. I don't know that it'll ever be. Every time I see him unexpectedly, my heart still skips a beat, and even when I know what to expect, like now, I can't keep from smiling.

He pulled the helmet off his head and smiled back. "Afternoon, darlin'."

"Same to you," I said, a little breathlessly. He has that effect on me, even fully clothed and in the middle of the day. "Any problems?"

"Did I take too long?" He kicked the stand down on the bike, and got off, and hung the helmet on one of the handlebars.

I shook my head. "You're here exactly when you said you'd be here. I'm just happy to see you."

"I'm happy to see you too, darlin'." He took the wide steps up to where I was standing two at a time, and bent his head to kiss me. He smelled of wind and leather—from the black jacket he was wearing—and his own spicy scent, and I drank it in while I wrapped my arms around his waist and held on.

When he lifted his head again, his eyes were dancing. "Your mama's watching."

"Let her watch," I said, but I did remove my arms. He kept his hand on my back until he knew my knees were steady enough to support me, and for good measure, he put the other hand on my stomach.

"Everything OK here?"

"As far as I can tell. My mother says the baby's dropped. My back is killing me." And the warmth of his hand right there felt good.

He was more interested in the stomach, however, and I guess I couldn't blame him. He took a step back to look at it. "I guess it looks like it's maybe a little lower."

"If Mother says so, I'm sure it is. She says it means I'll start having Braxton-Hicks contractions." In fact, I was having one right then. My stomach tightened for a few seconds before relaxing again. The baby responded by kicking me in the ribs. At least it was facing the right way. I guess that was one thing to be grateful for.

Although with more than two weeks to go, it might have turned right side up anyway, by the time it was ready to come out.

Rafe helped me inside, and then turned to greet my mother and his grandmother. Mother presented a smooth cheek for a kiss. "Rafael. It's good to see you."

"You, too, Margaret Anne," my husband said politely, and buzzed her cheek before turning to give his grandmother a hug. She beamed as brightly as my mother.

They dragged him back into the parlor for a chat. I sat by as Mother asked him questions about work—as if he went to and from an office every day—while Mrs. Jenkins just watched and smiled. Then the doorbell rang again, and I told Rafe to stay where he was while I went to let my sister in. She was carrying a big basket of fresh-baked rolls, and they smelled so good that I snagged one on our way to the dining room, where she left them on the table.

"I have news," I told her, once my mouth was empty.

"What about?" She was looking around the dining room.

"First of all, Mrs. Jenkins is wearing your blue eyelet dress with the cap sleeves, that you left in your closet when you went to college fifteen years ago."

She turned to look at me, eyebrows raised, and I added, "It was convenient. We went to Audrey's on the Square yesterday, to look for a dress for Mrs. Jenkins to wear today—we left Nashville in a bit of a hurry; long story—but before we could find anything," or even look at any dresses, really, "we discovered that Audrey's mother was Mrs. Jenkins's sister."

Catherine's jaw dropped.

"So we forgot about the dress. And we had to borrow yours instead. Sorry."

Catherine hiked her jaw up. "Audrey's mother was Rafe's grandmother's sister?"

I nodded.

"That's a small world," Catherine said.

"But it explains what Tyrell Jenkins was doing in Sweetwater when he met LaDonna Collier. I always wondered."

Catherine glanced toward the parlor. "How does Rafe feel?"

I glanced in that direction, too. "He seems to feel fine. No reason why he wouldn't. Audrey and Darcy are both nice."

Catherine nodded. "But Audrey must have known all along that he's her... whatever he is."

"Some sort of cousin. First cousin twice removed, or something like that." And I hadn't thought about that part of it. But I could see where that might be upsetting. If Audrey had known all along that he was her... let's just call it nephew, to make it simple, and she hadn't acknowledged the relationship—or him—in over thirty-one years, it might make him feel slightly unwanted.

Unless she hadn't known until yesterday. I didn't think Tyrell's name was common knowledge in Sweetwater. Rafe hadn't known who his father was until after LaDonna died a year and a half ago. So Audrey might not have connected Tyrell's visit to LaDonna's pregnancy or to Rafe until Mrs. Jenkins called her by her mother's name yesterday.

But no. She would have figured it out earlier than that. But only about a year ago. When Rafe figured it out and told me and I broadcast the news to my family and friends. So she'd probably only known for a year or so. And had kept that, like her relationship with my father, to herself.

My stomach tightened again, and I put my hands on it and breathed.

"How much longer?" Catherine asked.

I gave her the same numbers I'd given our mother this morning.

"Braxton-Hicks?"

I nodded. "It'll stop in a few seconds. Mother says the baby's dropped."

Catherine took a step back and examined me critically.

"Looks that way. Are you excited?"

"Terrified," I said.

She smiled. "You'll be all right. You can ask me and Dix for advice when you need it. Between us, we've been through this a few times."

More than a few. And don't think I wouldn't. I'd be calling her all the time, until she got sick of me, most likely.

The contraction did stop, and we headed back into the parlor. My husband got to his feet, politely, to greet my sister, and waved her into his place on the loveseat. "I'll go change."

"I'll go with you," I said.

My sister muttered something. I didn't ask her to repeat it, although I flushed. Rafe chuckled and put an arm around my shoulders. "We won't be long."

We'd be longer than he thought, since we had a couple of things to discuss. Although it wouldn't be for the reason Catherine imagined. I wouldn't engage in that sort of behavior in the middle of the day on Thanksgiving, with the house full of people. But that didn't mean I couldn't enjoy watching my husband change his clothes.

And a very enjoyable minute or two it was, too. I sat on the bed while he skimmed out of faded jeans and pulled the snug Henley up over his head. At that point, he stopped for a second and gave me a grin. "What's that you were saying?"

I swallowed. "We need to talk about your grandmother. Last night she made a break for it in the middle of the night. I'm not sure whether she was awake or not, but she was on her way out of the house, and we can't let that happen."

Rafe nodded, as he pulled a pair of dark gray slacks up over his hips and zipped them. Slowly.

"I don't want to lock her up. You know? And I hate the idea of doping her to the gills. But we can't have her wandering off. She gets herself in trouble."

"She's damned lucky she didn't end up dead in that water,"

Rafe agreed. He turned to the backpack he'd carried upstairs, and rummaged for a shirt. I watched his muscles move smoothly under the skin, and had to peel my tongue off the roof of my mouth.

He pulled out a pale blue shirt and shook it, eyeing it critically.

"You'll look great," I told him. Who cared if the shirt was wrinkled? The color would look amazing against his skin.

He shrugged into it, and then took his time buttoning the buttons. I imagined my eyes must have gone glassy, because he grinned wickedly. "Hold that thought, darlin'."

I told him I intended to. "We really do need to figure out something, though. I can't guarantee that I'll always wake up. Earlier this week I didn't. She made it out of the house before I woke up in the morning, and got all the way down to the Milton House before I caught up. And I was lucky I found her at all. She could have gone in the other direction. Or someone could have snatched her."

"With Fesmire dead," Rafe said, tucking the shirt into his slacks, "hopefully we don't have to worry about that no more."

Hopefully not. If I'd been right about Fesmire and Julia and everything else. "I don't suppose you ever figured out who made the phone call from the payphone on Tuesday afternoon? It was a woman, so it wasn't Fesmire himself. Did you ask his wife?"

"She was in Franklin," Rafe said. "I had the boys sitting on Fesmire's house and business, remember?"

Right. And José would have noticed if Mrs. Fesmire had left for any reason.

And if Fesmire had been sleeping with Julia, chances were he didn't have another girlfriend he could tap to do it. And since it had been made on-site, it wasn't like anyone could have done it, from anywhere. Whoever did it, had to actually be there.

So who had made the phone call?

"He coulda paid a stranger to do it," Rafe said, "for all we know. Plenty of people in that neighborhood would be happy to make a phone call for twenty bucks, no questions asked. And Fesmire had money to spare."

Maybe so. It wasn't anything to get hung up on, anyway. Especially if Rafe and Tamara Grimaldi weren't worried about it.

"Grimaldi's working today?"

"That's what she said," Rafe answered. "She's on call, and tying up loose ends on the Poole investigation. Did you need her?"

I didn't. I just wished she was here instead of there. But someone had to hold down the fort, even on Thanksgiving, and if she was willing, more power to her.

"I don't suppose she's said anything about Dix?"

"Not to me," Rafe said. "But if you want, I can talk to him. And ask his intentions." He grinned.

"Would you?" Dix might be more forthcoming with Rafe. We were close, my brother and I, but Rafe was another man. Dix might be more comfortable talking to him about Tamara Grimaldi.

"Sure," Rafe said.

"Thank you." I pushed to my feet, and stood swaying for a second, trying to find my equilibrium. Rafe put a hand under my elbow to steady me.

"You all right?"

"My center of gravity changes from day to day. It takes me a minute to find it." I smiled up at him. He smiled back, and put his palm against my stomach.

And frowned. "It's hard."

"Braxton-Hicks contractions. Nothing to worry about."

"If you say so." But he didn't sound convinced.

"We still have almost three weeks to go. This is normal."

He nodded. "Ready to head back downstairs?"

I guess I was. The show was over up here, and I wanted him to talk to Dix. While we'd been up here, I'd heard the front door open and close several times, so I figured the rest of the family had probably arrived by now. And Bob.

And maybe Todd. Oh, joy.

At that point, the party divided itself along gender lines. The women congregated in the kitchen, prepping food and drinking wine—and in my case, sparkling water—while the children parked themselves in front of the TV and the men took their beer into a different room where they could shoot the breeze without female ears listening in.

It took me a few minutes to notice that Mrs. Jenkins wasn't in the kitchen with the rest of us. But the children had taken over the parlor with the TV, so maybe she was in there with them. I excused myself and wandered down the hall to see.

The parlor was crawling with small shapes. Three were female: Dix's Abigail and Hannah, and Catherine and Jonathan's Annie. Annie even wore a pretty eyelet dress. But neither of them was Mrs. Jenkins.

I didn't think she'd be with the men, but I stuck my head into the room just to be sure. Dix frowned at me, and I withdrew again.

Maybe the excitement and all the people she didn't know had been too much for her. Too much stimulation, too much activity. Maybe she'd gone upstairs to her room.

I dragged myself up the stairs again, and had to stop halfway when another Braxton-Hicks hit. This time, it felt like it would never end, but it was probably just because I had somewhere to be in a hurry. I wasn't really worried—or not a whole lot—but Mrs. J did have a tendency to disappear. I just wanted to make sure she was safe.

Wherever she was, it wasn't in her room. That was empty.

Since I was upstairs anyway, I checked my own room, Dix's old room, the bathroom, and the master bedroom and bath, as well. Mrs. Jenkins was not on the second floor of the house.

I took the servant's staircase down to the first floor and into the kitchen. A quick look around told me that Mrs. Jenkins had not shown up in the five minutes or so I'd been gone. "Where's Rafe's grandmother?"

"She took the dog outside," Mother said.

"Pearl's in the parlor with the kids." Or she had been when I looked in. Or so I'd thought. But maybe I'd been wrong.

I headed back down the hallway to the parlor.

Yes, there she was. Curled up on the floor.

Pearl, not Mrs. J.

"Have you seen Mrs. Jenkins?" I asked the kids.

The looked at each other. "The old black lady?" Cole asked, and his older brother immediately shushed him. The kids all looked guilty.

I nodded. "Yes. Rafe's grandmother. Have you seen her?"

"She left the dog in here," Robert said, with a glance at Pearl. As always when her name or species is mentioned, Pearl's tail slapped against the floor and she gave me a canine grin.

"Did she take the dog out before she left it with you?"

The kids exchanged another look and a universal shrug. I looked at Pearl. "Go outside?"

She wagged, but didn't move. That usually means she's been out recently. If she has to go, she gets up and heads for the door.

I left them there and went to the door myself. It was open. Or unlocked, rather. Latched, but not locked. As if someone had gone out without a key, and not come back in.

I stepped out onto the porch and looked left and right. There was no one in sight.

I went inside again and closed the door behind me. And left

it unlocked, just in case Mrs. Jenkins was around the corner of the house. No sense in locking her out if she was on her way back.

"I can't find your grandmother," I told Rafe once I'd made my way to the room where he, Dix and Jonathan were nursing their beers. "I've been all over the house. Mother said she took the dog for a walk, but Pearl's in the parlor with the kids. They said your grandmother dropped her off. And the front door's open."

Rafe didn't say anything, but I could see his hand tighten around the beer bottle. If it had been a can, it would have crumpled.

"Sorry," I added.

His hand relaxed. "Not your fault. She musta left while we were upstairs."

Most likely.

"She's probably just out wandering around. Maybe she decided to go to Audrey's house. We drove home from there yesterday, so she might remember the way." Or think she remembered the way.

Rafe nodded.

"And like you said, at least Fesmire isn't a threat anymore." All we had to worry about was hypothermia and Mrs. J getting hit by a car.

He put the bottle on the table and pushed to his feet. "Let's go."

"You want us to come with you?" Dix asked. "The kids are fine here." He glanced at his brother-in-law. "Jonathan and I can take our two cars and drive around."

"We'll let you know." Rafe navigated around the table toward me and the door. "If we don't find her at Audrey's, or on the way there, it might come to that."

"For now," I added, "just keep the front door unlocked in case she comes back."

Dix nodded. "I'll check the house again. Just in case you missed something."

I didn't think I'd missed anything, but it couldn't hurt. And I moved slowly these days. It was certainly possible that while I'd made my slow way down the servant stairs, Mrs. J had nipped up the foyer stairs to her room. "Check the outbuildings, too. The carriage house and the slave cabin. Just in case she got curious and decided to take a look."

Dix nodded. "Take my car. It'll save you from having to go get the Volvo out of the garage." He handed Rafe the keys.

Rafe dropped them in his pocket. "Let's go."

He brushed past me and into the hallway. I smiled at my brother and Jonathan, and followed.

EIGHTEEN

Dix's car is an SUV with two booster seats in the back. If we found—when we found—Mrs. Jenkins, we'd have to take one of them out to make room for her. Or maybe she was small enough to fit. She wasn't a whole lot bigger than Abigail, Dix's oldest daughter.

Rafe took the turn from the driveway onto the road on two wheels. I didn't think Dix's car had ever seen that kind of treatment before, but it responded. Even if a warning light went on on the dashboard.

"'Tipping danger,'" I read. "Maybe take the turns a little more carefully."

Rafe glanced at me, but didn't speak. Not about that. "How far d'you think she mighta gone? How much of a head start did she get?"

At least ten minutes. And she was a nimble old lady when she wanted to be.

"She could be halfway to town by now," I told him. "At least if she's following the road. If she's crossing the fields, it'll take longer."

And we might not see her. There was no sign of her yet.

"Someone mighta picked her up," Rafe said.

"If so, she's probably at Audrey's already." If she was headed that way. "Sweetwater's a small town. Everyone knows who Audrey is. If your grandmother explained that she wanted to go to Audrey's house, anyone in town could have taken her there."

Rafe nodded. "If we're lucky, that's what happened."

He didn't have to spell out what would happen if we weren't lucky. Sweetwater tends to be a nice, law-abiding place, but bad things can happen anywhere. And Mrs. J might not remember Audrey's name. She might have asked for Oneida's house instead. And depending on who picked her up and how old they were, they might not remember Oneida. She'd been gone a while.

"Would you like me to call the sheriff?" I asked.

He hadn't shown up at the mansion yet. I knew he was expected, but since he wasn't part of the family, I guess he was waiting until closer to when dinner was supposed to be served, as befits an honored guest.

Or maybe something had happened at work that he needed to deal with. When you're the sheriff of a county, you're pretty much always on call. Even if it is Thanksgiving.

"Give it a couple minutes," Rafe said, and the way his knuckles whitened around the steering wheel were in sharp contrast to the calmness in his voice. "We could find her along the road. If we do, no need to involve the sheriff."

"Of course." I knew what he was thinking. For as long as we could keep calm and not call the police, we could pretend that maybe it wasn't a big deal that she was gone. "She's probably just on her way to see Audrey. Or already there." No need to panic yet.

Rafe nodded. "Keep an eye out on your side of the car. I'll check over here."

We drove another minute in silence. He was driving slower now, partly to give us enough time to look, and partly, I'm sure, because when we got to Audrey's, if Mrs. Jenkins wasn't there, we'd have to deal with the fact that this wasn't going to be easy. The longer he could put off the inevitable, the happier he'd be.

The houses started getting closer together, and there was still no sign of Mrs. Jenkins. On Rafe's side of the car, there was the stone wall surrounding the Oak Street Cemetery.

"We went here yesterday," I told him, pointing. "I can't imagine why she'd want to go back. Unless..."

He glanced at me.

"Oneida is probably buried there. She lived in Sweetwater. And I told your grandmother yesterday that everyone in town is buried at Oak Street."

Rafe hesitated. It was a tough call. If she wasn't at the cemetery, we'd be wasting time by stopping. Time we could use to find her. But if she was there, and we drove by and didn't look, we'd miss her that way, too. And she'd spend more time out in the cold, maybe catching a chill.

I made an executive decision. "Let me out. I'll go up and look for her. You keep driving. I have my phone, so if I find her, I'll call you."

Rafe pulled over to the side of the road with a screech of brakes. Dix would not have been happy about the treatment of his car. "Be careful."

"Always," I said, throwing his standard response right back at him.

But let's be honest: what was going to happen to me in the middle of a cemetery on Thanksgiving? The only other person who might be there, was Mrs. Jenkins. And it was broad daylight, so it wasn't like I was in any danger of stumbling over any gravestones or into any open graves. "Call me when you get to Audrey's. Either way."

He said he would, and I slammed the door and watched him peel off before I crossed the road—looking carefully both ways before I did—and through the gate into the cemetery.

Like I said, there was nothing creepy about it. Nothing at

all. Not at this time of day. And the Oak Street Cemetery isn't rumored to be haunted, either, so there was nothing at all to worry about. It was overcast, the sky heavy with low-hanging clouds, but it wasn't raining. Visibility was pretty much a hundred percent. And while there was a distinct chill in the air—I really hoped Mrs. Jenkins had thought to put on her coat before she left, but I had a feeling she hadn't—it wasn't as cold as it could have been.

I didn't know where Oneida and her husband were buried. I could have called Audrey and asked, I guess, but I figured Mrs. Jenkins wouldn't know either, so there was no point in actually finding out. If she was here at all, she'd either gone back to LaDonna's grave, which did know where was—if she remembered from yesterday—or she was wandering around, trying to find Oneida.

I decided to wander, too. In the direction of LaDonna's grave, to begin with, while I kept an eye out along the way for Mrs. Jenkins.

When the city of Sweetwater first acquired the land for the cemetery early in the 20th century, they started by burying people close to the road. That's a hundred years ago, give or take, and although we're a small town, we've had a few deaths since then. By now, there are graves all up and over the hill, with the new burials on the other side, out of sight.

I trudged in that direction. That's where LaDonna was, and for all I knew, Oneida as well.

There was no sign of life around me. As far as I could tell, I was the only one here. A couple of birds tweeted, and a squirrel chattered, but other than that, it was quiet.

When I got to the top of the hill, I turned around and looked out at the area I'd traversed. My stomach was doing its cramping thing again, and my lower back hurt. I put my fist back there and kneaded through the layers of clothes while I surveyed the terrain.

With the trees bare, I could see the road in both directions, and most of this part of the cemetery from fence to fence. There was no sign of Mrs. Jenkins, and no sign of anyone else, either. I dropped my hand and turned my back to the road and surveyed the other side of the hill.

And there she was. A small, blue figure weaving among the gravestones, over in the area where LaDonna was buried.

I pulled out my phone and dialed Rafe. "I've got her. Or rather, I see her. She's here. You can turn around and come back."

"Good," Rafe said, sounding grim, "cause I'm here at Audrey's house, and I ain't seen her, and they haven't, either."

I heard him explain to the others—Audrey and Darcy and maybe Patrick Nolan—that I was at the cemetery and that Mrs. Jenkins was here, too.

"I figure she's probably looking for Oneida's grave," I told him when he came back on. "I don't know where she's buried. Would you mind asking Audrey? I might as well show Mrs. J where it is, since we're here anyway. It's going to take you five minutes to get back here to pick us up, and we might as well keep moving. Your grandmother left without her coat again."

"Hang on."

I heard him pose the question to Audrey, and heard her begin to give directions for where to find Oneida's final resting place. I was listening to the faraway voice with one ear, and keeping the rest of my attention on Mrs. Jenkins, as I picked my way toward her. We were moving in the same direction, but she was moving faster than I was. She was probably cold, and anyway, she most certainly wasn't pregnant. My back was killing me, my feet hurt, and I felt like I was carrying a medicine ball strapped to my stomach. A medicine ball that was sitting squarely on my bladder.

For a second I contemplated the possibility of squatting behind a gravestone. Not *on* a grave, of course. Somewhere

where I could be sure that nobody was buried.

There was a nice, bushy line of trees near where Mrs. Jenkins was, along the perimeter of the cemetery. She wouldn't be there by the time I reached that spot, of course, but maybe I could duck in among the trees for twenty seconds.

Or maybe not. It was cold, and while I was squatting in the trees, Mrs. Jenkins might get away from me. I could just see myself trying to explain that to Rafe. And anyway, it's probably not a good idea to pee anywhere in a cemetery. Just in case. So I'd just have to hold it until we got home. Or back to Audrey's. Or wherever we were going once we'd gathered up Mrs. Jenkins and put her in the car.

"OK," Rafe's voice said. "Here's what Audrey said—"

"Hold on." Something was moving on the right. In that tree line I'd just been contemplating using for an impromptu bathroom.

"What?" He was instantly alert.

"Something." I had stopped, because one does, while Mrs. Jenkins was blithely moving forward. "I saw something move."

"Fesmire," Rafe began.

"Is dead. I know. I don't think it's Fesmire."

If he was haunting somewhere, it wouldn't be here.

"Prob'ly just a bird or something."

It was too big to be a bird. But before I could say so, it burst out of the trees and straight for Mrs. Jenkins. And it was considerably larger than a bird. What it was, was a fully grown man dressed head to toe in camouflage, including a hood covering his head.

I screamed—as one does—and he turned my way for a second. Just long enough for me to see that under the hood was a ski mask, the kind that only leaves two holes for the eyes and one for the mouth.

It looked like my presence made him falter for a second. He must not have noticed me until I screamed.

Too focused on Mrs. J, I guess.

And he still was, or maybe he'd been calculating quickly in his head, and determined that I was no threat. I was still far enough away that there was nothing I could do when he descended on Mrs. Jenkins and flapped the black thing in his hands open before pulling it down over her head.

It looked like a big, black trash bag.

I had just processed that when he yanked her off her feet and up over his shoulder, and set off down the hill with her.

I dropped the phone in the grass and gave chase down the hill. But whoever he was, he was in better shape than me, and I fell behind with every step. I was also moving farther and farther away from the road where Rafe and the SUV would be coming. The guy was moving toward the back of the cemetery, toward the service road back there. The bag with Mrs. Jenkins inside bounced up and down on his shoulder.

My spirit wanted to follow. Hell—heck—my spirit wanted to fly. To soar through the air and jump on the guy's back and knock him down and then beat him bloody and make him give me Mrs. Jenkins back.

My flesh, however, was weak. I couldn't keep up. And although it felt a lot like failure, I stopped and turned and started plodding back up the hill again, to where I'd dropped my phone. Rafe was probably already on his way here. Close by. If I could divert him, maybe he could reach the service road before whatever car was down there had a chance to leave.

It took a minute or two to find the phone in the dry grass. By the time I lifted it, Rafe was long gone, and I had to call back. While I waited for him to pick up, I turned once more, and started trudging in the direction of the service road.

The phone picked up. "Yeah."

I could hear from the echo that I was on speaker. Probably so he could have both hands free to drive.

"The service road," I said—or perhaps gasped is a better

word. "Behind the cemetery." I was seriously winded, and my back was screaming. My stomach chose that moment to have another contraction, too, one strong enough that I actually had to stop for a moment while I waited for it to pass. "Oh, shit. I mean... shoot." I leaned forward and braced my hands—or one hand; the other was holding the phone—on my thighs.

"What's wrong?"

Other than the obvious? "Nothing. Just another stupid contraction." I focused on breathing through it. "He picked up Mrs. Jenkins and threw her over his shoulder. And ran down toward the back of the cemetery. There's a service road there. If you hurry—"

"We're almost there," Rafe said, and I could hear the squealing of tires through the phone when he took another turn on two wheels. "Where are you?"

"On my way down there." Slowly. "If I can't get there by the time you do, and you see the car, follow it. I can call Dix for a ride home."

"What kinda car?"

I had no idea, and told him so. "When I couldn't keep up, I went back for my phone. So I didn't see the car. But I doubt they're on foot." The bad guy had been pretty quick, but he wouldn't be able to keep it up for long. Mrs. Jenkins isn't big, but she's still a hundred pounds or so, and that kind of weight starts to wear after a while. Just look at me and the baby. It was nowhere near a hundred pounds—even though it sometimes felt that way—and I couldn't run more than a few yards before I was out of breath.

"Did you recognize the guy?"

Nobody could have recognized the guy. "He was wearing camouflage from top to bottom. With a hood. And a ski mask."

"Army? Or hunting?"

The camouflage? What was the difference?

But I thought about it for a moment. "Hunting. Pretty sure.

It was pale tan, with those stripes that look like grass or twigs."

"Weapon?"

"I didn't see one," I said, as the service road came into view at the bottom of the hill. "Although it went really fast. He had a big, black bag—like a lawn and leaf bag—that he threw over Mrs. J's head. And then he picked her up and took off with her, like she weighed nothing."

"She doesn't weigh much," Rafe said. I could hear the squealing of tires in stereo now, from the phone and from down on the road to my left.

"I can hear you," I told him.

"We're turning onto the service road now. How long before you're here?"

I was so close now, that I didn't want to be left behind. I tried to move faster. "Thirty seconds. Less."

"I see you." Dix's SUV burst into view and came to a quivering stop. The back door opened as I huffed and puffed my way toward it. Someone else must be in the car. Rafe couldn't have opened that door from behind the wheel.

I staggered toward the SUV and climbed in. With a little help from Darcy, who grabbed my arm and hauled.

"Ooof." I smacked against the seat before I clambered to a sitting position and yanked the door shut behind me. "Go."

He went. The turn on the narrow road would have landed us in the ditch if anyone less skilled had been driving. And then we were on our way down the service road spurting gravel, with another two-wheeled turn onto the paved road that made Audrey, in the front passenger seat, squeal and grab for the chicken stick.

"You'll get used to it," I told her, although to be honest, I never have. I trust him, and trust that he won't get us into an accident, but I've not gotten used to it.

"We didn't see any cars." His voice was as calm as if he were driving down a nice, wide-open interstate at sixty miles an hour, instead of keeping that same speed on a narrow two-lane country road edged by trees limbs that slapped at the sides of the SUV. "They musta gone this way."

"This is the way to the river, isn't it?"

The Duck River runs through the Bog, or what used to be the Bog, but before it gets there, it also snakes along the southern perimeter of town.

Rafe nodded, his face grim. So did Audrey, the Sweetwater native.

"I'm guessing you're not happy about that."

Rafe glanced at me over his shoulder, as we flew down the road like it was a NASCAR race track. "Too much water in this story."

There was, actually, now that I thought about it. From the rain the night Mrs. Jenkins had shown up in our yard, to Julia Poole's car submerged in the Cumberland River, to the cops fishing Alton Fesmire's body out of the water.

And the river winding past the nursing home in view of the pavilion where Julia had been murdered.

"Mrs. Jenkins told me that one of the Bristols has a boat," I said.

Or not a Bristol, but someone in the Bristol family.

Rafe gave me a look. "Is that so?"

"She said they took Beverly out on the river."

"Who's Beverly?" Audrey wanted to know. She was gripping the bottom of her seat with both hands, her knuckles white.

I explained who Beverly Bristol was, and what had happened to her, and what—if anything—it might have to do with Mrs. Jenkins. Then I turned my attention to Rafe. "There was a truck parked outside the funeral home on Tuesday morning. It had an '*I'd rather be fishing*' bumper sticker and one of those balls in the back, that you hook things to."

"A trailer hitch." Even under the circumstances, his lips

twitched.

I nodded. "It probably belonged to one of the Bristols. Or whatever their names are. It wasn't Fesmire's and it wasn't ours, and it probably didn't belong to the staff."

Chances were they didn't drive hearses to work, but a truck with *'I'd rather be fishing'* seemed a little too frivolous. And anyway, the employees probably had their own parking lot. Or their own corner of one, away from the spaces in the front, where the mourners were likely to park.

"One of the Hammonds lives on the river in Madison," Rafe said. "With his wife."

"No kidding?"

He shook his head. "It ain't much of a place. A modular home on a half acre or so. But they do have a river view. Why?"

"I guess I'm questioning our theory that Fesmire killed Julia and then himself. I mean, it certainly wasn't Alton Fesmire in the cemetery. He's dead."

Rafe nodded. So did Darcy and Audrey.

"And nobody else has a reason to want your grandmother out of the way. Just the person who killed Julia, because he knows that your grandmother can identify him."

"So?" Rafe said.

"So what if it all goes back to Beverly Bristol? What if she was the main victim? We've been treating her like she was sort of incidental—like, she died because Julia Poole wasn't where she was supposed to be, too bad, right?—but what if it was all about her? I mean, there she was. Old and demented and childless. And while not rich, at least quite comfortably off."

"Quite," Rafe agreed.

"So maybe the Bristols wanted money. Or needed money. Or could use money. It wasn't doing Auntie Beverly any good, after all. She was down there in that facility in Brentwood, losing her mind more and more every day, while all that lovely money was just sitting in the bank."

"And you think one or more of'em decided to do something about it?"

"It's possible," I said. "It probably wouldn't be all of them. But it would have to be more than one."

We screeched around a bend in the road. "Lay it out for me," my husband said.

"Hold on a second. I'm having another contraction."

Darcy and Audrey both looked worried, and I added, "I have several weeks to go. They're just fake contractions. Not the real kind. Probably from all the running up and down the hill earlier." The baby had gotten bounced around quite a bit. Not as badly as Mrs. Jenkins, but I'd been jostling it more than usual.

We drove on in silence, just broken by the sound of the tires on the blacktop and the branches slapping at the windows.

"Shouldn't we have caught up by now?" Audrey asked, her voice worried.

Rafe shot her a look. "Depends. They're probably going fast, too."

I nodded. "He saw me. So he has to assume someone's coming after him. He probably didn't realize we'd be coming so soon, though."

My stomach relaxed, and I unclenched my teeth. "Anyway. The person who picked up Mrs. Jenkins and ran with her was a man. It couldn't have been a woman. She wouldn't have been strong enough to do that. And he was tall. And bulky."

Rafe nodded.

"But it was a woman who called me the other day. And while Fesmire might have bribed an innocent bystander to make that call, I doubt the Bristols would have thought of it. It was probably one of them."

"Mrs. Roberts," Rafe said, "Mrs. Wilkerson, or Mrs. Hammond."

"One of the twins is married? Which one?"

"Chet," Rafe said, hands on the wheel and eyes forward.

"Who isn't married?"

"Les. The thinner one."

Who had worn the gray suit at the funeral. "Lester and Chester Hammond? Are you serious?"

His eyes met mine in the mirror. "Their parents were."

Right. "Moving on. If Julia Poole was sleeping with someone, it was probably the single brother. So we can probably assume Lester is involved."

"Unless Chet and his wife did it all," Audrey said, getting into the game. "And she was OK with him seducing Julia for the good of the mission. She might have wanted the money enough to put up with that."

She might have. That would mean Mrs. Chester was the one who called me and got me out of the house on Tuesday. And it was Chester I'd seen in the cemetery, abducting Mrs. J, after he failed in Nashville.

"Here's what I think happened." Now that Alton Fesmire was dead and my whole big theory about him had gone up in smoke. "Chet and his wife, or Chester and Lester and Chester's wife, wanted Beverly Bristol's money. So one of the twins started making googly eyes at Julia Poole sometime when they were down there, visiting Aunt Beverly. Julia googlied back, and they arranged to meet at midnight in the pavilion on the night Beverly died. It might not have been the first time. Maybe they did a trial run, just to make sure it would work and they could do it. Julia probably gave whoever it was the code to the gate. Or maybe they didn't come by gate. Maybe they came by boat."

Rafe didn't say anything, but he arched a brow.

"That would mean Fesmire suspected something was going on, and came to the nursing home on Saturday night to see if he could catch Julia in the act. He's the one who came through the gate. And instead he ended up there when Julia was murdered."

"So did he see the murderer?"

He probably hadn't. It was hard to believe he wouldn't have mentioned that to someone if he had. Maybe he'd been too late. The code-in at the gate had come very close to midnight. By then, Julia might already have left the building and gone to the pavilion.

Or maybe he had known. Maybe his remark at the funeral, about things coming out, was a veiled threat to the Hammonds. Maybe he'd been trying to blackmail them.

"Sorry," Rafe said. "I sidetracked you. Go back to the night Beverly Bristol died. They come by boat. One of'em—maybe Chet, maybe Les—meets Julia in the pavilion. The other—maybe Les, maybe Chet's wife—goes inside, snaps Beverly's neck while she's sleeping, and then throws her and her walker down the stairs to make it look like she was out walking around, and fell."

I nodded. "Then Julia realizes what has happened—or more likely, she thinks Beverly fell because she, Julia, was neglecting her work by dilly-dallying in the pavilion while she should have been on duty."

"Uh-huh."

"She feels guilty, and she threatens to tell Fesmire the truth. Or she gets suspicious and wonders whether maybe Beverly's accident wasn't an accident after all. Either way, Lester and Chester can't let her live. So they arrange to meet her in the pavilion one more time, and—"

I raised my hand to my throat, but before I could make the cutting sound, Rafe stomped on the brakes.

"Hold that thought," he said. "We're here."

NINETEEN

We were. The road had ended in a small parking lot at the edge of the river.

It was deserted, which wasn't a surprise on Thanksgiving afternoon. Most of Sweetwater—most of the country—was at home, either preparing or already eating the turkey and dressing.

Except for this small group of us. We slid sideways into the parking lot, and saw the car parked at the far end—not too far away at all, given the size of the lot—by the boat ramp.

Yes, there was a boat ramp here, too. For most of its length, and it's the longest river located entirely inside the state of Tennessee, the Duck is a pretty narrow and shallow river, but it's home to more freshwater mussels and fish than any other river in North America. And if you follow it far enough, you end up at Land Between the Lakes, where you can transfer to the Tennessee River or the Cumberland, if you'd like.

This little park was the public access to the Duck River here in Sweetwater. But the car was not local. I recognized it.

"That's Fesmire's BMW."

Rafe nodded, his jaw tight as he fought to keep the SUV going in the right direction.

We'd made good time getting here. (I wasn't surprised. The tires of Dix's car had barely touched the ground.) The guy in the camouflage was still over by the car, trying to wrestle the bag with Mrs. Jenkins out of the trunk.

I don't know whether he was having a problem because she was fighting or because she was limp. Limp can sometimes be harder to deal with. But either way, he was hauling and not making much progress.

When we screeched into the parking lot, he glanced over his shoulder.

If it were me, I would have left Mrs. Jenkins where she was, and run. He didn't. He made one final herculean effort, and got her out of the trunk. And while Rafe stood on the brake and the SUV skidded across the parking lot on screaming tires, the guy in the camouflage ran to the edge of the river and jumped, still with Mrs. Jenkins in his arms.

Rafe let loose with string of expletives I won't repeat. Audrey threw her door open and jumped. The car was still moving, albeit not very fast, but she wasn't able to stay on her feet. Instead, she fell and rolled.

Beside me, Darcy screamed. She yanked on her door, but it wouldn't budge. Mine wouldn't, either.

"Child locks," I said, as Darcy launched herself forward instead, slithering through the gap between the front seats and out the door her mother had opened.

By now, Audrey was back on her feet and limping as fast as she could toward the water. Darcy caught up within just a second or two, blew past her mother, and over the edge. A second later, Audrey followed.

Rafe was still cursing fluently. But the car had come to a quivering stop, and he pushed his door open.

"Let me out!" I screamed. Unlike Darcy, slithering between the seats was not an option for me.

He shook his head. "You're not getting in that water. Stay here."

He was gone before I could tell him that I wasn't going to

go in the water. I just wanted out of the car. When—*if* was not an option—when they came back with Mrs. Jenkins, I wanted to be able to do something to help. Not be stuck in here.

And anyway, what if the bad guy doubled back around and decided that Dix's SUV, sitting here with the key in the ignition and the engine running would make a good getaway vehicle? I'd be stuck here, like a rat in a barrel, with no way out.

No sooner had the thought crossed my mind, than the worst happened. Rafe had disappeared over the edge of the river, and was nowhere in sight. Audrey and Darcy were gone, probably floating downstream after Mrs. Jenkins. Hopefully they'd gotten to her by now. Hopefully Rafe would get to them, and they'd all make it out of the water.

But they could probably use a little help. I pulled out my phone and called Dix, since I'd promised to update him anyway. "I'm at the Oak Street boat access ramp. Everyone but me is in the river. The bad guy threw Mrs. Jenkins in, and Audrey and Darcy and Rafe jumped in after her. You need to call 911 and— shit!"

I mean... shoot.

"What?" Dix said.

I peered out from behind the seat. "The bad guy just crawled up the ramp. He's going to take your car. And me. I gotta go."

I cut the connection, in the middle of an exclamation from Dix. Hopefully he'd call 911 instead of trying to call back. If the bad guy decided to take the SUV rather than the BMW, I'd like to pretend I wasn't here. And if my phone was quacking, I couldn't.

The bad guy stood for a second at the top of the ramp, breathing hard, with water sluicing off his coveralls and running back down the ramp to the river. He was breathing hard. I could see his chest heaving under the camouflage. It couldn't have been easy, fighting against the current to make it back up the ramp.

He looked from the BMW to the SUV. And like I would have done, he made the decision that taking the SUV, which was already running, with the door open, would leave Rafe and the others with no vehicle, if they made it back to the parking lot at all.

The thought that they might not—or that one or more of them wouldn't—was terrifying. But the bad guy had to be hoping for that. And he probably had good reason. It was November. The water was cold. The current was strong. And they'd keep looking for Mrs. Jenkins, maybe past the point when they really should stop and save themselves instead.

And on that note, as the bad guy came limping toward the SUV, maybe I should take my own advice and try to save myself, as well. Or at least do what I could so he wouldn't notice me.

I squeezed myself as far behind the seat as I could and tried to imagine myself very, very small. And it must have worked, because when he stuck his head in and surveyed the car, he didn't seem to notice me. He just got behind the wheel and shut the door behind him. I heard the locks catch. And then he engaged the gear shift, and we started moving.

And it occurred to me that I might have miscalculated. What if he actually had noticed me back here? And what if he'd decided to do me the way he'd done Julia Poole and Mrs. Jenkins last Saturday night? By rolling the SUV down the ramp and into the river, with me stuck in the backseat, unable to get out? Even if I rolled the windows all the way down, I didn't think I could squeeze through. I'd be stuck here, while the water slowly filled the car.

And while I was dealing with that, and while Rafe and the others had been swept away by the current, the bad guy could get in the BMW and make his leisurely way back to Nashville.

The concern was strong enough that I popped my head

over the back of the seat to see which way we were going. And the bad guy really mustn't have realized I was here, because he jumped, and his foot slipped off the gas for a second. "Shit!"

A pair of gray eyes met mine in the mirror.

"I'm nine months pregnant," I told him. "If you dump the car in the river, I won't be able to make it out."

He hesitated. I'm pretty sure he did. Or maybe that was wishful thinking on my part. If I was right, he'd already killed three people. Or conspired with his brother or wife to kill them. Aunt Beverly, Julia Poole, and Alton Fesmire. And maybe Mrs. Jenkins. She might have been dead by the time she went in the water. Black plastic bags aren't known for helping people to breathe. And if one or more of the others didn't make it out of the river alive, he was certainly responsible for that, too.

What was another murder or two at this point?

I wasn't surprised when he turned the nose of the SUV toward the boat ramp. If he hadn't been planning it all along, my comment, and my presence here, had given him the idea to do it now. And I could see his reasoning. If the car had been empty, he'd have had a good shot at getting away. With me in it... well, there was a chance that someone might track me down. By my cell phone signal, if nothing else. And while I was alive, and back here, there was a chance I could do something to stop the car. Or get someone's attention.

No, much safer to leave me and the SUV behind, and make his escape in the BMW. If the SUV—and I—were in the river, the coast was clear for him to get away.

I braced myself when the SUV started rolling down the ramp. I don't know why. It wasn't like the impact with the water was rough. We just slid right in, with very little resistance. Floated on the surface for a second, it seemed, and then started to sink.

The bad guy lowered the window by his seat and started to wiggle his way out. So far the interior of the car was dry, but his gyrations made the car rock—he was a big guy—and a little water splashed over the edge of the window. The SUV rolled a few feet farther into the river, and more water started coming in. My feet were getting cold, and when I looked down, I saw that the bottom of the car was starting to fill up. I guess the doors and joints and whatever weren't water tight.

The back windows didn't open either, of course. Another feature of the child safety package, probably. Dix wouldn't want Abigail or Hannah to open the window and—in a hissy fit—throw their backpacks or whatever out of the car.

I'd never get to see Abigail and Hannah again. I'd never get to see Dix again. Or my mother. Or Catherine or Jonathan or their kids.

Or Rafe.

The bad guy kicked his boots free from the front window, and used the roof rack to pull himself through the water back to the boat ramp. I saw the legs of his coveralls and his boots go by on the other side of the car. Then he let go and kicked off, and disappeared through the water toward the ramp.

I was alone. In a car that was slowly sinking into the Duck River with me in it.

I didn't think about Rafe. Or Audrey or Darcy or Mrs. J. I couldn't think about them. If I did, I'd probably just sit here and drown.

If the worst happened, and I never saw Rafe, or Mrs. Jenkins or Audrey or Darcy again, but I could get out of here and save myself and the baby, I'd have a piece of Rafe I could keep forever. It wouldn't be the same as having Rafe, but he could live on through our baby.

I couldn't let our baby die.

In water up to my ankles now, I stood up and started to maneuver my way to the front seat. But as I'd realized earlier, it was impossible. I couldn't fit between the seats the way Darcy and her skinny body had done, and with this unwieldy baby bump, it was hard to navigate over the tops of the seats, too. Not only were they tall, but I couldn't slide on my stomach over the seatbacks. I had to try to climb, and it wasn't easy.

And moving around inside made the car rock and shift. One of the tires slipped off of something that might have been a rock on the bottom of the river, and the front passenger side of the car did a nosedive.

I shrieked, and clung to the back of the seat and tried to stay very, very still so the car wouldn't move anymore. When it looked like it had settled back in, with water lapping at the front window, I turned my head, slowly.

The good thing was that now, the rear end of the car was higher than it had been before. I couldn't make it across to the front seat, but maybe I could make my way into the back of the SUV. And maybe there was a way to open the hatch. That probably didn't have a child lock on it. Abigail and Hannah weren't supposed to be back there.

I shifted my weight, very slowly and carefully. The car twitched, but stayed in the same position. I maneuvered onto the backseat, and contemplated the space between the seat and the ceiling, and calculated my chances for making it across.

They were fair to middling. There were two headrests, but they were spaced far apart. Same as the front. But unlike the front, where there was a long, narrow gap between the two seats, the backseat was one long seat all the way across, and the middle part was lower than the headrests. If I could haul me and my stomach across that, I stood a good chance of making it into the backseat.

I'll spare you a detailed description of the gyrations I made, but if someone had had a camera on me, we could have won a lot of money on America's Funniest Home Videos. I was sweating and cursing and crying a little, and the baby didn't seem to like the activity, because it kept kicking me in the ribs and elbowing me in the stomach. And in the middle of everything, I had another contraction that put me out of commission for a minute or so while I breathed and sniffed and cursed through it.

But I made it into the back of the SUV. It was neither easy nor graceful, and at one point my skirt was up around my waist—or at least above my hips, since I don't have a waist anymore—but I got there. I landed on my back with every intention of staying there long enough to catch my breath. Instead, I had to roll over immediately when it became clear that I'd landed on top of Abigail and Hannah's booster seats. Darcy must have shoved them over the seatback into the rear when she got into the car. Or when she saw me thundering down the hill in the cemetery, and realized she'd have to share the backseat with me.

I stayed on my side for a minute and breathed instead. Side-sleeping is supposed to be better for the baby anyway.

Once I'd caught my breath, I moved over onto my hands and knees and crawled the foot or two over to the hatch. And tried to open it.

And came quite close to tears again when I couldn't. It felt like it moved a little, but we're talking fractions of inches here, not inches. Certainly not feet. Or the yards I'd need to fit myself and the stomach through.

I sat back on my heels, panting. If nothing else, it was dry here. The floor of the rear was higher than the floor of the SUV. And the front of the SUV was deeper in the water than the back of the SUV. Unless the SUV moved again, I had a little time to figure this out.

There was a window across the back. What were the chances that the window opened independently of the door? I'd seen cars—or SUVs—with that feature.

Hadn't I?

I examined it more closely. And yes, there was a button. I pushed it. The window glass popped open, and I could push it out.

Unfortunately, it didn't seem to be big enough for me to fit through. In my normal state, I could have managed. I've never been skinny, but I could have sucked my stomach in and slithered through.

Now, that wasn't an option. I had to go through sideways, if I were to have any chance at all. And I didn't see any way I'd get my hips though that way. I could slide my shoulders through the regular way, then twist to get the stomach through sideways, but the rest was going to be a problem. I could perhaps hold onto the roof of the car and twist my body, as long as my posterior didn't get stuck...

"Savannah!"

My heart skipped a beat. That sounded like...

But no, it couldn't be. Maybe it was Dix. Maybe he'd driven here and had come to save me.

"Savannah!"

It didn't sound like Dix. I turned, in time to see my husband come running down the boat ramp. Two seconds later, he was in water up to his waist, wading toward me.

He was soaked to the skin. The leather jacket he'd put on as we ran out of the mansion was gone—he'd probably ditched it in the river, so the weight of it wouldn't drag him down—and the pale blue dress shirt he'd worn for Thanksgiving dinner was plastered to his body.

Under other circumstances, that would have given me a little thrill. But I was already as thrilled as I could possibly be that he was here at all, and alive and seemingly well, that the shirt passed mostly unnoticed.

"Savannah!" He wrapped his fingers around the top of the hatchback and peered in at me. "You all right?"

I nodded. And I'm not ashamed to admit I had tears streaming down my face. "I thought you drowned."

"I ain't that easy to kill," Rafe said. "Can you make it outta there?"

I sniffed. "I was just trying to figure out how. I think I'm too big."

"It ain't you. It's the window. It's too small."

It was nice of him to say so.

"Either way," I said, "I don't think I can fit through. And I can't get the door open."

"Is it unlocked?"

I told him I'd thought it was, but I still couldn't get the damn—darn—thing to budge.

"There's a lotta water in front of it," Rafe said, and he should know, standing in it up to his chest now. "I'll give it a try."

He dropped his arms into the water and fumbled around. "Gimme a hand. Push when I tell you."

I put my palms against the back of the door and prepared to push.

"Now."

He pulled. I pushed. I could see the muscles in his arms straining against the weight of the water. I put my shoulder against the door and leaned as hard as I could. Slowly but surely, the hatchback opened. Water started pouring into the back of the car.

"C'mon, darlin'."

He reached for me. I flowed—literally, but against the tide—into his arms and wrapped my arms around his neck. He was ice cold.

He didn't seem to mind. "Let's get you to shore."

"You, too," I said, hanging on.

"I'm all right." He kept wading.

I swallowed. "The others?"

"We came ashore half a mile or so farther down. They're on their way."

All of them, I assumed. If not, surely he would have said so.

We sloshed through the last of the water halfway up the ramp. "You can put me down," I told him. "I can walk."

"When we get to the top. You sure you're all right?"

I was sure. "Couldn't be better." Now.

He laughed. And although he was soaked to the skin, and his back teeth were chattering, he managed to make it sound good.

We got to the top of the ramp just as two things happened. Mother's Cadillac screeched into the parking lot, followed a second later by Catherine and Jonathan's minivan. And Audrey and Darcy staggered out of the woods at the far end of the parking lot, supporting Mrs. Jenkins between them. All three of them looked like drowned rats, with their hair and clothes plastered to their heads and bodies.

The passenger door on the Cadillac opened, and Mother ran to the trunk. It popped, and she grabbed a stack of blankets and hurried toward the three women. The minivan, meanwhile, also stopped, and Catherine jumped out and followed. Dix hustled over to the trunk of the Cadillac and grabbed a couple more blankets. For me and Rafe, as it turned out.

"I'm fine," I said when he got close enough to us. "It's mostly my legs that are wet. Rafe is soaked."

"You're soaked now, too, darlin'."

I guess I was, from the water flowing into the back of the car and from being carried against his body. Not as wet as he was, though. I was still wearing my wool coat, and while it had absorbed some of the water, it wasn't sodden. He was, from top to bottom.

Dix wrapped one of the blankets around him. "Let's get you back to the house. The others can go with Mother and Catherine in the van."

"The SUV..." I began, with a glance over my shoulder at the boat ramp.

"We'll get it pulled out. For now, the sheriff has to see it."

He started herding us toward the Cadillac. On the other end of the parking lot, Darcy and Catherine were wrapping Mrs. Jenkins in blankets, while Mother was sobbing on Audrey's shoulder. I guessed they'd made up. Nothing like the possible death of a loved one to align people's priorities.

I turned back to Dix. "Did you call him? Bob Satterfield?"

"I called everybody," Dix said. "911, Bob, Tamara."

"You called Grimaldi?" All the way in Nashville?

"I thought she'd want to know what was going on," Dix said, and he was probably right about that.

"Todd?" If I haven't mentioned that my brother and Todd Satterfield have been best friends since kindergarten, I'm mentioning it now. I wouldn't put it past Dix to think that Todd should know what was going on, too.

But Dix shook his head. "He's having Thanksgiving with Marley and Oliver. And anyway, I don't think he's getting to prosecute this one."

Probably not. The Bristols—or Hammonds, I guess—would be going on trial in Nashville. For the murders of Beverly Bristol, Julia Poole, and Alton Fesmire, and the attempted murder of Mrs. Jenkins. And me.

If Maury County wanted to pursue charges beyond that, Bob Satterfield could fight Tamara Grimaldi for the Hammonds.

"I don't suppose you thought to call Patrick Nolan?"

"As a matter of fact," Dix said, and opened the back door of the Cadillac for me, "he's down the road sitting on your friend until someone from the sheriff's office can haul him off to jail. This being outside the Columbia PD's jurisdiction, Patrick made a citizen's arrest. With a little help from his badge and gun."

Good for him. "I'm sure the bad guy didn't realize Nolan was out of his jurisdiction."

Dix shook his head. "We'll pass them on our way back to

the mansion. You can identify the guy then."

"I didn't see his face," I said. "He was still wearing the hood and ski mask when he got into the SUV."

"Don't worry about it," Rafe said, crawling in behind me, still hanging onto the blanket Dix had wrapped around him. "We all saw him. We all saw what he did. He ain't getting away with it."

No, he wasn't. I waited until he was settled next to me, and then I snuggled in next to him—I was already wet, so what did it matter?—and waited for Dix to start the car and take us home.

TWENTY

Fesmire's BMW was parked on the side of Oak Street just before we got to the main road. Patrick Nolan's Charger was in front of it, and when we rolled slowly past, we saw the outline of our bad guy in the back seat. And Nolan in the front, patiently waiting to be relieved of his prisoner.

Dix pulled over to the side of the road in front of the Charger, and stopped. Rafe opened his door, and I scrambled out after him. "Don't do anything stupid."

He shot me a look over his shoulder. "I'm not stupid enough to take a shot at him in front of a cop."

Maybe not. But it had to be tempting. This guy had put Mrs. Jenkins inside a plastic bag and thrown her in the river. *I* wanted to punch him.

"Besides," Rafe added, "he's cuffed. I don't hit people who can't hit back."

Good to know.

"I just wanna know who he is. Don't you?"

I did, actually. So when he made his way over to Nolan's car, I followed.

Nolan powered down the front window, and his eyebrows rose at the sight of Rafe's wet state. "You all right, Agent Collier?"

"Fine," Rafe said.

Nolan swallowed. His rather prominent Adam's apple bobbed. "Darcy? Her mother?"

"They're all fine," I assured him. "They're right behind us, in Catherine's minivan. Along with Mother and Mrs. Jenkins. Everyone's all right."

"We just wanted a look at your prisoner." Rafe bent and peered into the backseat. I bent, too. With a little difficulty.

Nolan had stripped the guy of the hood and ski mask, although he was still wearing the wet camouflage coveralls. And Nolan had the heat cranked, probably so the guy wouldn't freeze to death. Nice of him. I couldn't find it in myself to care too much, to be honest. This jerk had tried to kill not only Mrs. Jenkins, but me and my unborn baby. And in the process, he might have killed Rafe, Audrey, and Darcy, as well. Why shouldn't he freeze?

I recognized him. One of the twins from the funeral. The skinnier one, who'd been wearing the gray suit. Not the florid one who'd been yelling at Fesmire.

Although given that this guy had driven here in Fesmire's car, and we'd watched him throw Mrs. Jenkins in the river, meant that he was in this up to his eyebrows, whether he'd confronted Fesmire at the funeral or not.

Rafe, of course, had met him before. "Lester Hammond. I don't suppose you've got anything to say for yourself?"

Hammond just stared at him. Sullenly.

"Just as well," Rafe said. "You'll be booked into the Maury County jail for a bit. I'm sure they've got some charges they'd like to lay on you."

Like kidnapping and a few counts of attempted murder that had happened here in their jurisdiction.

"After that, you'll be transported back to Nashville where you'll be charged with the murders of Beverly Bristol, Julia Poole, and Alton Fesmire."

"I didn't do nothing to Aunt Beverly," Lester Hammond

growled. "And you can't prove I had anything to do with what happened to Julia or Doc Fesmire."

"I guess that means your brother did your aunt while you were keeping Julia busy." Rafe gave him a tight smile. "And then you did Julia while he took the boat back up to Shelby Park to pick you up."

Interesting. I hadn't considered that maybe the murderer had boated away from the park. I'd wondered whether he'd had a car parked there—risky, in case someone saw it and noticed the license plate—or whether he had walked home. Once Rafe had told me that neither of Beverly Bristol's family members lived in walking distance to the park, I'd settled on the parked car as the solution, risky or not. But this worked, too.

Worked very well, as a matter of fact. Ten minutes on the river, and you'd be in Madison.

I heard the sound of an engine, and then another. Catherine's minivan was making its way toward us from the river access. When it came alongside, Catherine slowed to a stop and the passenger side window rolled down. "We're going home," Mother said, with a look at me and Rafe. To Nolan, she added, "Come to the mansion when you're finished. Darcy will be there."

Nolan nodded. "Yes'm."

The window rolled back up and enclosed my mother, who I thought had done a credible job of imitating Queen Elizabeth. The van rolled on, all the way out on the gravelly side of the road to pass the squad car coming in the other direction.

It went past us, made an eight-point turn, and pulled to a stop beside the Charger. The door opened and sheriff's deputy Cletus Johnson emerged.

Cletus and Rafe have always had a contentious relationship, mostly due to Cletus's ex-wife, Marquita, who went to work for Rafe, minding Mrs. Jenkins, after she left Cletus and their kids.

And then she ended up dead, which Cletus blamed Rafe for.

I braced myself as I waited for the fireworks to begin. But Cletus didn't say anything. He gave Rafe a look, but addressed Nolan. "I'm here to transport the prisoner."

"He's all yours." Nolan gestured with his thumb into the backseat of the Charger. Rafe pulled the back door open.

Cletus gave him another look, but didn't tell him to keep his hands to himself. It was a step in the right direction, I thought. And it wasn't Rafe who reached in and grabbed Hammond. Cletus did that. Rafe just kept watching as Cletus yanked Hammond out of the car.

The thing is, Rafe simply standing there looking, is enough to make strong men wet their pants. Hammond's were already wet through and through, so I couldn't tell if he did, but it wouldn't surprise me.

"We'll talk later," Rafe told him. You could take it as a promise if you wanted, but it sounded more like a threat. And although Hammond tried to act like he wasn't worried, he couldn't quite pull it off.

Cletus shoved him into the squad car—making sure not to hit Hammond's head on the top of the door frame; we didn't want anyone to be able to scream about police brutality—and closed the door on him. "Thanks," he told Nolan.

Nolan nodded. "Sorry to make you come in to work on Thanksgiving."

Cletus shrugged. "Someone has to do it. And the kids are with my mama. They'll make a plate for me for later. You have a good one."

He gave Nolan a nod, gave me a nod, and grudgingly, gave Rafe a nod. And got in the squad car and took Lester Hammond away.

"We'll see you at the mansion," I told Nolan. He nodded. We got into the Cadillac again, and headed home.

It wasn't a long drive. Three minutes later we pulled to a stop behind Catherine's car. The minivan wasn't here yet, so it must have taken a left beyond the cemetery and gone to Audrey's house, most likely to give her and Darcy the chance to get out of their wet clothes into something dry. Mother's clothes weren't likely to fit either of them—she was too short or they both too tall—and mine weren't either, at the moment. Hopefully they'd find something to put on Mrs. Jenkins, as well.

"Can you take care of Nolan while we go change?" I asked my brother. "I want Rafe into something dry as soon as possible."

And I wanted out of my own wet booties and hose.

Dix nodded, as the Charger came up the driveway. "Don't worry. We'll find him a beer and make him comfortable. I'm sure Darcy'll be here soon, too."

Probably so. "She likes him a lot. So be nice to him."

"I was nice to your boyfriend," Dix said, "wasn't I?"

Rafe arched a brow but didn't say anything.

Dix added, "Even that jerk you married. The other one. I was nice to him, too."

I guess he had been. At least until Bradley cheated on me and wanted a divorce. "So you'll be nice to Nolan. And not screw things up for Darcy."

Dix nodded.

"Is Grimaldi coming?"

He checked his watch. "She'd probably halfway here by now."

Good. It wasn't how I had planned for things to go, but I was still happy that Grimaldi was coming. At least she'd be able to spend a little time with us before she had to interrogate Hammond, and maybe take him back to Nashville with her.

As the Charger pulled to a stop behind the Cadillac, Rafe and I headed up the stairs to the front door, and then—after greeting Pearl—up to the second floor.

"Strip," I told him in the hallway. "Go straight into the shower. Make it hot. Just drop your clothes on the floor. I'll get them."

"I think I should prob'ly strip down in the bathroom. I think your brother-in-law's here somewhere. With all the kids."

He had a point. "Maybe that's a good idea. I'll wait until I hear the water running and come get your wet clothes. Don't lock the door."

"You could join me." He winked.

I could. It was tempting. After worrying that I'd lost him, and almost being stuck in a sinking car myself, making love sounded nice. The closeness. His arms around me. But to be honest, I wasn't feeling that great. My back hurt. So did my stomach, a little bit, around the bottom. I'd probably banged it trying to get over the backseat in Dix's car. No surprise, the way I'd been twisting and turning. And I was feeling sort of nauseous. A result of the stress, no doubt.

Maybe I needed to eat something.

And anyway, satisfying shower sex was pretty much impossible at this stage of the game no matter how I felt. Bed sex was so much better.

"Tonight," I told him. "There are a lot of people here right now. I feel weird."

He gave me a closer look. "You all right?"

I smiled. "Fine. Just a little tired from all the activity. And stress."

He nodded. "I'll be out in a minute."

"I'll find some dry clothes for you," I said, and waited until he'd disappeared behind the bathroom door before I headed into our bedroom. He hadn't brought a change of clothes beyond jeans and T-shirts—the nice clothes he'd brought for dinner were now a sodden mess on the bathroom tile—so I laid out a pair of jeans and a long sleeved Henley with dry socks and underwear. When I made my way across the hall on bare feet, he was in the shower, humming.

"I'm taking your clothes," I told the shower curtain, gathering them up. "You have dry ones on the bed."

"I'll be there in a minute."

I took him at his word, and went back into the bedroom to wait. And lo and behold, a minute later he wandered in, with one of Mother's fluffy towels wrapped around his waist. Looking at him wasn't as good as making love in the shower, or on the bed, but it made me feel better to see him safe and whole. And the fact that he was mostly naked gave me a nice little tingle.

I smiled. He smiled back. "All right?"

"Fine," I said. "I just need some food, and some time to relax. And everything will be OK again."

He nodded. "You watching me change?"

I told him I thought I might.

"Wanna turn on some music before I get started?" He started humming the windup to *You Can Keep Your Hat On*, complete with hip movements.

"I think we can save that until we're in our own house," I said primly, "don't you? There are too many people here. And kids." And even if I would be happy to watch him strip, they wouldn't.

"We're gonna have to get used to that," Rafe told me. But he dropped the towel without music, other than the one he was making himself.

I smiled appreciatively. He chuckled, and reached for the underwear. He doesn't always wear it, but since we were in my mother's house, I didn't feel right about sending him downstairs without any. Even if Mother would never know the difference, I would.

He lifted the jeans next, and looked at them. "Guess I won't be impressing your mama this year."

"My mother's already impressed," I said. "And is probably more impressed now than she was before. I don't think you have to worry."

He pulled the jeans up and reached for the zipper. "I wasn't exactly worried."

No, I didn't imagine so. "I was. Not about that. But about you not making it out of the water." About any of them not making it out of the water.

And about me not making it out of the water. And the baby.

"We were all right," Rafe said, pulling the Henley over his head and down over all those lovely muscles. "We didn't go far. Darcy's a strong swimmer. Audrey's all right. They didn't need help. So we could all help my grandma."

"I can't believe he'd do that!" Hammond.

"I can," Rafe said grimly. "Anybody who'd snap his eighty-year-old aunt's neck and toss her down the stairs—for money!—is capable of anything."

When he put it like that. "I think the other brother probably did that. While this one was entertaining Julia and keeping her out of the building."

"Don't matter," Rafe said. "They planned it together. They were in it together. And anyway, this is the guy who slit Julia's throat and left my grandma to drown. He'd done it before. I ain't surprised he'd do it again."

Maybe not. I shuddered, and then smiled. "I'm glad it all worked out."

He nodded. "Ready to go on downstairs?"

I guess I was. "Give me a hand?"

"Sure." He took the one I extended and pulled me to my feet. "You sure you're all right?"

"We're fine," I said. "My back hurts. My stomach hurts. I keep having those stupid fake contractions. But I'll be all right once I eat something. We all survived. We're all together. That's the important thing."

Rafe nodded. "Let's go. The sooner we do this, the sooner we can get you off your feet and into bed."

I grinned. "I like the sound of that."

"I bet you do," Rafe said, and steered me toward the door.

We came back downstairs just in time to greet the minivan and the other women.

Patrick Nolan had driven up right after we did, of course, and Dix had done what he said he'd do, and pushed a beer into Nolan's hand. When the door to the minivan opened and Darcy came out, Nolan put the beer down and went outside and wrapped her in his arms. She dropped her head on his shoulder, and they looked very sweet just standing there for a moment.

Both Darcy and Audrey had changed their clothes. Out of Audrey's closet, I guess, since Darcy looked a bit more dramatic than she usually does. Like Grimaldi, she's more of the sporty type. This green silk dress was something more like what her mother would wear. But there's no question that Darcy looked great in it. And judging from the way Nolan's hand moved up and down on her back, he seemed to like the texture, too.

Audrey was in black from head to toe. Slacks and a long sleeved sweater. And while nobody was embracing her, Mother kept close. I guess the idea that Audrey might not make it out of the Duck River alive, had made Mother realize what she'd be losing. It was all right to be angry with Audrey when Audrey was right down the road and aware that Mother was angry with her. It was something else to maybe never seen Audrey again. They'd been best friends for more than half my mother's life. I was glad she'd finally come to her senses, even if it had taken something like this to do it.

Mrs. Jenkins was still wrapped in a blanket. Under it, Catherine's sodden blue dress was gone, and a fuzzy bathrobe had taken its place. It dragged along the ground when Mrs. Jenkins moved. Chances were, Audrey hadn't had anything in her closet that would fit Mrs. J, and had done the best she could to keep her warm until they could get her home. Or back here.

I opened my mouth to tell Rafe to go get her, but he was already moving. He scooped Mrs. J up into his arms and strode up the stairs with her. I scurried after, to the degree that I could scurry. "She has dry clothes in her room. If you'll just put her down on the bed, I'll take care of her."

"I'll do it," Audrey said calmly. She was keeping pace with me up the stairs and across the foyer. As we reached the staircase to the second story, she passed me and kept going. "Just stay down here, Savannah. I've got this."

Fine by me. The stairs were getting harder and harder to manage, anyway.

So I stayed downstairs with the others. Rafe came down after a minute, and joined us. And then another vehicle pulled up out front. Bob Satterfield's off-duty pickup truck.

As he opened the door and stepped down, yet another car turned off the road and into the driveway.

"She made good time," Rafe remarked.

I nodded. It might feel like the beginning of today had gone on forever, but it wasn't that long since I'd called Dix from the parking lot down by the river to tell him what had happened. And yet it was Tamara Grimaldi's burgundy sedan coming up the driveway, and Grimaldi herself, in her usual business attire of suit and crisp shirt, who came out of the driver's side door.

By now, the foyer was getting crowded. Mother was greeting Bob Satterfield and sobbing a little against his chest, probably about Audrey. Darcy and Patrick Nolan were still sticking close to one another, although Nolan had picked up his beer again, and Darcy had found a glass of wine somewhere. She probably needed it. I could use some, too, to be honest, but of course that wasn't possible.

Dix was catching Jonathan up on everything that had happened while Jonathan was minding the kids, and every so often, one of them would stick his head into the parlor to make sure that those same kids were still OK.

And Pearl was winding her way through the forest of legs and feet, sniffing a little here, snuffling a little there, and skipping out of the way whenever someone moved.

"I need to sit down," I told Rafe.

He nodded. "C'mon." He put an arm around me, and gestured to Tamara Grimaldi with his other hand. She looked like she really wanted to talk to the sheriff—probably preparing to fight him for custody of Lester Hammond—but since Bob was busy cooing at Mother, Grimaldi followed us down the hallway to the second parlor, the one not occupied by the kids. On her way past, she gave Dix a quick glance. Neither of them said anything, but I wasn't surprised when, three seconds later, Dix left Jonathan and followed the rest of us down the hall.

TWENTY-ONE

"Tell me what happened," Grimaldi said when we were installed in the second parlor.

It was a long story. I started, then Rafe continued, and I took over again, at the part where Les Hammond came out of the river and got into the SUV.

"I should have just kept my mouth shut, you know? When I look back on it, I don't think he planned to drive into the river. I think I gave him that idea when I said something about it. And when he realized he wasn't alone. At first, he probably just wanted to take the SUV—it was standing right there, empty, or so he thought, with the engine running—and get away. He had the keys to the BMW, so nobody could take that and follow him—"

Rafe made a face, and I nodded. "I'm sure you could have hot-wired it if you had to."

"In about ten seconds," Rafe said, "if I'd gotten back there and you were gone."

No doubt. "But then he realized I was in the backseat, and he didn't want to drive off with me. More for his own sake than mine, I'm sure. And I opened my big mouth and told him that if he drove into the river, I wouldn't be able to get out. So that's what he did. I don't know if he would have, if I hadn't said anything."

Rafe muttered something. Grimaldi gave him a look. "For

purposes of charging him, this is good info. He knew you wouldn't be able to get out. And he drove the car into the water anyway. That's deliberate. Not something he can wiggle out of by saying he thought you'd be able to escape."

Good that one of us was happy. "If Rafe hadn't shown up," I said, "I'm not sure I would have. I had the window open, but I'm not sure I would have fit through it."

Grimaldi nodded. Over by the door, my mother made a distressed sound. She'd come in in the middle of the conversation, and I think this was the first time she'd heard what had happened to me when I was left behind in the SUV.

Bob was with her, and Grimaldi looked at him. "I'm sure you'd like to string this guy up from the nearest tree for all this, but we need him in Nashville. You have a handful of attempted murders here. I have actual murders in Nashville."

Sheriff Satterfield nodded. "I'll give him to you. Tomorrow."

Grimaldi opened her mouth, and he added, "It won't hurt him to spend the night in the county lockup. You can take him in the morning. After you've had some turkey and a good night's sleep."

Grimaldi didn't look happy about this. "Listen, Sheriff Satterfield—"

"And I'm charging him, too," the sheriff continued. "You get first dibs. But he doesn't come into my county and try to kill my people and get away with it. If you get him put away for long enough up where you are, these charges won't matter. But it might make the difference for him ever seeing the light of day again. I don't want him to."

Mother shook her head.

Grimaldi sighed. "Fine. Keep him until tomorrow. File charges. But he's going to answer for the murders he committed in Nashville first. I'll tack yours onto the back end."

The sheriff nodded. "Good enough." He looked hopefully

at Mother. "Time to eat?"

She smiled and patted his arm. "Come along. You can help me set the table."

Since the table had already been set by the catering crew yesterday, I didn't know what she planned to have him do, but they headed out and down the hallway. Grimaldi turned back to me. "You all right?"

I nodded. "Fine. A little achy here and there. It could have been worse." A lot worse.

"You made good time getting here," Dix commented.

Grimaldi made a face. "I used the sirens. And now I want to talk to this guy ASAP."

"Have some food first," Dix told her. It sounded more like an order than a request. "If I know Mother, she's rearranging the table to make room for all the extra people we weren't expecting."

"Probably setting a separate table for all the kids instead of having them at the main table." That would solve the problem. We had five kids, and we had added four extra adults, unless my math was off. Putting the children in the kitchen for their own dinner would solve the problem.

"We'd like you to stay," I added, to Grimaldi. "Not just Dix, but all of us. We wanted you to be here from the start. It's nice that you could make it, even if the circumstances aren't as happy as they could have been."

She'd opened her mouth when I started talking, and shut it again. Now she opened it a second time, when she was sure I had finished. "Someone has to be on call."

"And it's nice that you're willing to do that. But I'm glad you're here with us now."

Dix nodded.

"So what's going on in Nashville?" Rafe wanted to know.

Grimaldi looked relieved at the change of subject. "Spicer and Truman are sitting outside the Chet Hammond house in

Madison, waiting to see if anyone moves. So far, no one is."

"It's Thanksgiving," I said. "The family's getting together." And I felt bad for Officers Spicer and Truman, who had to spend Thanksgiving in a squad car somewhere in Madison.

"So far it's just Chet and his wife and the kids," Grimaldi said. "But here's an interesting fact: Lester Hammond drives a Ford Explorer. It's parked outside his brother's house."

So while Lester Hammond was sitting in the Maury County jail, his car was somewhere else. With people who would no doubt swear up and down that he'd been there with them all day, if anyone asked. Even the neighbors would be able to say that yes, Lester's Ford Explorer had been parked outside Chester's house all day on Thanksgiving.

"Giving himself an alibi," Rafe commented.

Grimaldi nodded. "We haven't moved on Chet and Brigitte yet. Part of me wants to. Part of me wants to pick them up and put them behind bars before they can eat their turkey and be thankful for all this money they're getting now that Aunt Beverly's dead. Or at least have someone knock on the door and establish, officially, that Les isn't on the premises, even if his car is. Put the fear of God in them."

"Would that mean you'd have to go back to Nashville right away?" I asked.

Grimaldi indicated that it would. I guess Spicer and Truman weren't 'fear of God' enough, and for it to work properly, she'd have to do it herself.

"Then wait a little," I said. "Stay here and have dinner with us. Talk to Les Hammond later, if you want. See if you can get him to roll on his brother. And pick up the others then."

"He won't roll," Rafe said.

Grimaldi shook her head. "I don't expect him to."

"Even if he doesn't," I said. "Just stay here with us for a couple of hours. It would make us happy."

Just one big family. Everyone together.

Grimaldi sighed. "No way I can say no to that without sounding like the Wicked Witch of the West."

No. "They're all under observation. Lester in jail and Chester in Nashville. Neither of them is getting away. And you relaxing for a couple of hours won't matter."

"If somebody gets murdered," Grimaldi warned, "I'll have to go."

I was aware of that. "We'll just hope really hard that that won't happen."

"Dinner's ready!" Mother's voice called from across the hall in the dining room.

I planted my feet and reached for Rafe. "Take me in?"

"Course, darlin'." He hauled me off the sofa and presented his arm for me to hold. Behind us, Dix did the same with Grimaldi. She rolled her eyes, but tucked her hand through the crook of his arm. And I think she might even have blushed a little when he covered her hand with his. Although by then things were getting a little too personal, so I looked away to give them some privacy. There wasn't much of that to be had in this house at the moment.

I'd been right about the seating arrangements. Mother had taken the path of least resistance, and had set the table in the kitchen for the children so she could fit the additional adults at the dining table.

It worked out fairly well, even if we didn't have enough men to manage a proper male/female rotation all the way around. Rafe sat between his grandmother and me, while across the table, Patrick Nolan was flanked by Audrey and Darcy. Jonathan was on Darcy's other side, then Catherine. I had Dix on my right, with Grimaldi following. Mother and Bob sat on the ends: Bob with Catherine and Grimaldi, and Mother with Mrs. Jenkins and Audrey.

Mrs. Jenkins didn't say much, but Mother and Audrey kept

the conversation going all by themselves. Now that they were together again, I guess they had a lot to catch up on. Mother got a little teary-eyed from time to time, and Audrey pretended like she didn't notice. Mrs. J, meanwhile, was eating. Her tiny body had the capacity to process an incredible amount of food.

I didn't have much appetite myself, even though the dinner was excellent. Mother's a good cook, and so is Mrs. Jenkins, and of course most of the dishes had been prepared beforehand by the catering company. The extra time before dinner hadn't hurt any of the food noticeably.

I just wasn't feeling it. It tasted good, but it was hard to get it down. I felt a little nauseated, something I had chalked up to stress and exertion and the time since I'd last eaten. I'd thought once we sat down to eat, I'd feel better.

But the food didn't help.

Rafe leaned closer to speak in my ear. "You all right, darlin'?"

I nodded. "I think so. I just don't feel great."

"It's been a big day. Lots of things happened."

Yes, indeed. Lots of things, most of them deeply upsetting.

"I thought I'd feel better once I ate something," I told him, "but I don't."

"You wanna lie down? D'you need to rest?"

That actually sounded good, but I wasn't going to go upstairs in the middle of Thanksgiving dinner with my family to lie down.

"I'll be fine," I said. "I just wish my back didn't hurt. And my stomach. And that I didn't feel sick. And that these damn Braxton-Hicks contractions would stop!"

I must have spoken a little too loud, I guess, because Mother looked over with a frown.

"Sorry," I added. Mother doesn't like cursing at the table. Or anywhere else.

Her face cleared. "Of course, darling. Are you not feeling

well?"

"Just tired," I said, since it's OK to tell the truth to my husband, but not to my mother in the middle of a dinner party. "It's been a big day."

She nodded and went back to her conversation with Audrey. They were giggling like two teenage girls. It was nice to see them happy again. I wasn't sure whether Mother even realized how much she'd missed Audrey.

"They're gonna be OK," Rafe said softly.

I nodded. "I figured they would be, once Mother got over herself and her bruised ego. Although for a while there, I wasn't sure she ever would."

Rafe slid his eyes the other way, in the direction of Dix and Grimaldi—who was conversing with Bob, probably talking police procedure or something equally dry; perhaps how they were planning to do the transfer of Lester Holland. "They'll be OK, too."

"I think so." Dix still needed more time to deal with the loss of Sheila. It had only been a year. And from what I knew about Grimaldi, I didn't think she was ready to give up crime fighting to be a wife and mother in Sweetwater. They lived very different lives, and what Dix needed wasn't at all what Grimaldi offered. But there was something there, between them. And I didn't think either of them was quite ready to give up on it yet. Not without a fair chance to make it work.

Another of those stupid contractions tightened my stomach, and I braced my feet and breathed through it. Annoying things that just wouldn't let up. I really hoped they wouldn't keep going like this for the next two-and-a-half weeks, because I really didn't think I could handle that. They'd been coming and going all day, and I was already sick and tired of it. Two more weeks of the same, and I'd be ready to rip that baby out of my stomach just to make it stop.

"Another contraction?" Rafe asked.

I nodded.

"When was the last one?"

"I've had them all day. The last one... I guess maybe in the parlor earlier, when we were talking to Grimaldi?" And before that, it had been upstairs, while I was waiting for him to get ready. "But I'm sure it's just a reaction to everything that's been going on. The running in the cemetery, and landing on my stomach when Darcy hauled me into the car, and then climbing over the seats into the back of the SUV while it was in the water..."

"Not that far apart," Rafe said. "Let me know when you feel the next one coming, OK?"

I blinked at him. "I'm not in labor. They're Braxton-Hicks contractions. Fake. We have almost three weeks to go." Or at least two-and-a-half.

"Humor me." He didn't say anything more about it. I didn't either, since I didn't want Mother or any of the others to hear what we were talking about. If there was any question at all about me being in labor—which was ridiculous, because I wasn't—I'd find myself packed off to the hospital so fast my head would spin.

I was tempted not to tell him when it happened again. I mean, they were just practice contractions.

OK, so maybe they came a little stronger and a little closer together now than they had yesterday, or this morning, but that was just because of all the activity today. Anybody would have contractions after everything that had happened. Even people who weren't pregnant.

So when the dessert course arrived, and with it another contraction, I thought about not saying anything. He'd never know the difference, after all.

Except he did. The contraction started, and Rafe glanced over at me. And frowned. "Another one?"

I gritted my teeth and nodded.

He glanced across the table at Nolan's wrist. "Eleven minutes."

Nothing to worry about, then.

Not that they were real contractions. But even if they had been, they needed to be under five minutes apart before we could go to the hospital.

"Don't worry about it," I said, when I could talk again. "I'm not in labor. Nothing's going on. We have weeks to wait."

"Sure, darlin'." But he kept watching me. Surreptitiously.

"Knock it off," I told him.

"Just trying to decide whether it's safe to leave you."

Leave me? "Where are you going?"

"I thought I'd go with Tammy and the sheriff to talk to Hammond after dinner. I told him I'd see him again."

"Sure," I said. "If you're willing to miss the football game with the other guys."

He smiled. "I doubt it'll take that long to get a confession outta him. I'll be back by the third inning. Unless you need me to stay with you?"

"Why would I need you to stay with me?"

He arched a brow, and I added, "I always want you to stay with me. But I realize you have things to do. It's fine. I'm not in labor. You can go."

"How about you just keep an eye on that clock and time your contractions while I'm gone? I don't really wanna have to deliver the baby on the side of the road as we're driving home tomorrow."

I would prefer to avoid that, too. "I'll do my best to make sure that doesn't happen."

"You do that," Rafe said.

TWENTY-TWO

After dinner, he and Grimaldi prepared to leave in Grimaldi's sedan. The sheriff was going to go with them, in his own truck, to unlock the jail and add his own charges to the litany coming out of Nashville.

"Can I come with you?" I asked.

Rafe arched a brow. Grimaldi arched both.

"I thought you were gonna stay home and time your contractions?" my husband asked me.

"I can time my contractions at the sheriff's office."

He didn't say anything, and I added, "I told you, I'm not in labor. It's too soon. And this guy tried to kill me. And Mrs. J. I'd like to hear what he has to say."

They both turned to the sheriff, obviously waiting for him to lay down the law.

I smiled. "You have one of those interrogation rooms with a two-way mirror, don't you, Sheriff? I can stay outside and see what's going on inside?"

The sheriff reluctantly admitted that he did.

"With a chair, I bet? So I don't have to stand?"

The sheriff nodded.

"So can I come? I won't interfere." Not that I thought either of them would give me the chance to. But I'd had plenty of theories about this case. I'd like to know how close I'd come to some of them.

Grimaldi looked at Rafe. He shrugged. "It don't bother me."

She looked at the sheriff. He shook his head. "Whatever the lady wants."

Grimaldi threw her hands up. "Fine. Get in the car."

"But if you go into labor in my sheriff's office," Bob Satterfield told me, "I'll have your head."

I shook my head. "Don't worry. I'm several weeks away from my due date."

Rafe looked extremely cynical, but he didn't speak up. Just picked up my coat and held it.

"Thank you," I said and let him put it around me.

He didn't speak, just gave me a jaudiced sort of look.

"If you really don't want me to come..." I began. And trailed off before I actually offered to stay home, since I had no intention of doing that.

"That ain't it. I don't care if you wanna look through the window and see what happens. It's the sheriff's jail. If he don't mind, I don't mind."

"But?"

"You're in labor, darlin'. I wish you'd just get off your feet and take it easy."

"If I'm in labor," I told him, "and I'm not, because they're Braxton-Hicks contractions and I have more than two weeks to go until my due date, and first babies are never early. But if I'm in labor, I might as well be in labor doing something I want to do. With something to think about other than the contractions. And I'd like to hear what this guy admits to when you interview him."

"Then that's what you'll do," Rafe said and nudged me toward the door. "But I'm making sure you have a chair to sit on."

That would be very nice. I had no problems whatsoever with that.

"We'll take our own car," Rafe told Grimaldi.

She nodded. "I'll see you there."

My car was the only one that was in the garage, of course, since it hadn't been out yet today. It took a minute to get it, and then Rafe helped me, solicitously, into the passenger seat. "Buckle up."

I did, even if the belt pushed on the sore part of the underside of my stomach.

It wasn't a long drive. Nothing in Sweetwater is far from anything else in Sweetwater. In less than ten minutes, we were parked in the lot behind the county jail, and on our way through the door.

It isn't a big place. Just three little cells, mostly used for people pulled over for DWI or disorderly conduct on a Saturday night. Sweetwater's a pretty low crime area, or I guess I should say that traditionally, it always has been. Since Rafe started showing up again, Sheriff Satterfield has had rather more to do than usual.

Although that's a bit unfair of me. The biggest case in recent history, the Skinner murders earlier this fall, had had nothing to do with Rafe, other than that the sheriff called him in to help solve the case. And the other big crime spree, in connection with my high school reunion in the spring, had had nothing whatsoever to do with Rafe. Or with me, for that matter. I'd just happened to be here, since it was my reunion, and Rafe had shown up after the bodies started piling up, to provide me emotional support. He'd had no connection to either victims or killers in that case.

He had been responsible for bringing Lester Hammond here, though. As Lester made clear once they got him into the interview room.

"Sure." He smirked. "I followed you. You didn't even look around."

I found that hard to believe. Rafe is usually very good at looking for tails. He had to spend years doing it, so it became second nature. Although in this case, with everything pointing to Fesmire and Fesmire being dead, he might have relaxed his vigilance a little.

At any rate, I was happy it wasn't me who had neglected to notice the tail. I'd been worried about that. But if Hammond had followed Rafe instead, I was off the hook.

"So you waited outside the house for Mrs. Jenkins to come out," Grimaldi said, and Hammond turned his smirk on her.

"Yeah. I figured she was gonna wander off sooner or later. She usually did."

I wondered whether Julia had told him that. Or maybe his Aunt Beverly. Someone must have, because I didn't think he'd been around Mrs. J enough to figure it out on his own.

"And then she came out with the dog."

Hammond nodded. "I wasn't gonna do nothing while she had the dog. Vicious-looking beast woulda probably bit me."

Pearl was the sweetest dog on the face of the earth, but I had no doubt that if Lester Hammond had tried to grab Mrs. Jenkins away from her, Pearl would have ripped him limb from limb.

"So I waited some more. Until she came out on her own. But she didn't walk on the road. She was going across the fields and into people's yards. So I followed along, and when she got to the cemetery, she went across the road and inside. I didn't wanna park where anybody could see me, so I went around the back and parked on the service road there. And I watched her."

"And when she came close enough you put a plastic bag over her head and picked her up and ran."

Hammond nodded. "I didn't know the fat bitch was there until she screamed. If I'd known, I'd have figured out a way to get her, too."

"She's pregnant," Rafe growled, "not fat. You moron."

Hammond smirked. "That your ball and chain, is it? She probably looks pretty good when she's not knocked up."

Grimaldi sent Rafe a warning glance. "You're single, aren't you, Les? I guess that meant when somebody needed to seduce Julia Poole, you got that job?"

Lester Hammond's face closed up. "I dunno what you're talking about."

"Julia Poole." Grimaldi enunciated clearly. I didn't think the problem was that Lester hadn't understood what she said. More that he didn't want to talk about it, because he hadn't been caught red-handed doing that. "The woman whose throat you slit last Saturday."

"You can't prove I did that," Lester said. Which was not exactly a denial. Although it wasn't an admission, either.

"I can make a good case for it. When you and your brother decided that your Aunt Beverly's money would look so much better in your bank accounts than in hers, you discussed how to get rid of her. And of course it made more sense to do it at night, when everyone else was asleep."

"Except for Julia Poole," Rafe said.

Grimaldi glanced at him. "But if someone could distract Julia, someone else could go in and take care of Aunt Beverly. And since your brother's married, distracting Julia fell to you."

"I'm better looking," Hammond said with a smirk.

"You're identical twins," Rafe told him.

Hammond gave him a look. "I'm still better-looking. My brother's let himself go. Gotten fat. Like your wife."

He seemed to have a real obsession with fat people. Whether they were fat or not. Or just pregnant.

"So you met Julia in the pavilion," Grimaldi yanked the conversation back on track, "while your brother snapped Aunt Beverly's neck and pushed her down the stairs. And when it came time to kill Julia, it was your turn."

Hammond shook his head. "You can't prove I did that."

"I can prove one of you did it. Your DNA was found inside Julia's car."

This was the first I'd heard of any DNA, but maybe she was just bluffing. I think cops are allowed to do that.

"That don't mean you can hang it on me," Hammond said.

Grimaldi smiled sweetly. It's a very scary look for her. "I don't really care whether I can prove which one of you did it. I'm charging you both with conspiracy, which means you'll both go down for all of it, whichever one of you did what. But since you don't seem inclined to want to share with me, I'll just tell you what I think."

She waited. And when Hammond didn't tell her not to—I'm sure he was curious just how close she'd come to the truth, just as I was, when it came to my own theories—she continued. "You wanted Aunt Beverly out of the way so you could get your hands on her money. It wasn't doing her any good. Most of the time she didn't even remember she had it. So you used Julia to get your brother into the nursing home. He killed Aunt Beverly, and you both went home. But Julia either suspected something, or just felt guilty for neglecting her job when she should have been available for Aunt Beverly, and she threatened to talk to Doctor Fesmire. So you made another appointment with Julia, and you slit her throat. And then you went to get her car. But while you were gone, Mrs. Jenkins showed up and found Julia. You told her Julia was hurt, and you needed to get help for Julia, and she crawled right into the car. You drove to Shelby Park, put the car in neutral, and pushed it down the ramp to the river. And then you got into your brother's boat, and the two of you headed up the river to Madison. He tied up the boat, you drove home, and neither of you thought of it again. Until the news started talking about Julia Poole's body being found. And nobody mentioned Mrs. Jenkins."

Hammond was doing his best to look nonchalant, but he couldn't quite pull it off.

"You realized she must have made it out of the car. You

could hope that maybe she'd gotten washed away, and her body would surface in a couple of days, but you were probably worried. She'd seen you. She could identify you. And you had no idea where she was."

"Until she showed up at the funeral," Rafe said. "And walked right into your confrontation with Doctor Fesmire."

Grimaldi nodded. "And suddenly you had two threats to deal with. Mrs. Jenkins, who had seen you with Julia's body, and Doctor Fesmire, who was saying things that made you suspect he knew something about what had happened. About what you'd done."

"No time to waste," Rafe said. "You went after Fesmire while your brother and his wife went looking for my grandmother."

"We have a witness," Grimaldi said, "who saw your sister-in-law make the call from the payphone on Ulm and Dresden, that brought Mrs. Collier out of the house."

I had no idea whether that was true, either, but it sounded good. And it might be true. If Grimaldi had continued canvassing the neighborhood after Mrs. J and I left Nashville, she—or the uniformed officers she'd sent out to do the job—might have discovered someone who'd seen something.

"But Mrs. Jenkins evaded your brother, and Mrs. Collier came back early. Your brother ran, and was picked up by his wife. Meanwhile, you dispatched Fesmire and threw the body in the river. And decided to hang onto his car."

"Nice car," Rafe remarked. "A damn sight better than that piece of crap Ford Explorer that's parked outside your brother's house right now."

Hammond flushed.

"You parked there," Grimaldi said, "so it'd look like you were at your brother's place for Thanksgiving. And then you took Fesmire's car and followed Agent Collier down here. Where you got lucky and caught Mrs. Jenkins alone in the cemetery."

"Kidnapping," the sheriff said, rolling his tongue around the word. Up until now, he'd been standing quietly in the corner with his arms folded, just listening to the conversation, and I'd pretty much forgotten that he was there. "Attempted murder. And four different people who watched you do it, and can testify to same in court. Plus another attempted kidnapping and murder."

Hammond looked annoyed. "I wasn't trying to kidnap the heifer, for God's sake. I didn't know she was in the car. I just figured I'd use it, since it was sitting there."

"And attempted grand theft auto," the sheriff added.

"And when you realized she was there," Rafe said, in a very soft voice, "and she told you she was pregnant and wouldn't be able to fit through the window of the car, you decided to try to drown her. And her baby. *My* baby."

"Another attempted murder," the sheriff said. "It's adding up."

Grimaldi nodded. "If I were you, Mr. Hammond, I'd start pinning whatever I could on your brother. You're looking at a lot of charges of your own. But you don't have to go down for the things he did."

"I'm not ratting on my brother," Lester Hammond said, seemingly offended that she'd even consider such a thing.

"That's fine. But the police in Nashville is picking up your brother and his wife as we speak. And you'd better believe Brigitte will do what she can to keep what sticks to the two of them to a minimum. And you know as well as I do that the DNA points to both of you. If Brigitte says you did it all, and Chester was with her when it happened, there's nothing we can do to prove it wasn't so."

"Effing bitch," Lester Hammond said.

Grimaldi nodded pleasantly. "If you want to take the fall for your brother, you go right ahead. But if you want some company in prison, it would help us all out if you'd just let us know what you're responsible for, and what your brother did. We've already got you for everything that happened here in Maury County, with eye witnesses. You're not getting out of any of it. But I don't see why you'd have to take on anymore than what you actually did up in Nashville."

Hammond hesitated. And seemed to come to the conclusion that this made sense. "Yeah."

Grimaldi spread her hands as if to give him the floor. And Hammond performed.

In the end, it turned out that we'd had it pretty well figured out already. He admitted to developing a relationship with Julia Poole after he and his brother decided to kill their aunt. "All her money was just sitting there. She didn't need it. And we were getting it anyway, once she died. All it was, was getting it a little sooner."

And murder. Let's not forget that.

"So while you were with Julia, your brother killed your aunt and threw her body down the stairs to make it look like an accident."

Hammond nodded.

"Did Julia guess what had happened, and threatened to turn you in? Or did she just feel bad about one of her patients dying because she'd walked off the job in the middle of her shift to meet you?"

"Stupid cow," Hammond said. "She didn't suspect a thing. Just kept talking about how horrible of a person she was for leaving her post and letting something happen to Aunt Beverly. And how she needed to talk to Doctor Fesmire and confess. And Fesmire wasn't stupid. If she talked to him, he'd figure it out."

"He'd already figured it out," Grimaldi said. "He was there the night you killed Julia."

"He didn't see nothing. But I saw his car when I went to the parking lot to get Julia's car. Stupid bastard hadn't even locked it. So I put the knife in his glove box. I figured it'd give him something else to think about." He smirked.

Neither Grimaldi nor Rafe looked surprised by this. I was. It was the first I'd heard of it. And since Rafe and Grimaldi hadn't told me, I had to assume it was the first they'd heard of it, too.

I wondered whether Fesmire had found the weapon, and whether that was why he'd been so unhelpful in trying to locate Mrs. Jenkins last Sunday. Maybe he thought she'd put it there, and that was why he'd been upset when he saw her at the funeral on Tuesday morning. Because he thought she'd been trying to frame him.

Inside the interrogation room, the conversation had moved on. Hammond explained how he had taken Julia's car and driven it back to the pavilion to load up the corpse for the drive to the river. "When I got there, the old bat was standing over the body."

He sounded unreasonably put out about this. Apparently it was just fine for him to do whatever he wanted, up to and including murder, to get what he wanted, but if anyone inconvenienced him in any way—as Mrs. Jenkins had done that night, or as I had done earlier today—all bets were off.

"That's my grandmother you're calling an old bat," Rafe informed him gently, and Hammond huffed.

"So you took Mrs. Jenkins with you," Grimaldi prompted, and Hammond went on with the story. He'd driven to the park, his brother had boated up there and picked him up, and they'd both gone home. And gotten a little worried when they didn't hear about Mrs. Jenkins being dead along with Julia. But then they'd seen her at the funeral on Tuesday morning, and used my name to figure out where she lived.

"I couldn't be in two places," Hammond said, sounding like everyone left all the work to him all the time, "so Chet and

Brigitte went after the old bat, and I contacted Fesmire. To talk." He smirked.

"Was he trying to shake you down?" Grimaldi sounded sympathetic.

Hammond snorted. "Not him. He told me he was going to call the police, because he thought I'd killed my aunt and Julia. So I grabbed a brick and hit him over the head." He shrugged.

"And tossed him in the river."

Hammond nodded. "Later, yeah."

"And kept his car and drove it here."

"My brother effed up with the old lady," Lester said. "And ran like a rabbit instead of finishing the job." He sounded exasperated. "He had'em both locked in the basement. He coulda just set fire to the kitchen before he left, and been done with it."

Rafe growled. I wanted to growl, too, even as I was very grateful that Chet Hammond was more squeamish than his brother.

"By the time I got back there after dumping Fesmire," Lester said, "the old lady was gone. And there were cops everywhere. So I waited. And kept an eye on the place. And today," he smirked at Rafe, "I followed you here."

"Where you tried to drown my grandmother and my wife and my unborn child," Rafe said. "And failed. For which you should be very, very grateful. Cause if you'd done any of that, you wouldn't be on your way to prison right now. You'd be on your way to the morgue."

Hammond tried to sneer, but he couldn't quite pull it off. I wouldn't have been able to, either. It was more than obvious that Rafe meant every word.

My husband turned to Grimaldi. "We done here?"

"The sheriff and I have some paperwork to take care of. Then we'll arrange to have Mr. Hammond transferred to Nashville. We don't need you for any of that."

Rafe nodded. "If the TBI can be of any assistance with any of this, you know where to find me."

He nodded to Grimaldi, nodded to Sheriff Satterfield, gave Lester Hammond a last look of the sort that should have made Hammond very happy to be alive, and walked out.

Two seconds later he walked into the room where I was sitting. "Everything all right?"

"Fine," I said. "That's not a nice man."

Rafe shook his head. "But he's off the streets until he goes to trial. No judge in his right mind's gonna give this POS bail he can afford. And with the evidence we have, no jury's gonna think he's innocent. So we don't have to worry about him no more."

Good. "We may have something else to worry about," I told him.

"What's that?"

"You know those fake contractions I've been having?"

"Yes," Rafe said.

"I'm not sure they're fake." They were coming regularly, and getting stronger all the time.

"No kidding." He didn't sound surprised at all.

"It's more than two-and-a-half weeks until my due date. I'm not supposed to have contractions yet." Not the real kind.

"Then maybe we should get you to the hospital, so they can check you out," my husband said.

"My OB/GYN is in Nashville. I can't give birth here."

"Not sure the baby cares," Rafe said, and hauled me to my feet and steered me toward the door. "But if they can give you something to stop the contractions, we can get you home and to the hospital in Nashville, and maybe wait a little closer to term."

"I don't have my hospital bag." I'd left it in Nashville when I took Mrs. Jenkins and ran for Sweetwater. After all, I was more than two-and-a-half weeks away from my due date.

"You'll have to make do with what you've got," Rafe said and opened the door. "Let's go have a baby."

"We're not having a baby! You said they could give me something to stop the contractions. We can't have a baby now. It's too soon. And I don't have my bag!"

Rafe patted my back and steered me toward the parking lot, making encouraging noises.

EPILOGUE

"Have you picked out a name?" my mother asked.

It was the next day, and I was still in the hospital. The doctor hadn't given me anything to stop the contractions. Not only did they consider thirty-seven-and-a-half weeks to be full term, but I'd also waited too long to get there. By the time Rafe walked me through the emergency room door, things had progressed too far. As the doctor told me, it was too late to put the pin back in the grenade. I was exploding whether I was ready for it or not.

So we had a baby. And if that sounds simple and easy, I can assure you it was not. It took hours, and a lot of effort. I moaned and cried. I vomited. I felt unspeakably sorry for myself, and very envious of Rafe, who'd had all the fun of making this baby, plus the countless times we'd practiced before conceiving, but he didn't have to go through any of the pain now.

I managed to refrain from yelling at him, though.

I didn't even want to, to be honest. He was right next to me the whole time. He held my hand and helped me breathe through the contractions. He held the little kidney-shaped bowl when I threw up—and let me tell you, it isn't every man who'll cheerfully dump his wife's vomit and come back into the room to tell her how beautiful she looks.

He was lying through his teeth, of course. I looked awful.

All sweaty and blotchy and red-faced. I knew it, but I didn't have the energy to argue, or call him a big, fat liar. I was too busy gritting my teeth and breathing and counting and—eventually—pushing.

"Just a little longer," Rafe told me, hanging onto my hand while the doctor and nurse got in position. "You can do this."

I shook my head. Weakly. "I'm not sure I can."

He bent to kiss me. Softly. On the lips. "I know you can. You can do anything. Compared to the other stuff you went through today, this'll be easy."

Easy for him to say.

But I did it. I pushed, and pushed again, and pushed some more.

And after one of those pushes—I'm not sure which one, because I lost count—the nurse said, "One more should do it."

And after one more, they all started moving around really fast, and nobody told me to push again, and I closed my eyes and enjoyed the tranquility until a shrill, irate cry cut through the peace and quiet.

My eyes popped open and I looked up at Rafe, horrified. "Is that our baby?"

He nodded. His eyes had tears in them.

I struggled to sit up. "What's wrong?"

"Nothing." He shook his head. "Everything's perfect."

"It doesn't sound perfect. The baby sounds angry."

"She was comfortable," the nurse said, approaching the bed with an impossibly tiny, blanket-wrapped bundle in her arms. A bundle so small it shouldn't have been able to make the ear-splitting shrieks I was hearing. "And then someone yanked her out here, in the cold and the light, and started slapping her around. She'll calm down in a minute."

She lowered the bundle toward me. I reached for it, automatically. "She?"

The nurse smiled. "You have a baby girl, Mrs. Collier."

A baby girl.

I looked up at Rafe. He was smiling, with tears still in his eyes. Obviously a baby girl was OK with him.

"We'll just finish up down here," the nurse said, "while you visit." She wandered off.

I didn't even look at her. And I had no need to know what finishing up down there entailed. I was holding a baby. Rafe's baby. Our baby.

He reached out and used a single finger to pull down the blanket so we could look at her.

She hadn't been cleaned up yet, so she was still a little sticky. Her hair was wet and black. Her face was small and wrinkled and a shade darker than mine, but lighter than Rafe's. Her nose was tiny and her eyes big. And blue.

"She's beautiful." My voice shook.

He nodded. "Like her mama."

To me, she looked more like her daddy, but I wasn't going to argue about it. I yawned. "I'm beat."

Rafe smiled. "They'll come take the baby in a bit. To clean her and weigh her and all that. I'm gonna go get a shower and tell everyone the news. When they wake up."

"What time is it?" I'd lost count of that too, as the night progressed.

"Going on five."

In the morning. "Long night," I said. "Why don't you try to get a couple hours sleep and come back later?" And maybe I could do the same. If he left me alone for a while.

He nodded. "I'll stay here until they take the baby away, and then I'll let you get some rest."

"That works." I put my head on his shoulder and looked down at our baby.

Things continued to be blurry after that, to be honest. They finished whatever they had to do, and then they took the baby away. Rafe left, and I drifted off to sleep. At some point, they brought the baby back, and I had to stay awake so I could try to nurse her. That happened a couple of times, I think. And eventually Rafe came back, as the first of the family.

He'd managed to get a few hours of sleep, and looked pretty good, considering. He's always been able to get by on little sleep, so he'd probably be OK. And he was freshly showered and dressed in clean clothes, including the blue shirt that had taken the plunge into the Duck River yesterday. Mother must have laundered it for him.

He brought Grimaldi, who bent and gave me a hug. She's not very demonstrative usually, so this was big.

"Congratulations." She gave the baby a dubious look.

I grinned. "Thank you. Want to hold her?"

She actually took a step back. "No. Thank you."

"Don't you like babies?"

"I like them better when they're old enough that I can reason with them," Grimaldi said. Which made sense, I guess. And probably meant that she got along fairly well with Abigail and Hannah, who are both old enough to be talked to.

"I'll take her." Rafe swooped in and scooped the baby out of my arms. "Hi there, beautiful." He smiled down at her.

So from now on, she was going to be the beautiful one. Not me.

I turned back to Grimaldi. "What's happening?"

"I'm headed back to Nashville. Lester Hammond is being transported this morning, and we have Chester and Brigitte in custody. I have to go wrap up my case."

"Good luck with it."

"It's mostly just the details," Grimaldi said. "We have Lester's confession implicating Chester. We know what they each did, and how they did it. I'll have to interview Chester and Brigitte, but we already know what happened. This is just ticking off the boxes."

"I don't expect you'll be back?"

"Not for a while," Grimaldi said. "Your brother invited me to Christmas dinner. And your mother told me about the Christmas Eve party she has every year."

"Any chance you could let someone else take Christmas duty this year, and come spend the holiday with us?"

"I'm thinking about it," Grimaldi said, which was probably the best I was going to get. "When are you coming back to Nashville?"

I'd be in the hospital one more day, from what they'd told me. But I also had a feeling Mother would try to keep me in Sweetwater for a bit longer.

"Not sure. Maybe not for a few days."

She nodded. "Let me know when you do."

I promised I would, and she headed out. Rafe moved over into the chair next to the bed, still holding the baby. "Morning, gorgeous."

He leaned in to kiss me. So I was still gorgeous—and that was still a complete lie. But nice of him to say so.

"I need a bath," I said.

"We'll get you one." He looked down at the baby. "She's beautiful."

She was. Nice and clean now, as opposed to me. Her tufts of black hair were curly.

"Do you have to go back to Nashville, too?" I asked. He'd been involved in the Poole investigation, if only because of Mrs. Jenkins. Maybe he'd have to go back and help clean things up.

"Not right away. But I should probably check in on Monday."

Probably so. "Are any of the others stopping by?"

"Your mother's setting up a schedule," Rafe said, with a grin. "She oughta be here soon."

Gah. "I'll have to clean up." Birth was no excuse for not looking great. Mother would expect me to be neat and polished, with fluffy hair and makeup in place. She'd probably want to take photographs. And she'd never forgive me if I looked less than presentable in them.

"C'mon." He shifted the baby to the crook of one arm, like he'd always been doing it, and used the other to help me out of bed and over to the bathroom door. "You gonna be all right in there?"

I'd have to be, since I couldn't take him with me. "I wish I had my hospital bag. With my pretty nightgown." Instead of this faded hospital gown I was forced to wear in lieu of anything personal.

"I brought your nightgown from your mother's house," Rafe said, nodding to the plastic bag he'd dropped on the chair next to the bathroom door. "And your shampoo and cream and stuff."

"Bless you." With any luck, there was enough in there to make me look halfway decent for Mother and the pictures.

"I aim to please," Rafe said with a grin, and got back to admiring his daughter while I closed myself in the bathroom and did my best to repair any visible damage from the night's excesses.

By the time Mother walked through the door, I was as presentable as I could expect to be. My hair was clean and dry, and wavy around my shoulders. I was dressed in a nice nightgown, and I had makeup on. There wasn't much I could do about the bloodshot eyes, but I'd managed to cover the dark circles under them. And anyway, as it turned out, nobody was all that interested in me.

Mother brought Mrs. Jenkins and Audrey with her. While Mrs. J and Audrey descended on Rafe and the baby, Mother came over to the bed and gave me a kiss on the cheek. "Good morning, darling."

"Good morning," I said.

"You look well."

She sounded vaguely disappointed. "I feel well," I said. A

bit sore, but it's amazing what a difference being clean makes. "And I have a baby."

I pointed to it. Mrs. J and Audrey were making cooing noises over Rafe's shoulders.

Mother nodded. "So I hear. How long are you staying in the hospital?"

I told her what I'd told Grimaldi, that they'd probably let me leave tomorrow, and she did what I expected her to do: tried to convince me to come back to the mansion for a few days. "Wouldn't that be better than being in that big, empty house by yourself?"

It probably would. If I stayed here, I wouldn't have to worry about doing anything for myself. I had a whole family I could dispatch to do my bidding.

On the other hand, Rafe was my husband, and we had a home together. And he might have an opinion on this, too.

"I hope you'll stay a few days, Savannah," Audrey said from where she was clucking over the baby. She glanced at Mrs. Jenkins, and took a deep breath. "We wanted to talk to you about something."

"What's that?" She looked uncomfortable, which isn't like her.

"Aunt Tondalia and I," Audrey said, "have been talking. She'd like to spend some time here in Sweetwater. With me. And I'd like to have her. I don't know what your plans were, after what happened..."

We hadn't really talked about it. Although I guess the plan had been that she'd either stay with us, so I could keep an eye on her and make sure she didn't wander off again, or we were going to find another facility for her, where she'd be happy and safe. I was more in favor of the latter, both because I was afraid I would lose her, and because I honestly thought she might be better off under the care of professionals. Although I was open to other suggestions.

Like this one.

I looked at Rafe. He shrugged. "If you're sure that's what you wanna do. You're gonna have to make sure she don't wander off. She has a habit of doing that."

Audrey nodded. "We'll make sure everyone in town knows who she is. That way, if anyone finds her, they'll know where she belongs."

"She's safer wandering off here than in Nashville," Mother added.

No question. And with the connection to her sister here, and her niece and now a great-niece, she might be happy in Sweetwater. And of course we'd come and visit frequently. We did that anyway.

There was a question I thought needed to be asked, though. "If you start introducing Mrs. Jenkins as your aunt, doesn't that mean people will know that your mother was... you know...?"

"Black?" Audrey said. "Yes. I assume so."

"That doesn't bother you?"

"It never bothered me," Audrey said. "It bothered my mother. But my mother's gone. And we've been hiding it long enough."

I glanced at Mother. How was she handling this?

But she was nodding and smiling. Hard to believe, considering the mother I'd grown up with, but I'd take it.

"I guess we'd be OK with that," I said, and looked at Rafe. "I mean, we could try it and see how it went. It's really up to Rafe, though. He's her next of kin. It has to be his decision."

Both Audrey and Mrs. J looked at Rafe. He focused on his grandmother. "This what you wanna do?"

She nodded. "Yes, baby."

"And you'll stay with Audrey and not wander off and get lost?"

She nodded. I have no idea whether she knew what that even meant—when she wandered off and got lost, she probably didn't see it as wandering off and getting lost—but if she wanted to be here, and if Audrey was willing to take on the responsibility for her, I didn't see any reason why we shouldn't give it a shot.

Rafe nodded. "Then let's see how it goes."

Audrey beamed. So did Mrs. J, whether she understood or not.

"So have you picked out a name yet?" Mother asked, peering at the little bundle in the crook of Rafe's arm.

I looked at him. He nodded.

"Carrie," I said. "Her name is Caroline Collier."

Mother nodded. "That seems fitting."

I thought so. And as Carrie scrunched up her tiny face and let out an eardrum-piercing cry, and my husband hurriedly dumped her on the bed so I could take care of whatever need she had, I looked around at my husband, and his grandmother, and my mother, and her best friend, and my new baby, and knew that I was the luckiest woman in the world.

Or at least I would be, if I could just get the baby to shut up.

# # #

ABOUT THE AUTHOR

New York Times and *USA Today* bestselling author Jenna Bennett (Jennie Bentley) writes the Do It Yourself home renovation mysteries for Berkley Prime Crime and the Savannah Martin real estate mysteries for her own gratification. She also writes a variety of romance for a change of pace.

For more information, please visit Jenna's website:
www.JennaBennett.com